VIRAGO
MODERN CLASSICS
725

© *Evening Standard/Getty Images*

Nancy Spain was a novelist, broadcaster and journalist. Born in Newcastle-upon-Tyne in 1917, she was the great-niece of the legendary Mrs Beeton. As a columnist for the *Daily Express* and *She* magazine, frequent guest on radio's *Woman's Hour* and panellist on the television programmes *What's My Line?* and *Juke Box Jury*, she was one of the most recognisable (and controversial) media personalities of her era. During the Second World War she worked as a driver, and her comic memoir of her time in the WRNS became an immediate bestseller. After the war she began publishing her acclaimed series of detective novels, and would go on to write over twenty books. Spain and her longtime partner, Joan Werner Laurie, were killed when the light aircraft carrying them to the Grand National in 1964 crashed close to the racecourse. Her friend Noël Coward wrote, 'It is cruel that all that gaiety, intelligence and vitality should be snuffed out when so many bores and horrors are left living.'

R IN THE MONTH

Nancy Spain

Introduced by Sandi Toksvig

VIRAGO

This paperback edition published in 2022 by Virago Press
First published in Great Britain in 1950 by Hutchinson

1 3 5 7 9 10 8 6 4 2

Copyright © Nancy Spain 1950
Copyright © Beneficiaries of Nancy Spain 1964
Introduction copyright © Sandi Toksvig 2020

The moral right of the author has been asserted

*All characters and events in this publication, other than those
clearly in the public domain, are fictitious and any resemblance
to real persons, living or dead, is purely coincidental.*

All rights reserved.
No part of this publication may be reproduced, stored in a
retrieval system, or transmitted in any form or by any means, without
the prior permission in writing of the publisher, nor be otherwise circulated
in any form of binding or cover other than that in which it is published
and without a similar condition including this condition being
imposed on the subsequent purchaser.

A CIP catalogue record for this book
is available from the British Library.

ISBN 978-0-349-01402-9

Typeset in Goudy by M Rules
Printed and bound in Great Britain by
Clays Ltd, Elcograf S.p.A.

Papers used by Virago are from well-managed forests
and other responsible sources.

MIX
Paper from
responsible sources
FSC® C104740

Virago Press
An imprint of
Little, Brown Book Group
Carmelite House
50 Victoria Embankment
London EC4Y 0DZ

An Hachette UK Company
www.hachette.co.uk

www.virago.co.uk

MARGERY ALLINGHAM'S BOOK

With love

... Still the shops
Remain unaltered on the Esplanade –
The Circulating Library, the Stores.
Jill's Pantry, Cynthia's Ditty Box (Antiques),
Trecarrow (Maps and Souvenirs and Guides).
Pale pink hydrangeas turn a rusty brown
Where sea winds catch them, and yet do not die.

JOHN BETJEMAN, *Beside the Sea Side*

Introduction

'The world of books: romantic, idle, shiftless world so beautiful, so cheap compared with living.'

NANCY SPAIN

I never met Nancy Spain, and I've been worrying that we might not have got on. It bothers me because I'm a fan. That's probably an odd start for someone writing an introduction to her work, but I think it's a sign of how much I like her writing that I ponder whether we would have clicked in person. The thing is, Spain loved celebrity. In 1955 she wrote, 'I love a big name ... I like to go where they go ... I always hope (don't you?) that some of their lustre will rub off against me ...'

I don't hope that. I loathe celebrity and run from gatherings of the famous, so I can't say I would have wanted to hang out with her, but I should have liked to have met. I would have told her what a brilliant writer she was, how hilarious, and I'd have said thank you, because I also know that I might not have had my career without her. I've been lucky enough to earn a crust by both writing and broadcasting, and I do so because Nancy Spain was there first.

During the height of her fame in the 1950s and early 60s she did something remarkable – she became a multimedia celebrity at a time when no one even knew that was a desirable thing. She was a TV and radio personality, a novelist, a journalist and columnist for British tabloids. She did all this while wearing what was known as 'mannish clothing'. Although her lesbianism was not openly discussed, she became a role model for many, with the closeted dyke feeling better just knowing Spain was in the public eye being clever and funny.

I am too young to have seen her on TV, but the strange thing about the internet is that people never really disappear. Check Nancy Spain out on the web and you can still see and hear her performing in a 1960s BBC broadcast on the panel of *Juke Box Jury*. She has the clipped tones of a well-bred Englishwoman of the time, who sounds as though she is fitting in a broadcast before dashing to the Ritz for tea. It is a carefully contrived public persona that suited Spain as a way to present herself to the world but, like so much of her life, it skirted around the truth. She was selling the world a product, a concept which she would have understood only too well.

In 1948 Spain wrote a biography of her great-aunt, Isabella Beeton, author of the famous *Mrs Beeton's Book of Household Management*. Although it was an encyclopedic presentation of all you needed to know about running the home, Isabella Beeton was hardly the bossy matron in the kitchen that the book suggested; in fact she wrote it aged just twenty-one, when she can hardly have had the necessary experience. Isabella probably knew more about horses, having been a racing correspondent for *Sporting Life*. The truth is that she and her husband Sam saw a gap in the book market. So, rather than being the distillation of years of experience, Mrs Beeton's book was a shrewd marketing ploy. I wonder how many people know that Isabella never did become that wise old woman of the household because she died aged just twenty-eight of puerperal fever following the birth of her fourth child? There are parallels here too, for Spain's background was also not what it seemed and she, like Isabella, lost her life too early.

Far from being a posh Londoner, Nancy Spain hailed from Newcastle. Her father was a writer and occasional broadcaster, and she followed in his footsteps quite aware that she was the son he never had. Her determination to come to the fore appeared early on. As a child she liked to play St George and the Dragon in which her father took the part of the dragon, Nancy marched about as St George while, as she described it, her sister Liz 'was lashed to the bottom of the stairs with skipping ropes and scarves'. No dragon was going to stop Spain from being the hero of the piece.

From 1931 to 1935 Spain was sent, like her mother before her, to finish her education at the famous girls' public school, Roedean, high on the chalky cliffs near Brighton. It was here that her Geordie accent was subdued and polished into something else. She didn't like it there and would spend time getting her own back in her later writing. Her fellow classmates seem to have varied in their attitude toward her. Some saw her as exotic and clever, while others found her over the top. It says something about the attitude to women's careers at the time when you learn that in his 1933 Prize-Giving Day speech to the school the then Lord Chancellor, Lord Sankey, congratulated Roedean on playing 'a remarkable part in the great movement for the higher education of women', but added, 'In spite of the many attractive avenues which were now open to girls', he hoped 'the majority of them would not desert the path of simple duties and home life'.

Deserting that path was Spain's destiny from the beginning. It was while at school that Spain began writing a diary of her private thoughts. In this early writing the conflict between her inner lesbian feelings and society's demand that she keep them quiet first stirred. She began to express herself in poetry. Some of her verse-making was public and she won a Guinea prize for one of her works in her final year. This, she said, led her to the foolish notion that poems could make money.

Her mother harboured ambitions for Spain to become a games or domestic science teacher, but it was clear neither was going to happen. Her father, who sounds a jolly sort, said she could stay home and have fifty pounds a year to spend as she pleased. She joined a women's lacrosse and hockey club in Sunderland because it looked like fun, but instead she found a fledgling career and her first love. She became utterly smitten with a fellow team member, twenty-three-year-old Winifred Emily Sargeant ('Bin' to her friends) a blonde, blue-eyed woman who could run fast on the field and rather glamorously seemed fast off it by drinking gin and tonic.

The *Newcastle Journal* decided to publish some reports about women's sport and almost by chance Nancy got her first job in journalism. Touring with the team meant she could both write and spend time with Bin. When she discovered her feelings for Winifred were reciprocated, she was over the moon.

> *Dearest – your laughter stirred my heart*
> *for everything I loved was there –*
> *Oh set its gaiety apart*
> *that I may feel it everywhere!*

She bought herself a second-hand car for twenty pounds and began making some local radio broadcasts, getting her first taste of fame when she played the part of Northumberland heroine Grace Darling in a local radio play. Meanwhile she and Winifred found time to escape. It was the 1930s and they were both supposed to be growing into 'respectable' women. The pressure must have been unbearable as there was no one with whom they could share the excitement of their feelings for each other. They went off for several weeks to France on a touring holiday, which Spain described as idyllic. It was to be a one-off, for they returned to find Britain declaring war with Germany. They both joined up, with Spain enlisting in the Women's Royal Naval Service, the Wrens.

She would later describe her time in the service as the place where she found emancipation. She became a driver, scooting across the base and fixing the vehicles when they faltered. Based in North Shields, where many large naval vessels came in for repairs, it was often cold and there was no money for uniforms. Some trawlermen gave her a fisherman's jersey, and she got a white balaclava helmet that she was told was made by Princess Mary. She also got permission to wear jodhpurs on duty. It was the beginning of her feeling comfortable in men's clothes.

At the end of 1939 news reached Spain that Winifred, aged twenty-seven, had died of a viral infection. Unable to bear the grief, she didn't go to the funeral, but instead wrote poetry about the efficacy of drink to drown sorrows. The Wrens decided she was officer material and moved her to Arbroath in Scotland to do administrative duties. It was here that she began to shape the rest of her life. She became central to the base's many entertainments. She took part in broadcasts. She wrote. She was always busy. She did not talk about her life with Winifred. Years later, when she wrote about their dreamy French holiday, she wrote as if she had gone alone. Her only travelling companions apparently were 'a huge hunk of French bread and a slopping bottle of warm wine'. The descriptions of the trip are splendid, but they mask the painful truth.

After the war, Spain was set to be a writer. An outstanding review by A. A. Milne of her first book, *Thank you – Nelson*, about her experiences in the Wrens, gave her a first push to success. She sought out the famous, she lived as 'out' as she could in an unaccepting world. I don't like how the tabloids sold her to the public.

The *Daily Express* declared about its journalist, as if it were a selling point: 'They call her vulgar . . . they call her unscrupulous . . . they call her the worst dressed woman in Britain . . . '

She called herself a 'trouser-wearing character', with her very clothing choices setting her apart as odd or bohemian. I suspect she was just trying to find a way to be both acceptable to the general public, and to be herself. It is a tricky combination, and was much harder then. She may not have known or intended the impact she had in helping to secretly signal to other lesbians and gay men that they were not alone. She lived with the founder and editor of *She* magazine, Joan 'Jonny' Werner Laurie, and is said to have slept with many other women, including Marlene Dietrich. Fame indeed.

I am so thrilled to see her work come back into print. Her detective novels are hilarious. They are high camp and less about detecting than delighting, with absurd farce and a wonderful turn of phrase. Who doesn't want to read about a sleuth who when heading out to do some detective work hangs a notice on her front door reading 'OUT – GONE TO CRIME'? Her detective, Miriam Birdseye, was based on Spain's friend the actress Hermione Gingold, whose own eccentricities made her seem like a character from a novel. Miriam's glorious theatricality is complemented by her indolent sidekick, the (allegedly) Russian ballerina Natasha Nevkorina, who has to overcome a natural disinclination to do anything in order to do most of the actual detecting. They work incredibly well together, as in this exchange:

'And she is telling you that you are going mad, I suppose?' said Natasha.

'Yes,' said Miss Lipscoomb, and sank into a chair. She put her head in her hands. 'I think it is true,' she said. 'But how did you know?'

'That's an old one,' said Miriam briskly. 'I always used to tell my first husband he was going mad,' she said. 'In the end he did,' she added triumphantly.

There is something quintessentially British about these detective novels, as if every girl graduating from Roedean might end up solving a murder. The books contain jokes that work on two levels – some for everyone; some just for those in the know. Giving a fictitious school the name Radcliff Hall is a good queer gag, while anyone might enjoy the names of the 'intimate revues' in which Miriam Birdseye had appeared in the past, including 'Absolutely the End', 'Positively the Last' and 'Take Me Off'.

Seen through the prism of modern thinking, there are aspects of Spain's writing that are uncomfortable, but I am sad if they overshadow her work so thoroughly as to condemn it to obscurity. P. G. Wodehouse has, after all, survived far worse accusations. Thomas Hardy is still recalled for his writing about 'man's inhumanity to man', even though by all accounts he wasn't nice to his wife. Should we stop reading Virginia Woolf because she was a self-confessed snob? I am not a big fan of the modern 'cancel culture', and hope we can be all grown-up enough to read things in the context of their time. Of one thing I am certain – Spain was not trying to hurt anyone. She had had too tough a time of her own trying to be allowed just to survive the endless difficulties of being other. My political consciousness is as raised as anyone's, and I see the flaws, but maybe it's okay just to relax in her company and succumb to being entertained.

Nancy Spain died aged forty-seven. She was in a light aircraft on her way to cover the 1964 Grand National when the plane crashed near the racecourse. Her partner Jonny was with her and they were cremated together. Her friend Noël Coward wrote, 'It is cruel that all that gaiety, intelligence and vitality should be snuffed out, when so many bores and horrors are left living.' She was bold, she was brave, she was funny, she was feisty. I owe her a great deal in leading the way and I like her books a lot. They make me laugh, but also here I get to meet her alone, away from the public gaze, and just soak up the chat. Enjoy.

Sandi Toksvig

To find out more about Nancy Spain, you might like to read her memoirs, *Thank you – Nelson*, *Why I'm Not a Millionaire* and *A Funny Thing Happened on the Way*. Also the authorised biography, *A Trouser-Wearing Character: The Life and Times of Nancy Spain* by Rose Collis.

Contents

Characters in the Story

Lt-Commander Anthony Robinson, RNVR	*Proprietor of the Oranmore Hotel*
Celia	*His wife*
April ⎫ May ⎭	*Their daughters*
May	
Connie	*Cook at the Oranmore Hotel*
Tommy	*Kitchenmaid*
Maggie Button	*Chambermaid*
Major Reginald Bognor	*Resident in the hotel*
Mrs Eithne Bognor	*His mother*
Miriam Birdseye	*A genius*
Frederick Pyke	*A poet in love with Miss Birdseye*

Mrs Ada Greeb	*Of Harrogate, mother-in-law to Tony Robinson*
Colonel Charles Rucksack	*Of Cherry Pickings, Brunton-on-Sea*
Dr Stalag-Jones	*Of the Plot, Mitre Road, Brunton-on-Sea, a doctor of medicine*
Bob	*Hall porter at the Warhaven Arms*
Graham Micah	*A chemist*
Mrs Micah	*His wife*
Charles Bodger	*A butcher*
Mrs Bodger	*His mother*
Ezekiel Twigg	*A greengrocer*

Frontispiece

'And so to sum up,' said Mr Justice Mayhem. He leant back behind his desk and shut his old, old eyes. The court-room was warm and filled with air that had been used many times by other people. 'To sum up. In order to understand all that faced the accused you will have to put yourselves to a certain extent in the same place.

'Murder is a most horrible crime. One (I feel certain) that you, members of the jury, might never find it in your hearts to commit. I do not (no matter what the circumstances) look upon it as the normal solution to a difficult emotional problem. I may feel sympathy for someone who has become entangled in an emotional net outside his or her control. I do not see how I can feel sympathy for someone who has used force to extricate himself from that net.

'In order, therefore, that you may consider your verdict and bring in such a decision as you may all unanimously find, I must ask you yet once more to consider the evidence of the Crown's witnesses that we have all had placed before us. And much of this evidence relates to the accused's behaviour on the 23rd of February last . . .'

BOOK ONE

ALONG THE BRINY BEACH

'O Oysters come and walk with us!'
   The Walrus did beseech.
'A pleasant walk, a pleasant talk
   Along the briny beach.
We cannot do with more than four
   To give a hand to each . . .'

LEWIS CARROLL: *The Walrus and the Carpenter.*

CHAPTER ONE

The road to the sea from Brunton-on-Sea railway station vibrates with trolley-buses. It is dominated by two house-agents, a wine-shop, a horrid little tea-room called the Blue Parrot and the Sussex and Provincial Bank, Limited, with its black double door. Brunton has only recently been included in the Southern electric circuit. It is healthily situated alongside Beachy Head and is one of the most hideous watering-places on the South Coast. Persons retiring there with the intention of dying have lingered on for years, feeling better than they have ever felt in their lives. It has the highest sunshine percentage of any town in Great Britain.

Nevertheless, on this morning in February the English Channel was at its worst. It had been churned up all night into a series of frothing waves caused by a south-westerly gale. Andrew Cathcart, the manager of this branch of the Sussex and Provincial, paused at the double doors and shivered. The worst of the weather was over, the rain had passed on towards London; the horizon was now a clear pale green, but the sea was still upset. Mr Cathcart's face slowly turned purple. He straightened his tie and shrugged his shoulders. Half past ten.

He expected 'young' Tony at eleven. Funny thing, he always thought of Tony Robinson as 'young', though by now he was well into his forties. Funny thing. Shaking his head, Mr Cathcart went into his office.

II

Half-way down Station Road a foolhardy terrace of villa residences shot off at right angles. It had been an attempt at a refined residential quarter. Here, Joshua Mabberly (the old jobbing builder) had run up villa after villa to the specifications of Anglo-Indian colonels and colonials, wishfully retiring. After many years the colonels had died. They had usually spent their capital, because they had lived longer than they intended. And the colonels' ladies had not cared to live on, among the Burmese gongs and Benares brassware, without the money to keep these things in the manner to which they had been accustomed.

Soon the colonels' ladies had gone away, no one knew where. The colonials had died, too; and because no one had ever married them, they left no woman to cherish the groups taken at Blauwildebeestefontein and Wallamaloo and Pretoria, with a white fox terrier in the foreground. So the Warhaven Sale Rooms, behind the house agents in Station Road, were filled with exotic bric-à-brac that changed hands once a month, wittily mocked by Ronald Cathcart, auctioneer and valuer and brother to the bank manager. And Durbah Villas, shamefaced, lurked behind signs announcing Gelthorne Guest House, Bolinbroke private and Price's family and commercial hotels.

Mabberly died in 1926. His interest in this story is only that he set the scenery. He had once been proud of the vast rich Durbah Villas, so much the same size and yet (as he would have said) so individual. And each (as he would also say) according. They all had their own atmosphere, but the richest and most sinister example of Edwardian Gothic in the whole terrace was the Oranmore. It stood on the much-coveted corner site. Six of its thirteen bedrooms possessed sea views.

The Oranmore Private Hotel (unlicensed) had once been *two* houses: Pondicherry Lodge and Burma Villa. Mabberly had enjoyed himself building these for their original owners, Captain Fortescue-Sykes (who had since tried to corner the pepper market, had gone broke and shot himself) and Mr Dunlop, who was dead. Neither of these men had wanted (in their lifetime) any damn' nonsense. Both of them had paid twice, through the nose and up to the hilt. Pondicherry Lodge had a sloping lawn and hydrangea bushes. Burma Villa had rockeries, fore and aft. So the Oranmore had the advantage of both of these rare types of garden. It also enjoyed the late Mrs Fortescue-Sykes' collection of cacti, which clustered obscenely in a corner of the Pondicherry Lodge back garden near the garden-seat.

Anthony Robinson stood in the porch of the Oranmore Hotel, complacently looking at his new writing-paper and billheads. They had arrived from the printer's that morning. (The printer also was a Cathcart: they had quite a stranglehold upon the neighbourhood.) *The Oranmore Private Hotel – Prop. A. Campbell-Robinson* appeared in Gothic letters at the head of a beige, deckle-edged sheet. The envelopes were also beige and deckle-edged. Anthony was pleased with them. The fresh air came from the sea, with salt in it, and ruffled the paper in his hands. Anthony looked at his watch. Half an hour before he

5

was due at the bank. As he went back into the house, moving his shoulders against the cold, he wondered if Connie the cook had swiped that gin he had hidden last night in the kitchen. Then suddenly in the little room above the door he saw his wife, holding up a twin to be admired. He waved and gestured and his face broke into happy, handsome lines.

III

Tony Robinson was the sort of man that women consider 'attractive' and of whom men are consequently jealous. He gave a general effect that was tall and willowy. He had a pale, thin face with darting blue eyes and eyelashes like tangled, unpruned hedges. He was intensely friendly and obviously delighted in human beings, expecting them to delight in him also. He wore cheap sports clothes; in some unbelievable way, on his lean figure they appeared well-cut. He loved to cut a dash. He very much admired gamblers and bookmakers. He was often in their company, imitating their slang, buying round on round of expensive drinks and sometimes picking up a tip for a selling plate. These people said Tony was a 'good scout' and (amongst themselves) a bloody fool. They could not (they said) credit it that a man could have that much bad luck on the track, but there, look at the luck he'd had with women.

Tony Robinson's father had been a clergyman – the Reverend Thomas Robinson of St Biddulph's, Brunton, no less. His mother, one of the rich Misses Pringle of Sheffield, had provided money for all her sons' educations. Andrew Cathcart (in those days a teller at the Sussex and Provincial) had enviously observed Mark, Luke, Tony and Edward going away to their prep schools, coming home from them frail and white and nervous, and then going away again, to Rugby. Edward, the youngest and most sensitive, had died of all this. Andrew had nevertheless been sick with envy. He looked forward to a day when a Cathcart might also smile, product of a public school education. His daughter Rosemary he had brought up as a lady. Perhaps also his brother's kid Kenneth ...

Sunk in this feckless dream, behind his desk in the nicely partitioned manager's office, old Cathcart heard Tony Robinson's entrance at five past eleven.

It was as though some subtle wind had come into the place. Cathcart could hear the tellers answering greetings. He could even hear one or two customers saying 'Good morning' gaily. He got up from his chair in spite of himself and advanced, blinking, through the door.

'Come on in, Tony,' he said, in a rush of warm feeling. 'Come in.' In spite of everything, he was fond of the boy.

'Sit down,' said old Cathcart. He pointed to the massive mahogany chair beyond the desk in the sunlight. Tony sat down and scowled like a little boy, screwing up his eyes. Old Cathcart drew the ledger towards him, mumbling a little. Tony had had his £4000 by his mother's will. The Oranmore had been in the market for 10,000. Let's see now, the bank had taken up that mortgage for him ... Tony wasn't beginning to pay his way yet. He'd have to stick in at it a bit more. Knock off spirits or something ...

'Well?' said Tony, faintly truculent. He looked at his shoes. They were cheap suède, but on Tony's long, flat, trim feet they seemed like shoes made by Lobb of St James's. 'You wanted to see me?'

His voice, which had been that of a country gentleman calling his dogs, had sunk to a whisper. He *must know* his financial position, thought old Cathcart, peering forward at him above his glasses. Suddenly he saw Tony's future plainly. He saw him a spiv, probably a hanger-on in a bookmaker's gang, probably known as The Duke or The Marquis. Cathcart spoke more sharply than he had intended. No doubt he remembered Tony's mother and that good old man the Reverend, Tony's father.

'It's your overdraft,' he said harshly. 'You're over your limit again, you know. This has to stop. It isn't the first time ...' He seemed to be making no effect on Tony. He raised his voice a little. 'This has got to *stop*,' he repeated. 'Banks aren't run like this, y'know. It's a pretty poor show. If your poor mother were alive ...'

Tony Robinson's thick eyelashes fluttered. His brows came together in a heavy line. One thin, long hand opened and shut on his knee.

'You keep my mother out of this,' he said, very rudely indeed.

Mr Cathcart trembled. He pushed back his chair. He could feel his heart rising in his throat, thumping in his wrists, banging in his stomach.

'Very well, then!' he cried. 'I'll teach you a lesson. I'll show you we aren't a philanthropic institution made to keep *your* pockets lined, so you can stand drinks to all the touts in Brighton. Pay off your overdraft by next Monday, or ...'

And, trembling foolishly, Andrew Cathcart rose to his feet. He stood there swaying, his face going darker and darker. Tony stood up too, and towered over him, glowering.

'Good morning,' said old Cathcart, and turned his back. He heard the inner door slam. It was as though the daylight left the building. He heard the outer door slam. Tony's angry feet went stamping past the window. Sunk back in his chair, Cathcart imagined Tony's entry into the Warhaven Arms. With a sour smile, he wondered how he would contrive to pay for his first round of drinks.

IV

Tony crossed the road. He walked furiously, with his head down. His face no longer showed a blaze of temper. He looked preoccupied and his mouth was twisted in a tight line. As far as he remembered, his overdraft was £142. £142. His own age, plus a hundred. His own blood pressure, or what his own blood pressure *ought* to be.

Here his brows unknotted and he was suddenly delighted with himself. The sun came out and the sea danced. The waves were tipped with gold. Station Road and Durbah Villas had a background like beaten brass – like one of the brass gongs from Burma . . .

'Hullo, Tony,' said the hall-porter of the Warhaven Arms, leaning on his brush in the porch. '*You're* in good form. Got a winner or something?'

'Not much, old boy,' said Tony. He was suddenly electric with enthusiasm. 'It's the spring. The spring, I tell you. Yes. And seeing your old face. How *are* you, you old devil? How's Mrs Bob? Any new whippets?'

He followed Bob through the plate-glass doors, past the manager's office to a little, warm, stuffy pantry.

'Ar . . .' Bob became confidential. 'Needs worming, I tell you, she does. Not the missus. The new bitch. These dogs I been getting sent down from Hoxton, they're in a shocking state . . .'

The sun warmed the window. There was a strip of thread-bare carpet on the floor. There were several cases of beer and a worn iron beer-opener.

'The journey, Bob,' said Tony. He hoisted himself on to a wooden kitchen table and sat with his long, strong legs dangling. 'It's the journey, that's what it is.'

Bob's miserable grey face now seemed alight with pleasure. He propped his broom against a case of beer and reached into a cupboard for a bottle of gin.

'Not today, Bob,' said Tony. He lifted one hand, flat, and wagged it from side to side. 'Not today. I tell you, it's the journey puts those dogs back. Now, if you were to travel from Hoxton, tied up and whining in a guard's van, *you'd* know it, I can tell you. If you'd only let me run up there in the station wagon now, I'd fetch them back to your little place and they'd never be so pulled down. It's that guard's van.'

Tony's feet swung to and fro. He was genuinely delighted by Bob's company and fascinated by his whippets. He would have been astonished if anyone had suggested that he was working hard for his gin.

'Narsty dirty stinkin' places,' said Bob, grinning from ear to ear. He poured out two double gins, utterly disregarding Tony's hand and his apologetic manner. 'Don' be a fool, Tony,' he said, under one quirking eyebrow. 'You'll never go off the drink.'

A fly buzzed and whacked its nose against the window glass. The air in the pantry was cosy with spilt beer and old sherry.

'I will, you know, when I can't pay for it.'

Tony threw back his head and roared with laughter. He laughed at himself, and Bob's sad face and the two double gins and his own regrettable weakness of character.

Bob looked at him. He plucked his upper lip between finger and thumb and his whole face changed and crumpled as he watched him.

'You short, boy?' He pushed the gin violently towards Tony along the kitchen table. 'You drink that up.'

Tony looked up. Something darkened his eyes.

'Ye-es,' he said slowly. Then he smiled directly into Bob's face. 'I'm a bit short.' He picked up the gin in his hand. He swilled it round and it slopped in the glass. Bob turned his back.

'Five any good?' he said, fumbling at his waist. 'Get you more tonight if you like ...'

'Oh, I say ...' Tony began to wave the money away. Bob shook his head. He had unbuckled a heavy soldier's money-belt.

'No,' he said. 'You *take* it, Tony. It's awful for people like you to be short. 'Tisn't like *me* ...'

Tony looked at the five crumpled pound notes. They lay in the sun where Bob had put them. There was a little pool of beer beside them. He suddenly drank his gin.

'Go *on*,' said Bob. 'You *take* it.'

'Well ...' There was another pause of indecision. Then the money was on the table no longer. It had been tucked into Tony's pigskin wallet. 'Thanks, Bob,' said Tony, and laughed pleasantly. 'Of course,' he added slowly, 'money's only a symbol ...'

'Any time, Tony, any time.'

'*Now* we can have one on *me*.' Tony produced a pound with a caricature of rustling banknotes. Bob poured two more double gins. He cocked an eye anxiously at the door. He heard footsteps, he thought. He was right. Major Bognor's bogus head came sidling round the door. Bob hated his thick moustache and his eyeglass and his pompous trashy manner. Bob turned his back.

'Hullo-ullo-ullo,' said Major Reginald Bognor. 'Any gin going? Oh, it's *you* in here, Robinson. Might have guessed it, what?'

'Trapped by one of my own tenants,' said Tony, waving his drink. 'But you're in time to catch up on the round . . .'

Bob poured another gin, muttering to himself. The back of his neck plainly resented his money buying drinks for a swine like that Major. Why, the Major'd been in here yesterday on the old touch himself. *And* he didn't get it . . .

'Well,' said the Major and lifted his glass. 'Mother's had to go into the station for a parcel, so I escaped. Here's fun.' His eyeglass fell back against his little checked waistcoat. He drank the gin greedily. Bob hid his glass behind the beer. Later, he would sell that drink again to someone else. Or ('Have a drink, Bob?') he might accept it gratefully, over and over again through the morning, with a clear profit of two-and-fourpence every time. Certainly he would never touch it. He looked at Tony with little sad eyes. He thought it a ghastly thing that men like Tony should keep hotels for beasts like Major Bognor to live in. With his *mother*. Bob snorted and began to mop up the spilt beer with a dirty rag.

'Quite comfortable, I hope, in your new room?' said Tony kindly to Bognor. The gin had made its effect. He was increasingly the owner of a very successful, extremely well-run private hotel, *far* better than home, my dear, and (thank God) the proprietor is a gentleman. The Major showed discreet false teeth. His glass had rattled against them as he drank.

'Oh yes,' he said. 'Your wife calls it The Slot, I believe.' He screwed in his eyeglass and looked fixedly at the mark that the beer had made on the table. 'Mother says she has a *draught* in hers.' He laughed blandly, inviting Tony to sneer also at his mother's discomfort.

'Oh, dear!' Tony was genuinely distressed. 'And with her sciatica. I've got some felt. I'll fix it round the door.'

Bob gazed dreamily out of the window. The conversation (as he would have been the first to tell you) was none of his business. He suddenly remarked that Tony had better get cracking.

'Saw your missus come up them steps just now. Looked a bit on the rampage, too.'

Tony sprang up and finished his gin. Bob nipped the glass away and hid it behind his back. The Major stirred and muttered something about 'Women in our hour of ease, what?' Tony said, 'Thanks for everything, Bob.' Then they all straightened their backs and waited for the quick rattle of feet clattering over linoleum, muffled by rugs, coming nearer and nearer to Bob's little pantry.

CHAPTER TWO

Mrs Tony Robinson was not a shrew, as we might imagine from the guilty herding together of men at her approach. Indeed, although her looks and charm were under the treble strain of a tendency to anaemia, of living in Brunton and of running the Oranmore Private Hotel, she was a young woman with all the gaiety that comes from a proper enjoyment of life. She had married Tony, for example, quite gaily during the war, when she had been in the Ministry of Industrial Warfare and he had been a lieutenant-commander in the RNVR. In the parties that followed their betrothal and marriage she had led the rout, and had been (as Tony's bookmaker friends would have said) a 'thorough-going little sport'. She was small and untidy. Her natural pale good looks were often spoilt by messy hair round her cheekbones. Her shoes were often covered in dry mud. Her name was Celia. She was sensitive and tried extremely hard to be practical. She had a provincial degree in science. Before the war she had taught chemistry in a girls' public school for a term and a half. She was thirty-six and looked at her best in trousers.

All women, they tell us, are happy to be mothers. If this is a universal rule there is an exception to it, and this exception was Celia Robinson. She had never really been happy since the birth of April and May, their two twin daughters. These had been born a quarter before midnight and a quarter after midnight on April 30th and May 1st two years before.

During the seven months before this date, Tony had visited the saloon bars alone, and had returned home with many fine, unsatisfactory tips at six to four on. Since this date Celia's morning always began badly. She had no nurse. April and May were inclined to fling objects from their cots and bawl for love and companionship. They were indistinguishable, with very little hair. Tony alternately spoilt and slapped them, and they adored him. Celia brought them up with a reference-book in one hand, as though she were failing in a very difficult practical chemistry examination. Consequently they rather disliked her. She was terrified of *them*.

II

She had slammed the Oranmore gate behind her and hurried along Durbah Villas with the benevolent impulse of helping Tony with the shopping. Tony was so good and cheerful with the tradesmen. April and May had not been too frightful this morning. They had been quite quick over their morning toilet and Celia for once had an opportunity to snatch some fresh air before returning to the torture of luncheon.

Connie (who preferred to be called Chef) was difficult, to say the least of it. Celia was positive she drugged or something. Chef was a huge, powerfully built, pear-shaped female with close-cropped hair. She derived a mysterious social *cachet* from the fact that she had once owned a guest-house. It had gone bankrupt. She had arrived five weeks ago in answer to an advertisement. She had brought Mrs Thomson, her own kitchenmaid, with her and would use no other. She had a large, weak, obstinate face with heavily hooded cobra eyes. Sometimes she became rather drunk and sang that she would 'Tell the World She had a Pretty Talent for Loving'. Celia, when she still possessed her sense of humour, found this pathetic and rather funny. Lately, however, things had not seemed such a scream. She had begun to find Connie sinister.

As she hurried towards Twiggs the greengrocer's her mind was filled with Connie as she had been that morning – grim in a green brace and bib. Celia hoped that perhaps Connie would pull herself together over the sweet just for once, and do a little better than pour 'hundreds and thousands' over some mauve blancmange. Also it appeared that 'Tommy' (as Connie called her) was in One of Her Moods and had said that Chef could do her own veg. Celia enjoyed peeling potatoes and had suggested (smiling pleasantly) that *she* could do it, then. Apparently this was not the point. The point was some obscure private quarrel between Chef and Tommy. The veg had merely been the breaking-point. It had originated in the arrival of Mr Thomson (Tommy's husband) next weekend. Really, Chef and Tommy would have to go. She would tell Tony *again* to sack them. He hadn't done so last time, in spite of agreeing with her so enthusiastically. He had given them another fortnight's trial. Celia sometimes didn't understand Tony ...

She had now arrived at Twiggs the greengrocer's, on the corner of Station Road, opposite the Sussex and Provincial Bank. There were boxes outside the window with ready-boiled beetroots and other root vegetables in them. A large black-board was leaning under cover. It said:

REGISTER FOR ORANGES. THEY'RE IN

The sun came out. She saw Tony cross the road, recover his good humour, smile and greet Bob, the hall-porter. Celia's mouth, fixed cruelly in contemplation of Chef and Tommy, relaxed into happiness. What a handsome creature Tony was!

'Darling Tony,' she said, completely happy. 'Yes. I'll have to winkle him out of there.'

She turned into Twiggs. He probably hadn't even *started* to do the shopping. Mr Twiggs came towards her rubbing his hands on his neat, fawn cotton overall, delicately licking his lips under his thin moustache. What could he have been eating?

'Good morning, Mr Twiggs,' said Celia. Her manner was very slightly patronizing, her tone very slightly over-refined. Mr Twiggs began to bristle very slightly. (Who was she to give herself airs? Now *him* he didn't mind ...) 'Has Commander Robinson been in here yet?' said Celia.

Mr Twiggs leant on a crate of oranges and said, well, yes and no, in a manner of speaking.

'I mean,' Celia began again, more apologetically, 'has he given you the *order* yet? – because we've two rather important guests arriving tonight and we're down to our last two pounds of potatoes. In fact we need—'

Mr Twiggs went very slowly to the till. He picked up a bill from a spike and stared at it. Then, rubbing it slowly across the seat of his pants, he moved back to Celia and spread it among the oranges. He said he hated to disoblige a lady, see, but that

17

no more goods could be supplied to the Oranmore Hotel until this here little account between him and the *Commander* (the sneer in Mr Twiggs' voice on the word 'Commander' was most unpleasant) had been squared up, see? Little matter of twenty pound. He hated to disoblige a lady.

Celia took this news like a blow in the face. She stared a long time at Mr Twiggs, not understanding him. She opened her mouth. Speech failed her. She put out a hand for the bill and husked. No words came. Eventually, half strangled, she thanked Mr Twiggs. She said, gasping, that the account would be settled that night. Mr Twiggs smiled. It was the little, cold, disbelieving smile of someone who has taken a lady down a peg.

'Thank you, madam,' he said. He turned and walked to the back of the shop.

Then Celia followed Tony into the Warhaven Arms.

III

Mrs Eithne Bognor, permanent winter resident of the Oranmore Hotel, and Major Reginald Bognor's mother, came out of the parcels-office of the station. She had been 'meeting' a small parcel of minced horse-meat for her cat. She walked daintily down Station Road towards the sea. She was worrying, as she always did, about her son Reginald. What would happen to him when she was gone? If *only* she was able to leave him the money on trust . . .

Mrs Bognor was an old lady with snow-white hair and snapping black eyes. She leant rather heavily on an ebony stick. She was muffled in sables against the sea wind. She was seventy-nine. She had often been called the Last of the English Gentlewomen. Knowing this, she kept her back straight and flat and her fine, high-arched nose proudly raised. The air came in from the sea like champagne.

The parcel of minced horse-meat was tucked out of sight in her bag. She really did not care to be seen carrying a parcel. Her husband, the late Engineer Rear Admiral Bognor, had often said it was a practice contrary to Good Order and Naval Discipline. She believed him. It was a marvellously fine morning for February.

She turned in at the door of the Sussex and Provincial Bank, much preoccupied by thoughts of Reginald. He was so *very deeply* in love, poor boy, with this actress. But what a delight for him it was that she was at last consenting to marry him! Reggie was always at his best when married. Or so he said. It was sad that this Miss Birdseye was an actress, but there ... No wonder Reggie was always so 'pushed for cash', as he called it in his witty way. And writing her those interminable letters. Why, he must spend a small fortune in stamps alone ...

And so, preoccupied, Mrs Bognor wrote out her cheque to 'self' and signed it and tucked away her money beside the minced horse-meat. She was so preoccupied that she did not notice the astonishment of the teller as he pushed two hundred one-pound banknotes across the mahogany counter. Nor did she observe him calling to Mr Cathcart to come from his inner office, and she did not know that they watched her back as she left the bank. She walked very upright, as usual. The bright fickle sunlight swallowed her as she paced away down Station Road.

'Well, I'm damned!' said Cathcart, as her stick tapped past

his window. 'Two hundred, eh? Wonder what the sweet hell she wants with 'em.'

IV

Connie, the Chef, sat on one side of an enormous wooden table in the kitchen. Her muscular forearms were propped upon it. Every now and then her head sank on a level with the table and she gave a gigantic yawn. Opposite her sat Tommy, the kitchenmaid. The kitchen was well below street level. Above their heads, outside the window, the green lawns and the rockery sloped away. At least, however, they were not distressed (as guests were distressed when dining in the front of the house on the same level) by the feet and legs of people passing and re-passing the windows. Connie and Tommy were quite absorbed in their own rather shabby little affairs. There was nothing inside the room to relieve the monotony as they grew steadily upon each other's nerves.

'Don't know what you see in him, Tom, I'm sure,' said Connie. She referred to the visit, that weekend, of Mr Thomson, Mrs Thomson's no-good husband. 'I'd give him the old go-by desert, if I were you.'

Tommy retorted that the old go-by desert didn't pay a percentage. Connie sighed. She turned a teacup in her hands.

'Please yourself, dear,' she said. She put her chin on her hand. 'Wish I could tell the cup. I must say, when we set out on the old Cook's tour like this, I never thought we'd end up in a *grave*. I feel like a suicide. How much is it Tony owes us, dear?' The sun, which had been shining on the lawn, went in behind a cloud. The kitchen was indeed drain-like, tomb-like, suicide-inducing.

'Two weeks,' said Tommy laconically. ''Bout time you cleaned out that old gas oven if you want to put your head in it.'

Connie clicked her tongue. 'That's you,' she said. 'Cruel.'

Tommy spoke again rapidly.

'Except what *you* lost with him betting yesterday,' Tommy went on furiously. 'You old fool! Why can't you stop doing things like that? You're old enough, heaven knows. And there's no need for you to put any money on for me, thanks very much. *I* know how much you know about horses all right . . .'

Connie put her head flat on the table.

'Nag, nag, nag,' she said. 'Nothing but dirty, rotten, filthy—'

Tommy left her chair, came round the table and kicked her hard on the shin.

'You stop calling names, Connie Watson,' cried Mrs Thomson harshly, 'or I won't do your veg.'

Connie's small piggy eyes filled slowly with tears.

'Dirty, rotten . . .' she went on. Her underlip wambled slightly.

'All right, all right.' Tommy's voice was still rough, but it was more friendly. 'Dry up. So you've come down in the world since you an' your Glory of a partner ran Wortleberry Down together. So what?' Her tone suddenly changed again. She glanced furtively towards the window. 'Know what? I got another of His Highness's letters today.'

Connie raised her head, but her eyes still lacked lustre.

'Who to? Where from?' she said.

The tears went on running sorrowfully down Connie's face. They were rain on an unheeding building, the tide coming in over the flats, the wash of a steamer going to be broken up . . .

'Not to Miss Birdseye this time,' said Tommy triumphantly. 'Imagine. That old Major, with his glass eye, is two-timing.'

'No!'

Life returned to Connie Watson. Her last tears fell from her like spray. She reached across the table. Her hand was vast and white, like a mandrake root.

'Let's have a look-see,' she said. 'Come on. Let's have a decko.'

Mrs Thomson looked around her furtively. Then she drew a letter, creaking, from her bosom. It emerged from a smart print overall.

'Classy paper,' she said angrily. 'Carlton Club indeed. H'm – smells of lavender water, don't it?'

She spread the letter on the table and read it slowly aloud, pausing wherever she pleased. She disregarded everything but her own bronchial convenience.

'My dearest little girl – my own Rosie-Posie,

'Only be patient and I will square this thing out. I must marry her (and she is rather a poppet, really), you know that, for the credit we should have, to say nothing of the sum I am sure she will settle on me.

'After all Clara made me an allowance 400 p.a. when I was married to her, so I should say a successful actress . . .'

'I say,' Connie looked up, breathing heavily. 'Livin' off women. I say! Filthy brute! That's a bit thick . . .'

'Think so?' said Tommy idly. 'Men are ever so expensive. And I ought to know, too . . .'

'Silly bitch,' said Connie, without expression. She lifted her terrifying head and blinked her eyes. 'Got comp'ny,' she said, and jerked her head towards the door. She could hear feet coming down the stairs. 'Not fit for comp'ny,' she added. Her kitchen chair scraped back across the floor. 'Goin' to take a Benzy,' she concluded.

And she lurched out of the room, banged her hip on the latch as she went, and tore quite a large piece out of her dungarees. For five days she remained quite unaware of this.

CHAPTER THREE

Miss Miriam Birdseye, the famous actress, twirled her small black motor-car round the mews at the back of Baker Street, where it had been garaged all night. It darted in and out of the dust-bins, like an exotic insect. The occasional sun blazed for a moment on its sleek, blunt nose and produced squirts of reflected light from the windscreen. Through the roof (and it gave the impression that Miriam had opened it for this reason) protruded Miriam's steep black hat and its scarlet feather. One of her associates had asked her, the day before, if she could get China on that aerial. Coiled beside her in the front of the car was a very beautiful young man with golden hair.

The motor-car came out daintily into Baker Street and flirted with the traffic at Marble Arch and Hyde Park Corner. Miriam was an excellent driver. She was on her way to pick up Frederick Pyke, the poet, outside the Grosvenor Hotel. They were going away together to write a play. It was to be a play in verse, and based on one of the more obscure of Zola's novels. She told the young man with golden hair about it as they cavorted through the Park. She would set *him* down when she picked up Pyke, she said. The young man looked cross.

Miriam made a face at herself in the windscreen. She was not good-looking by the usual standards. Her attraction (which no one denied) lay in an infinite capacity for enjoyment and a naive pleasure in her own existence. These moods alternated alarmingly with moods of depression when she believed that the end of the world would be any minute now. Miriam was more than a popular actress. She was loved by all her friends to the point of idolatry. Also, her mind was so good and so original, and her effect on the impressionable young (and particularly young men) so immediate and inspiring, that she had often been described as the greatest influence in London. She had already inspired the young man with golden hair to write a play for her. Playing in it she had made a fortune for herself and a great many other people. Added to all of which, she was a perfect darling. The play had been running for a year, but Miriam was already sick of it. This was to be her first forty-eight hours away from the theatre in six months.

II

Frederick Pyke, the poet, stood outside the Grosvenor with his suitcase at his feet. He pouted with annoyance as he saw the motor approaching, with Miriam's feather through the roof, looking like an antenna. She had kept him waiting for ten minutes, and that blond boy who wrote *I Heard a Vampire Sing* was sitting beside her. It was too bad. Pyke had been in love with Miriam for five years.

The car stopped and Pyke's heavy face broke up into amiability. The golden young man (briefly introduced by Miss Birdseye as 'a ne'er-do-weel') bowed like a clasp knife and said

25

he was terribly impressed to meet Mr Pyke, because he had always admired *Rouge on Parnassus* more than absolutely *anything*. Then he idled off towards the railway station, looking like Apollo, and Pyke put his suitcase in the back of the car.

'Where did you say we were going, my dear?' he said. The little car creaked slightly as he sat down. He was a big man. He stammered slightly. He arranged his legs fretfully. 'Th-this motor of yours,' he said, returning to his petulance, 'is more like a g-gramophone. A p-portable gramophone,' he added, scowling.

Miriam tapped him lightly on the knee with a long and beautiful hand, where an opal ring flashed and several rubies caught the light. She looked down for a second to admire it. Then she continued to concentrate on the traffic on Battersea Bridge.

'Brunton,' she said. 'Brunton-on-Sea. Of course, I *would* drive you about in a Rolls,' she added suddenly. 'If you would buy me one.'

Pyke's laugh was an attractive bass-baritone. It was intended for a barrister's rather than a poet's. Poets (or so we are taught) sing and laugh in a reedy tenor. But Pyke had a stammer and so he had left the bar after two years' misery.

'Brunton,' he repeated slowly. 'For God's sake, why Brunton?'

Miss Birdseye frowned.

'There is a man there,' she said, 'who wants to marry me.'

III

Their journey, with pauses for drinks at Hayward's Heath, East Grinstead and Brunton (the old and beautiful Regency village of which Brunton-on-Sea was a hideous offspring), was unscarred by distress or scenes of jealousy. Pyke drank dry martinis and laughed a lot, and Miriam (with evident enjoyment) ordered (and drank) several glasses of milk.

'Why aren't we st-staying here, dear?' said Pyke, plaintively looking around him at the Cap and Bells, Wardown. 'It looks comfortable. I agree that we have to write the bloody play *s-somewhere* – but why not here? It's quiet, too. And I like the garden. And the rain-water butt. I probably won't be able to write a s-single *line* at Brunton-on-Sea for the howling ...' He paused and stuttered richly, 'Of the p-p-pierrots ...'

'Pierrots are very inspiring,' said Miss Birdseye severely. She looked out at the garden where the sun shone suddenly on Christmas roses. 'I was madly in love with a pierrot once.'

Pyke put his glass on the table and sighed.

'You have been madly in love with everyone,' he said sadly.

'Oh no.' Miriam was quite sure about it. 'I have never been in love with Clement Attlee.'

IV

Twenty minutes later Frederick Pyke looked up at the Edwardian Gothic gables of the Oranmore Private Hotel and groaned.

'Worse than I thought,' he said. 'Worse than I could have imagined. It is the most d-depraved d-design I have ever seen. And that p-pattern of oyster shells spelling out the name m-merely increases the h-horror. Worse than the holiday camp you made me stay in when you wanted me to re-write *Ghost Stories of an Antiquary* for you as a musical comedy. Far worse.' A child's face appeared at an upper window and Pyke shut his eyes. 'Your boy friend lives here, you say?' he went on, opening them again.

'He is not my boy friend,' said Miriam. 'He thinks he is going to marry me, which is not the same thing. He writes to me every day. Sweet, isn't it?'

The grey sea could be seen between the houses on their right moving sullenly. Pyke scowled.

'*Are* you going to marry him?' he said.

'How should I know, dear?' said Miriam lightly. 'Now, don't just *sit* there, Pyke. Take up your suitcase and see if you can't find someone – and get us rooms.'

V

Pyke came back in a minute or two and said as far as he could see there was absolutely *no one* in the hotel, but he could hear voices in the kitchen underfoot. He pointed downwards, towards the pavement. Miriam climbed out of the motor-car. Her hat miraculously remained on her head as the wind whipped at it from the sea. The feather alternately bent itself double and shot back into place.

'Like clockwork,' said Pyke, watching it. 'You are extraordinary, Miriam.'

'Aren't I?' said Miriam. She went happily up the steps of the Oranmore Hotel. 'Let's find the kitchen. I'm really very fond of kitchens . . .'

Pyke followed with the suitcases, grumbling about the cold. Ahead of him Miriam disappeared down the stairs to the basement.

VI

Tony Robinson, his shoulders hunched to his ears with annoyance, marched beside Celia. The wind, freshening every minute, blew his grey flannel trousers against the front of his legs and whipped his thick hair up in a crest on the top of his head. Celia, trotting beside him, with her hair blown all over her face like a Yorkshire terrier, said that if the wind kept up the sun would stay out. She plunged her hands in her pockets and managed to look like a defiant small boy.

'Glad you think so,' said Tony. There was an unpleasant silence between them. Then Tony suddenly stopped and faced her. 'What the hell do you mean,' he began furiously, 'by bursting into the Warhaven Arms, snatching me out like that, in front of Bob and the Major? What's the priority? Mrs Bognor dead or something?'

Tony was very angry indeed. All his fury against old Cathcart added to his irritation with Celia. His usual carefully modulated voice began to crack and break. Celia stopped walking too, and held her ground. She set her round chin firmly and one foot tapped on the pavement as she replied.

'No, Mrs Bognor's not dead, you plastered idiot,' she said explosively. 'She's right behind us. It's far more serious than that. Why the hell didn't you tell me that we owed Twiggs twenty pounds? You've made an absolute pot mess of our account there.'

They were both breathing heavily. Their eyes seemed to beat against each other. Their eyes were hard and bright and full of anger quite out of proportion to the matter between them. Tony plunged his two fists in his jacket pockets and turned slowly round.

'You think of nothing but money,' he said as he did so. 'It's a thoroughly middle-class way to behave.' Then his whole voice changed. 'Good *morning*, Mrs Bognor,' he said charmingly. There was no longer any anger in his eyes. They were as soft and welcoming as doves.

Nevertheless, something made Mrs Bognor stand still, staring from one to the other. She seemed abnormally surprised. And then, oddly enough, her bag slid from her hand and fell heavily to the pavement. It was a big, black, plastic bag, and as it hit the ground it burst open and scattered its contents at Tony's feet. There was the parcel of minced cat's meat, and a lipstick in a golden case, and a cheque-book payable on the Sussex and Provincial Bank, Ltd, and finally there fell the two hundred one-pound notes that Mrs Bognor had withdrawn that morning, done up in a white paper binder.

Tony remained upright, staring down at the money as though he had been fixed by an electric shock. Celia was already crouched on her hands and knees picking everything up.

'Thank you, my dears, thank you,' said Mrs Bognor. 'How very careless of me!'

CHAPTER FOUR

When Tony went on he pranced with anger. He went towards the middle of Brunton. Celia went with him. She had to trot to keep up.

'Are you going to the butcher's?' she said, panting. 'Do we owe money there, too? Tony, do *say* something. You *can't* go on like this.'

Tony, whose life, ever since he had invested it in the Oranmore Hotel, had become a dream world of sycophantic shopkeepers and satisfied clients who were so *glad* that Mr Robinson was a gentleman, stopped and stared down at his wife. He resented this interruption in his dream. His eyebrows were drawn together in a thick line. Under them his eyes blazed with rage. He did not show any guilt. He was bitterly angry with Celia. How dare she intrude on him like this? She was a thoroughly tiresome woman and she looked very untidy indeed. Not at all the thing for a successful hotel-keeper.

'Do shut up!' he said explosively. 'Whining on like that. You give me the sick, you do really. Always have. Just like your mother. Whine, whine, whine. *I* can manage these people. *I* never have any trouble with the shopkeepers. It's you they

31

don't like. You're rude to them, that's what. After all, they're human beings . . .'

His disconnected, badly expressed resentment poured over her. Things he had disliked (ever since he had married her) seemed to hang in the air between them like a cloud of angry, swarming gnats.

Celia was not frightened. She was surprised. Why had he married her? she wondered vaguely, aware of a piece of hair that strayed across her face and tickled her nose. Her unspoken thoughts were answered, uncannily, in Tony's next verbal attack. It was so violent that she stepped backwards, as though she had been struck across the face.

'I didn't marry you to have a blasted stuck-up prig running round after me fussing about my overdraft. I thought you were a jolly little kid, that's what I thought. Not a pocket edition of your *mother*.'

He walked on again furiously, while Celia stood uncertainly, wondering whether to follow him or not. He turned into Bodger's the butcher's. He wagged his hips with rage. Celia did not think how foolish he looked. She was frightened. She stood on the corner of Station Road and Arnadale Road, where Bodger lurked behind his cool blue and white tiles and a strange, meaningless china cow, and thought carefully about money. 'I mustn't panic,' she said.

She had £68 in the Post Office savings. No, £63, because Tony had taken £5 to buy her that birthday present – those lizard courts that hadn't fitted. If necessary, all *that* could go. Tony could have the whole lot if only he wouldn't be so angry with her. He sounded as though he didn't love her a *bit*. And what is more, as though he had never loved her.

If only he wasn't so restless. If only he didn't have to drink *quite* so much to show what an awfully good chap he was. They mightn't spend quite so much. Every guest that arrived Tony snatched. He escorted them down the road to the blasted Warhaven Arms and there they'd stay, hour after hour, shut away in Bob's stuffy little cubby-hole, talking about nothing, running away with pounds and pounds. It wasn't even as if they had any decent intellectual conversation like she used to have with the girls in the Poly that time they went to Paris. About the ballet and Moira Shearer and that ... It was just racing, racing, racing and dogs, dogs, dogs until Celia could scream. She bit her lip. She could almost *hear* the scream.

She had now stood in Arnadale Road for so long that she was most conspicuous. Several passers-by looked at her curiously. A child in a red wool hat ran its Kiddycar into her leg. Celia turned and began to walk sadly back to the hotel. She decided she didn't understand Tony at all.

II

Tony leant confidentially against the little glass cage where old Mrs Bodger made up the accounts. 'Thank God,' thought Tony, 'that Charlie Bodger's not here. *He* wouldn't let me get away with it.'

Mrs Bodger looked up from her ledger and saw Tony's candid sunburnt face laughing at her beyond the glass. Her heart sprang up. Of course, the Oranmore. That young devil Robinson. Still, he was a gay spark. Knew a good old piece when he saw it. Mrs Bodger preened herself and supported her fine bust on the till.

'How's my best girl?' said Tony.

'Oh, get along with you, do,' said Mrs Bodger. She was very pleased.

'You get better-looking and younger every day,' said Tony. He put his marketing-bag on the floor at his feet.

'Oo, you are awful. You say that to every woman in Brunton,' said Mrs Bodger, like a vast character study from Dickens. She laced her plump fingers together and leant further forward on the till.

'I don't, you know.' Tony's voice had acquired a subtle shading of Cockney, so that Mrs Bodger shouldn't consider he was giving himself airs. 'Have you heard the one about the old man who married a young wife?' Tony's head came through the little window and he told the story, enjoying himself very much indeed. He writhed with his long legs and every now and then did a quick double shuffle among the sawdust. The shop lay cool around him; the dissected sheep, the evil pieces of kidney, the tins of corned beef like bright tin battlements, made a smooth background for him. 'And she's going to have a baby, too ...' It was the triumphant pay-off line. He straightened his back and laughed gaily. Mrs Bodger's heavy old walrus's head tilted backwards as she too shouted with joy. She wheezed. She slowly returned to normal, but her face was an awful glazed purple ten minutes later when she placed his meat in his shopping-bag. He went away blowing her a kiss. Then Mrs Bodger remembered.

Charlie had said not to give that shyster another quid's worth without we get the account paid. Mrs Bodger went into her little glass cage and pulled the Oranmore account out of the drawer of her desk. Thirty-five quid. My God! Maybe Charlie had something after all. She shrugged her fat old shoulders and slowly added 'Sirloin, best cut, seven shillings and sixpence' to the list. Then she scowled round her cage, looking like an angry old goldfish in an aquarium.

'I don't care,' she said. 'Tony's a gen'man. He'll pay – eventual.'

III

Tony went on, his dream restored. He swung his shopping-basket and whistled one of his favourite tunes. He didn't know its name, but it was 'Musetta's Waltz Song' from *Bohème*. He saw himself in the dark-green-painted window of the wine shipper's on the next corner and straightened his shoulders. Fine figure of a man. Who had said that? He wondered if Mrs Bodger thought so. Yes, he was almost sure she did.

Vegetables. He'd have to get vegetables *somewhere*. Blast Twiggs – cutting up rough about the bill. Still, there were at least twenty greengrocers' shops in the town. Just a question of taking a butcher's hook and having a chat. To convince someone who wanted to supply a decent quantity of fresh greens to the hotel every day that it would be a privilege to supply the Oranmore. Should be like falling off a log. What was this little place on the corner? Stanley Wool? Stanley Wool would do.

IV

'Good morning!' The voice behind the screens at the back of the shop was sour and masculine and efficient.

'Mr Wool?' Tony raised his voice, sniffing the strong earthy smell of potatoes, the pleasant stench of onions, the dark scent of the cabbages. Tony loved shops.

'At your service.' The voice was still sour and suspicious.

Stanley Wool appeared, moving between his wooden boxes and the difficult display trays of turnips and carrots and swedes. He was a thin, scraggy little man with a leaping Adam's apple and a string tie.

'Nice shop you have,' said Tony cheerfully. 'Corner site. Clever'f you to buy it.'

Outside, the February sun winked and fled, pursued by swift clouds.

'Think so?'

Wool scowled. Tony realized his manner had been patronizing.

'Oh, 's nothing. Just that I have a corner site myself. The Oranmore Hotel.' Tony jerked his head sideways, as man to man. 'Just moved. My wife and I hope to get cracking soon. Make it a real nice place. Home from home. *You* know.'

Mr Wool evidently knew. He relaxed a little. He rubbed his hands down his shirt.

'Well ...' He spoke slowly, lugubriously. 'Suppose business must look up. Couldn' be worse.'

'Got to get worse before it'll get better.'

Tony stared round him at the bottles of brown malt vinegar, the salad cream and tins of diced beetroot, the old, old shabby tins of peas.

'Never get well if you pick it,' said Wool suddenly.

Tony stared at him. They both laughed.

'So *you* were in the Service, too ...'

'Certainly *was*.' Stanley Wool now stood up very straight indeed. 'Torpedo gunner's mate, First Class. Had me ship sunk under me. *Duke o' York*. Chatham man myself.'

'Ah!' said Tony. 'Devonport.'

From this point their conversation became so hopelessly technical, and involved so many proper names of ships and admirals, that it would be idle to record it. After twenty minutes' steady gossiping, Tony left the shop. His bag bulged with greengroceries. His ego was in splendid shape. It was only when he was half-way along Durbah Villas, walking very straight and fast, pulled slightly over to the right by the weight of his bag, that he recollected his £142 overdraft.

'Oh, the hell with it!' said Tony Robinson. 'Something will show up. It always does.'

CHAPTER FIVE

Mrs Ada Greeb, upright in the corner of an empty first-class Pullman car (non-smoker), peered out of the window with cold, sharp eyes. Sussex, in all its grey-green February horror, swam past the windows, appearing to vibrate a little as the carriage shook on the points and other irregularities in the line. Ada Greeb was over seventy. She was a thin, biting Yorkshirewoman who would stand no nonsense from anyone but her children. Her youngest daughter, from whom she had stood more nonsense than any of the others, was Celia Robinson. We have already met her.

Celia, Mrs Greeb now remembered, had always been wilful. As a child she had thrown expensive toys out of her pram. As an adolescent she had had a terrible craze for a girl called Noni Winterton. As a young woman she had (against fierce opposition) married Tony Robinson. Mrs Greeb sniffed and brought the corner of a well-laundered handkerchief to her eyes. Tony was obviously a rotter. On first acquaintance he had seemed dull. On second acquaintance (and this had been at Celia's wedding), through Mrs Greeb's tears, he had seemed to be drunk. On third acquaintance he had borrowed five pounds from Mrs Greeb and had bought her a drink with it.

Mrs Greeb shook her head a little from side to side. She was suffering from that unnatural internal misery that tells a mother her offspring is up to no good. She considered everything that she knew of Tony. He was a clergyman's son, and *that* was bad. In Harrogate (where Mrs Greeb had lived for a great many years in a small by-pass house called 'Flagstones') they took no account of clergymen, even. Clergymen's sons were obvious monsters of vice. Mrs Greeb and her friends, Mrs Goldberg and Mrs Proot, had only to read the novels that they had from Boots' library to know what was what about clergymen's sons. Moreover, he had been in the RNVR. Mrs Greeb knew what she thought of *that*. Neither gentlemen *nor* sailors. Why, Mrs Greeb came of seafaring stock herself and her grandfather had sailed madly backwards and forwards to Australia with clipper ships stuffed with tea. Mrs Greeb was very proud of him. A picture hung above her fireplace in Harrogate that showed the *Dawn* hull down from Australia, dipping through the tropics, with every stitch of canvas shown ...

The Pullman car attendant appeared in the doorway of the carriage. He pointed out that Brunton would be the next stop. Madam had best look sharp, too, else she might get carried on.

Mrs Greeb nodded and the young man went away. His white coat was stained under the arms. Mrs Greeb disliked squalor, so she clicked her tongue. The train ran into Brunton station very fast indeed and stopped, jiggling a little, opposite a lot of milk-cans and a folded mail-cart done up in brown paper. The legend 'Brunton' was everywhere: on seats, on lamps, on walls. Mrs Greeb picked up her small, zipping shopping-bag. It was slightly open and showed some grey, snarled knitting. She got stiffly down on to the platform.

She was, everyone had always agreed, a wonderful woman for her age.

II

Miriam Birdseye sat down at the kitchen table in the Oranmore Hotel. She said yes, she would have a nice cup of tea. Tommy's jaw dropped open and she looked at Miriam as though she were an apparition. Miriam stared brightly round her. She was in excellent form. She held her hand over the lip of her cup and said, 'Chib, chib,' when Tommy tried to give her more sugar. This made Tommy's jaw drop even farther open.

Miriam stretched in her chair and lifted her elegant feet on to another that stood beside her. She smiled at Pyke. Pyke was nervous. He had put his soft black hat on the floor and now took off his gloves, finger by finger, with great care. He threw the gloves into the hat and cleared his throat.

'Y-you have a n-nice little place here, haven't you?' he said, turning to Tommy, who scowled at him. 'C-cosy,' he added desperately.

Connie came back into the kitchen and stood silently by the door. She too was obviously transfixed by Miriam.

'Glad you think so,' said Tommy expressionlessly. 'We think it's a tomb, don' we, Con?'

'Hello,' said Miriam, looking idly at Con. Con slouched into a chair.

'It'll take a minute or two for me Benzy to work,' she said, without apology. She rested her head on her two mottled fists. 'Better comp'ny then. Pooh! I smell of dishwater.'

'Oh, good,' said Miriam. She waved at Pyke with an

introductory gesture. 'This is Fred Pyke,' she said. 'He is a poet.' There was a pause while Connie groaned unintelligibly and Tommy gasped. 'A *minor* poet,' added Miriam hastily. 'He is here to act as my mother.'

Tommy's eyes opened wider and wider. She was uncertain whether to laugh or not, and indeed, Miriam often had this effect on her audience. Tommy settled her bosom in its flowered overall covering and looked under her eyelashes at Pyke. Pyke lowered his eyes. Really, he thought, Miriam—

Connie suddenly rubbed her two fists briskly in her eyes and snapped upright, quivering with synthetic health.

'Told you so!' she said. 'Now I'm fit to speak up. *Who* are you? Pyke, you said? What are you both doing here?'

Outside, the sun shone on the green banks of the garden. It did not look warm. Inside the kitchen there was a great gas-cooker with several gas jets blazing. It was as warm as anything.

'Yes,' said Tommy, 'and if you're visitors, why did you come into the kitchen? Eh? Tony will scalp us when he hears. Thinks he's the only one allowed in the kitchen.'

'Too right,' said Connie sadly. 'Too right to be good.'

She leered and did an odd little shuffle with her feet.

'First of all,' said Miriam coldly, 'who is Tony?'

Under the window there was a table where fifteen little mauve bowls of blancmange, covered entirely with 'hundreds and thousands', suggested the sweet for luncheon.

'He owns the joint,' said Tommy vulgarly, 'for what it's worth.'

'And it ain't no sirloin, he-he!' cried Connie excitedly. The Benzedrine had worked. Her eyes were now wild and gay and not very sane. She flashed them round the kitchen. Miriam looked interested.

'Hotel not doing well?' suggested Pyke suddenly. His deep pleasant voice was a relief, and Miriam looked at him gratefully. 'Not even for Feb?' suggested Miriam.

'Oh, I dunno,' said Tommy, in her usual nasal Cockney whine. Her eyes were still on Pyke. Depression had settled on his face like a heavy plaster mask. 'Tony has *some* regulars. Bogus and his mum, for example.'

'Bogus?' said Pyke, with interest.

'Bognor,' explained Connie. '*She's* well off even if *he* isn't.'

'How d'you know Mrs Bognor's well off?' Miriam's voice was too silky and too caressing.

Several pots filled with bubbling potatoes boiled over. The water hissed on the gas jets and nearly put them out.

'All right, then,' said Connie. 'But she drew two hundred smackers out of the bank this morning. That's what I call well off.'

She swung back on one leg of her chair and neatly turned down the gas with one toe. She was wearing intellectual's sandals. The hissing stopped.

'Oo, Connie, she *never*!' Tommy was incredulous.

'She did *so*!' Connie swung back again to the table.

'How d'you know, then?' Tommy's voice was shrill.

'Yes.' Miriam was interested. 'How do you know?'

'Never you mind,' said Connie. She stood up and padded towards a large chromium machine that stood against the wall. 'This is what we keep your dinners hot in,' she remarked, 'after they're cooked. I think I've seen *you*' – she jerked a thumb at Miriam – 'before.'

'Oh no, darling,' said Miriam lightly. 'Not me. Two other ladies.'

'No,' said Connie. '*You.*'

She opened the vast chromium soup-holder and took out a battered magazine. It was called *Forces' Fluff* and had a large picture of a gentleman film star on the cover. Connie came back to the table, folding the magazine back as she did so.

'That's right,' she said, and slammed it down, face upwards on the table. Sure enough, Miriam's face peered up at them through a framework of hearts. It was a Valentine's Day number and Miriam had been billed as the 'Valentine of the Blue Network'.

III

Tony walked into the kitchen and slammed down his shopping-bag on the table. The faint thud as it arrived there, the clink of cups and saucers as the table shook, made no impression on Connie or Tommy. They sat, morosely gazing at the ceiling (Connie) or glumly staring at the floor (Tommy). Miriam flashed a bright smile at Tony, but only Pyke sprang guiltily to his feet and sent his chair crashing back behind him. He discerned, vaguely, that Tony Robinson had authority.

'F-forgive me,' said Pyke. His rich, damask stutter was suddenly in evidence again. 'We m-may be intruders. We h-hoped to stay in your h-hotel.'

To his credit Tony was not perturbed. He smiled broadly round the room.

'Quite,' he said. 'Quite. It looks as if we may have fun this weekend after all.' He went over to the window and looked

43

sadly at the mauve dishes of blancmange. 'Do you know what,' he went on. 'A taxi drew up just now, outside. Just as I was coming downstairs. Know who it was?'

'Yes,' said Connie. She seemed to have an infernal capacity for the inner knowledge of other people. She was an uncomfortable companion. 'Your mother-in-law. Your wife had a telegram from her this morning.'

There was a pause while Tony held himself up by the table and turned rather white.

'Seemingly,' said Connie, 'Mrs Greeb isn't satisfied with *how* the hotel runs. Seemingly, she's coming to see for herself how you and Celia get *on* . . .'

Tony's hands fell listlessly by his sides.

'Old *busybody*,' said Tommy suddenly. But whether she meant Connie or Mrs Greeb it was hard to tell.

Tony sat down on one of the kitchen chairs.

'This,' he said slowly, 'is too much. My mother-in-law. I shall now get stinking. And you, sir,' he turned to Pyke, 'and you, madam,' he turned to Miriam, 'will accompany me. The lunch here is never good.' He stood up and spoke harshly. 'Tommy,' he said, 'you must tell Mrs Robinson that I and—'

'Mr Pyke and Miss Birdseye,' said Connie with bright, twinkling eyes.

'Yes. Will not be in to lunch until *very much later.*'

Compelled by Tony's rather large, prominent blue eyes, Miriam rose slowly to her feet. And wherever Miriam went, Pyke sublimely followed. They went out of the kitchen and Tony stood on one side to allow them to pass. He propelled them gently forward with little pats from his large soft hands and gentle, friendly pressure on their shoulder blades.

'Better turn to the right,' he said. 'We'd best leave by the side door. My mum-in-law won't want to see *me*.'

IV

The open air might be achieved from the basement of the Oranmore Private Hotel by either of two staircases. One (used by the tradesmen and kitchen staff) was directly inside the front door. The other (supposedly used by guests) gave directly into the dining-room. The dining-room was a fine big basement room. It was a little dark, perhaps, but one couldn't have everything.

Tony led the way through the dining-room, waving at four pathetic little red-painted iron tables arranged under the front window. They had white tablecloths and red iron chairs to match them.

'For the guests,' he said.

'But *we* are guests,' said Pyke plaintively. Pyke was, perhaps, a little greedy. He did not care to think that he would not be allowed his luncheon until very much later.

'Hush, Pyke!' said Miriam, slapping at him. 'No one who sits in the kitchen is a guest.'

Tony Robinson went ahead of them up the stairs. They passed a bicycle, a very disagreeable go-cart with accommodation for two great strapping twins, and a bag of assorted golf-clubs. Beyond all this was a door and the street.

'What sort of place would you like to drink in?' said Tony suddenly. He stood on the top step. He looked very handsome. The sea wind blew his hair into its cockatoo's crest and his discreet RNVR tie burst from its moorings and flapped briskly, like the pennant of a yacht.

'The nearest,' said Miriam amiably, and tucked her arm warmly through Tony's. 'Not,' she added as an afterthought, 'that I drink. Haven't for years.'

'Ah . . .' Tony smiled down at her. The wind seemed cold to him. He was always grateful for human contacts.

'And do you think,' went on Miriam carefully, 'that you will be able to tell me any gossip about poor Reggie? Reggie Bognor?'

'I should think so,' said Tony lightly. 'He's lived at the Oranmore for six months. One of those mother's darlings. Pathetic to be a mother's darling at the age of fifty.'

'Oh, he's *not* fifty!' Miriam was indignant.

'We are all as old as we feel,' Tony said. 'And Bognor obviously feels at least fifty. He's sweet to all the old ladies, moustache and all.'

Miriam stiffened. She seemed incredulous. They were going towards the sea. It was slowly changing to a turbulent and disconcerting green.

'D'you m-mean the old l-ladies' moustaches?' said Pyke.

'Certainly not,' snapped Tony. 'Reggie Bognor's.'

'It is a fine moustache,' said Miriam gravely.

There was an enormous Palace Hotel ahead of them now, labelled on every available corner Rialto, Rialto, Rialto.

'Is that where we're going to drink?' asked Pyke gloomily. 'I m-must go h-home and put on m-my gaberdine.'

'Nonsense, dear,' said Miriam briskly. 'I'm sure they have spittoons – a big place like that.'

They turned in at a side gate. There were hydrangeas that had once been in flower, that now looked singed at the edges, obscuring the french windows of an obvious cocktail-bar. One might tell it was a cocktail-bar by the large and vulgar rooster painted in the primary colours that occupied the lower half of the windows. Outside, there were one or two cement pools, with cement nymphs guarding them. Pyke was glad when he came into the comparative peace of the bar itself. The walls were a faint *eau-de-nil*, the curtains were (savagely) scarlet and the carpet was a deep, deep unpleasant green.

'Do you think,' said Tony delicately into Miriam's ear as he opened the french window for her, 'that your boy friend could lend me five pounds? I'll stop it out of his hotel bill.'

CHAPTER SIX

Miriam and Tony and Pyke stood at attention in front of a curved *eau-de-nil* bar, where small cocktail-glasses, polished to an ecstatic radiance, stood in rows. Pyke saw himself reflected in the looking-glass background behind the till. He was horrified to observe that his mouth had gone into a small, nipped bud of disapproval. Like a rose, he thought, a cabbage rosebud, nipped by frost. And he parted with his five pounds to Tony and hardly noticed it.

Presently Tony had paid for three champagne cocktails and they had begun to sip them. Pyke had been gently deluded into a frame of mind where he truly believed that Tony had bought *him* a drink. The bar tender was an agile young man in a white coat. He told them in a low, hissing whisper that he was learning the hotel business from the bottom up.

'Oh, and Mr *Robinson*,' he went on, playing with the till, 'Major Bognor's *oysters* have come. From the Rucksack Beds, Whitstable. You must take them away with you. They arrived half an hour ago in little barrels.'

There were few things in the world more important to Miriam than oysters. She now said so.

'B-but how extravagant!' suggested Pyke. 'For example – you w-weren't to kn-know that *we* were coming?'

'It will cost you a pretty *penny*,' said Miriam darkly, scowling at herself in the looking-glass.

'Oh no.' Tony seemed to grow bigger as he drained his champagne cocktail and ordered three more, and dropped a pound note and a ten-shilling note on the bar counter as though they were dead leaves. He waved his loose prehensile hands round his face in alarming, meaningless gestures. 'Oh no, Bognor is the oyster king.' He smiled broadly at Miriam. 'Major Reginald Bognor. It's his mother's birthday today. Oysters are her favourite thing too, apparently.'

'If there is an oyster b-bed anywhere, B-Bognor will get into it?' said Pyke, on a question.

'He has buttered his bed and now he must eat it,' said Miriam. She drank her champagne cocktail. 'I used to think he was *rich*,' she added slowly.

'His mother is,' said Tony. 'Thank God.'

'D-drew two hundred pounds from her bank,' said Pyke. 'And that would make a nice refrain for a ballad,' he added, in a different tone.

Tony turned white. He looked at Pyke for the first time. His conversation and all his laughing, flirtatious glances had hitherto been Miriam's exclusive property.

'How did you know *that*?' he said.

'Common knowledge, dear,' said Miriam. She shrugged her shoulders. 'Everyone seems to know.'

II

The oysters were produced and handed over, in their barrels. Tony made a lot of fuss about portage to the Oranmore. A waiter appeared. He seemed to be a bosom friend of Tony and he had exceptionally dashing side-whiskers. He was called Roderigo. He said he would help and he would also get his chum to help as well. Tony was obviously extremely popular. As he left the hotel, Roderigo slapped him on the back and said Tony owed him thirty shillings. Roderigo's chum was comatose and silent and carried most of the barrels. They were a very fine type of Whitstable button oyster (Roderigo said), and he envied Tony and Tony's guests, if they were going to have a real slap-up feed.

'I will say that for Bognor,' said Miriam. 'He does have good, big, generous ideas . . .'

'Even if he can't afford to pay for them himself,' said Tony. He spoke in the sudden bitter tones of a successful hotel proprietor. Afterwards, Roderigo said to his chum that that was rich, that was, coming from Tony.

III

Oddly enough, Mrs Greeb had only a lukewarm welcome from her daughter. But when it is admitted that Celia (at the moment when she was imprinting the kiss of welcome on her mother's faintly lavender-smelling cheek) was also feeding both twins *and* supervising the movement of Major Bognor's 'effects' into the small room known as The Slot (it was above the boiler-room), Celia should really be congratulated on welcoming her mother at all.

'We've put you in the second nicest room,' said Celia. She looked sadly over her mother's head towards the Warhaven Arms, and then, despairingly, back to the Rialto. 'Tony shouldn't be long. He will be sorry he wasn't here to meet you. We would have come to the station, but ...'

'That feed blood heat?' asked Mrs Greeb. Her faint Yorkshire accent was in evidence. She pronounced 'blood' to rhyme with 'good'.

'I expect so. It's difficult to get it quite right.' Celia's forehead wrinkled. 'Nurse Vibart says in "Comfort for Kiddies of Every Age Group ..." Anyway, I must go back to Apey and Maysie-waysie.' She laughed unhappily. 'I'm in the midst, as ever ...'

'None of you ailed when you were tots.' Mrs Greeb sounded quite cross about it.

'No, we were ever so healthy, weren't we?' Celia picked up her mother's suitcase in one hand and began to climb the stairs ahead of her, waving the twins' feed and the twins' porringers on a tray in the other. She panted and shouted encouragement as she went. She had a powerful voice.

'Here you are.' Celia put down the suitcase on the landing and opened a door on her left. It swung back with a crash against a chair. Inside, the room looked pleasant enough. It seemed to be one of the six with a sea view. A girl called Maggie Button was on all fours between the beds, rubbing at the carpet with a duster. On the dressing-table under the window Major Bognor's sleeping-pills seemed triumphant, as though (in spite of everything) his personality had succeeded in imprinting itself on the room.

'Maggie's giving the final touch, as you can see,' said Celia.

51

Maggie stood up and smoothed her skirt.

'I shall be right enough here,' said Mrs Greeb. She thumped over to the window. Maggie escaped while Celia held open the door.

'I must get back to Apey,' said Celia, lingering. 'Lunch will be in ten minutes.'

Mrs Greeb said nothing. As the door shut behind her she stared out of the window at the Rialto.

'Take my word,' she announced, speaking loudly to herself. It had been her habit since her husband's death. 'Take my word but *that* Tony's out drinking.'

IV

Ten minutes later Mrs Greeb went down to the dining-room. Her hair was well piled up in silver heaps and nicely held in place with nets and hairpins. She crossed to the best table by the window, and bowed graciously to Mrs Bognor and Major Bognor, who were already settled in their places. Reginald was staring through his eyeglass at the bill of fare. Mrs Bognor was hardly paying proper attention.

Tommy, the kitchenmaid, shot into the room with plates of soup. She wore a black dress and a white apron and she had been prevailed upon to help out. 'For a few weeks until we can get a waitress – it *is* good of you.' She slapped a soup dish down in front of the Major and some tinned tomato soup swung dangerously about in it. Mrs Bognor said, 'Thank you,' and Tommy approached Mrs Greeb.

'Soup!' she shouted, in a strained baritone.

Mrs Greeb nodded. She didn't care for the atmosphere at *all*.

It reminded her of that place at Looe where Dick had insisted on their staying in 1912. She remembered that Dick had said the proprietor had committed suicide later. Dick was the late Richard Greeb, once Mayor of Harrogate. In his lifetime he had worn an Albert watch-chain. She jerked back her thoughts as Celia hurried in from the kitchen and brought two more plates of soup with her. Bad. Celia couldn't expect loyalty from the staff if she did all their work herself. And Mrs Greeb began to instruct Celia in the proper management of staff, while Celia crumbled her bread and looked miserably round the room for Tony. By and by, Mrs Greeb bent her head to her soup spoon and Celia had an opportunity to speak for herself.

'Your soup to your liking, Major?' she said, slewing half round in her chair.

Major Bognor screwed in his eyeglass.

'All soups are much alike,' he said pompously. 'What?' He seemed to collect his thoughts, and continued in a more social manner: 'Now, Mrs Robinson, you and your lady mother will be welcome at our oyster party tonight, in Mother's room. It's her birthday ...' Mrs Bognor smiled faintly. Major Bognor patted one of her plump, well-manicured little hands.

'My son and I always do things hindside foremost,' said Mrs Bognor, embarrassed. 'On *my* birthday I give him a present and on his—'

'She gives me another one, ha, what?' said Major Bognor, with an abrupt roar of laughter. 'Shocking state of affairs.'

'Still,' said Mrs Bognor vaguely, 'I don't know what I should do without him.'

'It's very kind of you to ask us,' began Celia doubtfully. 'I don't know if Mother *likes* oysters.'

She turned to Mrs Greeb, who sprang into action as though galvanized. Mrs Greeb adored oysters; it was very, very kind of Major Bognor to ask her, and Celia would observe that there was an 'R' in the month. Celia said, 'February,' slowly and gloomily to herself.

Mrs Greeb's self-respect was restored. She bent forward to sniff at the vase of pale early daffodils that stood in the middle of the table. They were nearly dead. She looked reproachfully at her daughter, who misunderstood the glance. Celia sprang from her chair and snatched the empty soup plates. She bolted towards the kitchen with them and knocked lightly into one of the chairs on the way.

'The flow-ers are thir-sty,' said Mrs Greeb, to no one in particular. Her North Country accent was much in evidence. 'I must water the po-ah de-ars.'

She picked up the glass water-jug from the table and walked round the room, officiously pouring water wherever (it seemed to her) it was needed.

At this precise moment Tony came back into the room. Pyke was with him. Miriam had gone upstairs 'to fix her face'. Mrs Greeb straightened her back and glared at Tony.

'The flow-ers are thir-sty, Tony,' she said. 'They all needed watering ... You ought to be ash-amed.'

Tony was furious. He had had more than enough to drink. His authority had already been deeply undermined, once by his interview with the bank manager and, more recently, in conspiracy, by Mr Twiggs and his wife. His blasted mother-in-law's interference was (so his unconscious told him) the very last straw. Something swelled and burst and throbbed in his neck as he stood, staring at her, his eyes glazing with

54

rage. Mrs Greeb bent forward and sniffed the air beside him sharply, twice.

'As I thought,' said Mrs Greeb.

And at that Tony appeared to go raving mad. His fists clenched and unclenched. He raised them above his head and shouted at the ceiling that it was *too much*, Celia, *too much*. Then he turned and ran out of the room towards the kitchen. Later the front door slammed behind him.

The subsequent scene: Mrs Greeb's refined surprise, Celia's shrieks ('My husband's on the drink again! My husband's on the drink again! It's all your fault!') could be heard all through the hotel. It rocked with the awful impacts of unbridled human emotions, clashing and jangling against each other. Tommy, the kitchenmaid, was so upset that she refused the washing-up, and, having too closely applied Celia's accusation, ran into the basement bedroom and locked the door. Maggie Button, the chambermaid, sat through it all with wide, uncomprehending eyes, solidly eating her lunch at the kitchen table. Pyke, going upstairs to Miriam's room, saw Mrs Bognor and Mrs Greeb leave the dining-room, much drawn together, and hissing a little. They already seemed fast friends.

V

Pyke knocked at Miriam's door and received one of her usual incoherent invitations to enter. She seemed glad to see him, and wanted to know, darling, quickly, what all the noise was about. 'It sounded as if there was a *brou ha ha*,' said Miriam. 'Like at the first night of *Hips and Haws*.' Pyke told his story happily. His stammer was non-existent as he rattled on, acting out each part in turn. He was particularly good as Mrs Greeb.

'You always loved other people's discomfiture,' said Miriam jealously, when he had finished. She tapped him with her hairbrush, then with a change of tone: 'What's the use of having any luncheon now? Mum's *missed* all the drama ... She pouted at herself in the glass and pulled up a handful of her pale hair to see if it made her look any better.

'You mean you've missed your *entrance*,' said Pyke unkindly.

Miriam's room was already very untidy. A suitcase lay half open on the floor. Miriam's clothes lay in sweet disorder on both beds, and one of her dresses had been shut half in and half out of the wardrobe. The place seemed (as they say) well *lived in*.

'Anyway, we've been asked to this oyster party,' continued Pyke, and suddenly resumed his defensive social stammer. 'C-can you l-last until then?'

'Last!' Miriam was furious. 'What a way to speak! You expect Mum to disintegrate?'

'No.' Pyke was quite calm. He studied the reflection of Miriam's pale-blue eyes in the glass. 'They're l-looking f-forward to you. *N-no one* expects you to disintegrate.'

Miriam swung round at him in a fury.

'You told Bognor that I was here?' she cried. She crossed the room, speaking viciously over her shoulder.

'Why not?'

Pyke shrugged. Then he blushed guiltily. Miriam sat on her bed and linked her hands in an agony of frustration and despair. It was, perhaps, a little overdone.

'What c-can be the matter?' said Pyke nervously, going to the door.

'Mum is going to bed,' said Miriam gaily. She was suddenly in a good temper. She had made her decision. 'Shut the door. No entrances for Mum until the party.'

Pyke went out and shut the door. When he was outside in the passage he sighed heavily. Really, Miriam ...

CHAPTER SEVEN

When Pyke stood on the landing outside Miriam's door he cursed a little to himself, quietly. In the first place, he didn't think he was going to find the Oranmore good to write in. Something told him that the scene between the Robinsons and Mrs Greeb was only the first of a great many. How could *anyone* write a play (particularly a play in verse) if he was constantly interrupted by shouts of 'My husband's on the drink again!', and 'It's all your fault!'? Pyke smiled his wry, unattractive little smile. Well, perhaps it was good copy. But it was *squalid* copy. Pyke had no use for squalor. As we know, he had a degree in law, had been a barrister once and had found it very squalid. 'Squalor,' he often said, in his attractive, slightly booming voice, 'is always so v-violent.' He therefore avoided contact with it – and whenever he met it (for the best-organized lives are inclined to slip sideways on occasion) he protected himself with a brittle artillery barrage of laughter. 'Distasteful' and 'disagreeable' were two of Pyke's favourite words.

Now he decided he would explore the hotel. Deprived of Miriam's company, he could indulge his curiosity about the way things worked and the manner in which backgrounds (or, as Pyke would have called them collectively, *décor*) affected people. This was a favourite theory of his. From Pyke's point of view, backgrounds were infinitely preferable to people. They rarely (except, of course, in the case of volcanic mountains in eruptions) offered him violence.

Pyke advanced towards a door that was half open. It showed a room facing north towards the back view of a lot of houses, the garden-seat and (presumably) Mrs Fortescue-Sykes' cacti. The room was empty, the beds were not made up. There were dust-sheets over each of them. The reading-lamp between the beds was of a morbidly unattractive modern design. Pyke came out. He found a bathroom on this floor, and a lavatory. They were heavily labelled in an unpleasant Gothic script, and he had no occasion to open either door. At the head of the stairs there was one more door. Pyke went towards it cautiously as though he knew that some social indecency was hidden beyond its bland ivory face. He turned the handle and peered in. The sun had made the little room warm and airless. Worse than this, however: on the floor, confined by a wooden play-pen that seemed distressingly inefficient, there crawled April and May, blowing bubbles at one another.

II

After this horrid experience Pyke did not linger on the top landing. He hurried downstairs accompanied by a feeling of unusual guilt. It was almost as though he had no *right* to be prying into other people's lives. Pyke did not understand this. He shook his head angrily.

On the next floor there was The Slot (where he could

hear Major Bognor plaintively complaining to himself as he 'stowed away his gear'), there were Mrs Bognor's two rooms (known as The Suite) and the room where Mrs Greeb had been installed. He knew Mrs Bognor's rooms by the faint smell of lavender water and Fuller's earth that he had already detected about her. The sitting-room door was half open and he could see a corner of Mrs Bognor's own tallboy and writing-desk, a green pot of ferns, and some Japanese fans. There was a mauve carpet on the floor. Pyke longed to go in. He could tell that the blinds were half drawn to protect the mauve carpet from the sun and to stop Mrs Bognor's yellowish snapshots of herself and Reginald's father from growing still more yellow. These were mostly of lawn-tennis parties, taken in the early years of the century.

Mrs Greeb's door was shut. Pyke, although he did not turn the handle, had the impression that she had locked it and taken away the key. Pyke's own room was on this floor, next door to Mrs Bognor's bedroom. He did not want anything at the moment. He went slowly down into the hall. He saw himself reflected in the looking-glass behind the Benares brassware tray. Tony had hung foxes' brushes from the top of it and had left his binoculars spectacularly on the tray. But the hall still looked like the hall of a rather badly ran private hotel.

Here, on Pyke's right, was the corridor that now connected Burma Villa and Pondicherry Lodge. Half-way along it Pyke detected the door of the common sitting-room. He supposed that he had better call it 'Lounge'. Indeed, the door, like the bathroom and lavatory upstairs, was very heavily labelled indeed. The murmuring inside – that could only be Mrs Greeb and Mrs Bognor, cooing together over their coffee – attracted him. Pyke liked old ladies. He pushed open the door and went in, and the two old ladies fluttered with pleasure.

III

'It is so kind of you to ask Miss Birdseye and myself to your party,' said Pyke, sitting down in an armchair by Mrs Bognor. He sighed. 'Miss Birdseye is a brilliant creature,' he said. 'A *brilliant* creature.'

Mrs Greeb's face now showed a strong mistrust of brilliant creatures. Even humming birds (or so her disapproving and tilted nose suggested to Pyke) could be a nuisance, flickering about like that – spoiling the intellectual treat of the conversation.

'Mrs Bognor,' said Mrs Greeb coldly, 'is a very kind woman. I am only thankful my *poor Celia* has her to turn to, when *necessary . . .*'

'Very nice of you to say so,' murmured Mrs Bognor. Pyke looked at her and decided it must have been Mrs Greeb's voice he had overheard in the passage. The room was very full of furniture. A grand piano sprawled across a good deal of it. A balcony (painted an unattractive green) ran round the outside of it. Every now and then the french windows rattled in quick blasts of wind from the sea.

'N-not an easy job r-running a hotel,' said Pyke, earnestly hypnotizing Mrs Greeb with his large brown eyes. In spite of herself, Mrs Greeb felt warmth and sympathy radiate from the large, carefully dressed young man. 'In f-fact I c-couldn't d-do it. You need r-real character to r-run a hotel.'

'My Celia has real character,' said Mrs Greeb.

'Oh, I'm s-*sure* she has.' Pyke was quite certain about it.

There were evil tiles in the fireplace that showed Dutch people and windmills in a horrid acid blue. It would need real character to endure them without going raving mad.

'Celia had a nice little fat bank-book when she married Tony. You know what Celia said to me?'

As neither Pyke nor Mrs Bognor had ever been in a position to know what Celia Greeb (as she then was) had said on her wedding day, they held their tongues. A grandfather clock in the corner ticked and ticked, showing a brass pendulum through a hole in its stomach.

'She said to me, "Mother," she said – and mind, when Celia used *that* tone of voice, I always knew something nasty was coming.' Mrs Greeb drew in her breath to savour once again the full horror of the past. 'She used the same tone in 1937 when she was so determined not to stay another year at St Padella's High. *And* she would have been head girl. Always a mistake, that was, with Miss Sandringham, the headmistress, thinking so highly of her, too. Celia said to me: "Mother, I don't care *what* you say, but Tony Robinson's a Gentleman. And I must marry a Gentleman."'

The grandfather clock whirred and languidly struck a quarter to three. Mrs Bognor stirred in her chair and her plump little hands refolded themselves.

'But *is* he a Gentleman, Mrs Greeb?' she asked. And her voice was a faint, faint sigh, like the wind in an empty champagne bottle whose contents had been consumed for health reasons only.

'That's what I say myself,' said Mrs Greeb. 'That's what I ask myself indeed. *Could* a Gentleman have behaved so just now in the dining-room?' Mrs Greeb leant forward, stabbing the air with a thin, knobbly forefinger. 'Mr Pyke, you're a Gentleman yourself ...' Pyke's warm sympathy had evidently penetrated Mrs Greeb's reserves. He was in. He was one of the family. He relaxed and crossed one shining shoe over the other. 'Is Tony Robinson a Gentleman, would you say?'

In the basement, muffled shrieks suggested that the scene was not yet over.

'Perhaps Mr Robinson was just overwrought,' said Mrs Bognor's faint little voice. 'There are, after all, a lot of *Neurasthenic* Gentlemen.'

'What do you say, Mr Pyke?' Mrs Greeb was sharply determined to have the male opinion.

'Well ...' Pyke's stammer came triumphantly to his assistance. 'I'm not really a j-judge of a g-gentleman. I'm m-more of a *poet*, myself, r-really ... Where did M-Mr Robinson go to school?'

'Rugby.' Mrs Greeb's mouth shut like a rat-trap.

'Ah ...!' said Pyke. He very much hoped the exclamation would convey meaning and understanding. Mrs Greeb seemed satisfied. She wagged her head and snapped her bag open and shut.

'And what is happening *now*?' said Mrs Bognor.

The heavy thudding of brisk, masculine feet approached the door. Reginald Bognor came in, bristling with military precision.

'Ah, there you are, Mother – sorry for butting in, what? Fact *is*, Tony Robinson and I've been tryin' our hand at the oysters and only opened six.' His face was flushed. A vein throbbed in the middle of his forehead. He seemed distressed, out of all proportion to the matter in hand. Pyke rose slowly to his feet.

'One of my f-few virtues,' he said slowly, 'is *oyster*-opening. I only got out of the way of opening them since I became a writer. Shall be g-glad to show you the kn-knack. Do you want to open them *now*?'

The two men, standing together, made the atmosphere restless. Mrs Bognor moved her feet anxiously, as though her son might tread on them. He seemed irascible.

'Well, I thought so, you know, what? Keep 'em on ice for tonight?' He slowly recovered and his angry flush faded. His cavalry moustache was left in complete command of his face.

Pyke said he thought it was a good idea. He bowed to Mrs Greeb and Mrs Bognor, and said he regretted that he could not continue their conversation. As he left the room with the Major, he heard Mrs Greeb say that she never did trust people who were too polite.

'When Celia married Tony Robinson she had three hundred pound saved. *Now* where's that gone, I'd like to know?'

'But Mr *Robinson* was *hardly* polite to you at luncheon,' said Mrs Bognor, in her soft, faint voice.

Pyke and Major Bognor faded away downstairs to the basement.

IV

The atmosphere that radiated upwards from the basement was most peculiar. Pyke, following the Major (and, oddly enough, the Major had taken off his jacket and now appeared in a highly striped grey-and-white silk shirt with a hard white collar), was very conscious of an unreality. The Major continued to talk all the time about the oysters – h'm, what? – and how he *used* to have the knack with the things. The oyster party was evidently very important to him. Pyke wondered jealously if he considered the whole thing as Miriam's betrothal. Yet the Major had not known about Miriam's coming down at all. Really . . . 'peculiar' was the word for the whole thing.

Meanwhile, the Major couldn't think what had gone wrong. He had managed to open half a dozen, but after that . . . He gestured with his shoulders. His narrative was very much complicated by his inability to speak about mere *oysters*. Sometimes they were 'bivalves', sometimes 'the jolly little Whitstables' and sometimes 'Ah! The Colchester molluscs, what! My favourites.' Pyke, gloomily taking off his own jacket, stared around him, wondering if he would make more sense of the basement *without* the Major.

Ahead of him, and cheek by jowl, were the servants' bedroom and the kitchen. Connie, the Chef, was sitting outside the bedroom door on a packing-case, occasionally striking at it with one foot and remarking, 'Let me in, you silly bitch, I won't do the washing-up alone,' in a tone of unvarying monotony. Occasionally a heavy thud on the inside of the door suggested that Tommy had thrown a boot at it. Through the half-open kitchen door Pyke now observed Maggie Button putting on her 'things' and dabbing at her long pink nose with a powder-puff. She was evidently huffed about something. Sitting at the table, sobbing as though her heart would break, was Celia. Her head lay sadly on her outstretched arms. Perfectly sufficient reason for her emotion was given by the piles of unattempted washing-up that surrounded her. There was no sign of Tony.

'The jolly old bivalves are *here* in the pantry,' said the Major, indicating a room on his left with a sink and more piles of washing-up. The oyster barrels, some formidable tools and a pile of assorted oyster plates with shell-shaped compartments for a dozen oysters each, were spread about.

'This *is* an odd hotel,' said Pyke, gazing round him.

'D'you think so?' The Major seemed surprised. 'These kind of emotional disturbances go on behind the scenes in most of them, as a matter of fact. I can tell you, when we lived in the Browning Court at Bexhill ...'

The Major's reminiscence of the set-up at the Browning Court lasted them through one barrel of oysters and half-way down the next. At this point Pyke (who had been doing splendid work with a sharp little potato-peeler) also began to have trouble. The Major was an industrious apprentice, but his temperament was more suited to the five-furlong burst than the long three-mile race. He often put down his knife and rested his hands on his hips and remarked that he was getting too fat, while Pyke worked steadily on, only too well aware of the fact that he was losing weight every minute. Soon Pyke's thumbs were both chipped and bleeding slightly, and the oysters seemed to become more and more obstinate. As Pyke finished each dozen the plates were packed one on top of the other on blocks of ice inside the doorway. Pyke suddenly estimated that he had opened twenty-four dozen. He would have about three more dozen to do before he rested. He put down his potato-peeler and sighed.

'I tell you what,' said the Major, straightening his back and screwing in his eyeglass for the fourth time. 'We can put these last ones on the kitchen stove, and when they gasp for air – what? – we can nip in quick with our snickersnees. Eh? What do you say? Remember a feller tellin' me that in the Crab Pit at Budleigh, come to think of it ...

Pyke was shocked beyond words. He thought it was extremely cruel and he said so.

'It r-reminds m-me,' he said, 'of the Bishop of wherever it was who killed those c-c-cockroaches with b-bicarbonate of soda; they *burst*, you see. A t-terribly painful death for a cockroach. I recollect the expert roach k-killers were t-terribly shocked.'

'Don't be silly,' said the Major, with a disconcertingly sadistic leer. 'What does it matter *how* they die? Big thing is to kill 'em. There's no such thing as cruelty to oysters. *Or* to cockroaches.'

He stooped and picked up the last half-empty barrel. Pyke shrugged his shoulders.

'A d-dangerous d-doctrine,' he said mildly. 'You m-might work your way up from cockroaches to dogs and children, for example . . .'

'Well, *you're* going to be very cruel to oysters if you eat all this lot,' said the Major accusingly. He somehow managed to give the impression that he could eat poets, too, if he had the chance. Pyke followed him nervously out of the door.

'Do you suppose that we shall m-manage all these?' he said vaguely.

'Poof!' The Major was contemptuous. 'My mother is a *famous* oyster-eater. Brillat Savarin (as you no doubt know) once ate thirty-six dozen. Well, my lady mother is in that class too. Five dozen last time we had a party. Not bad for a seventy-year-old, what?'

Pyke said he thought it was most *praiseworthy* for a seventy-year-old. The Major said yes, indeed. He went on to describe the special oyster plates which Mrs Bognor collected. She had five, it seemed, perfectly beautiful Dresden plates, with scallop shells arranged beautifully around groups of nymphs and shepherds.

'And that's another thing,' said the Major, walking past Celia Robinson as though she didn't exist and putting down his oyster barrel in the middle of the table. 'My mother's mad about Dresden china.'

And so, swept forward on the tide of the Major's heartily developed personality, Pyke found himself in the kitchen of the Oranmore Hotel for the second time that day.

V

The Major still ignored Celia Robinson. He moved purpose-fully to the stove. He placed the oysters on it in neat rows. He lit the gas jets under them.

Pyke turned away disgusted. His enormous pleasure at the thought of the number of oysters he was going to be allowed to eat that evening was completely spoilt. He decided it was his duty to comfort poor Celia.

'Er . . .' he began unhappily, 'it will all be the s-same a hun-dred years hence, don't you think?'

Celia's tears flowed, like unnoticed waterfalls, down her face. She did not seem to expect or welcome sympathy.

'Um . . .' said Pyke. He tried again. 'It will be the w-wash-ing-up, of course, that is upsetting you so much? I mean th-that th-there is so *much* of it? I do agree, you know. It is something quite extraordinary. I've never s-seen so much . . .'

Even the little glass bowls that had been standing under the window when Pyke had arrived that morning were back again. Some of them, moreover, were still full of mauve blancmange. It was a depressing sight.

'Chef refuses to do it,' wailed Celia. 'And Tommy has locked herself up in her bedroom. I suppose I shall have to do it all myself, as usual, and oh, I am so tired and the twins must be put to sleep, and . . .'

Pyke patted her gently on the shoulder. He was very surprised at himself.

'Don't cry,' he said; 'p-please don't cry. It will only m-make you m-more tired. I've noticed it's always like that . . .'

His voice continued to soothe her. He had no control over the things it said. And poor Celia, wiping her red and streaming eyes with the back of her hand, thought it sounded as though an archangel were speaking to her. An archangel who was saying: 'Don't cry, my child. *I* will do *all* the washing-up for you.' And nobody was more surprised at this remark than Frederick Pyke.

CHAPTER EIGHT

Pyke's many acquaintances, who usually enjoyed his ironic wit in the back bar of the Café Royal, would have been very surprised to observe him during the next twenty minutes, wrapped in an apron and smelling furiously of dishwater. His few friends would not have been at all surprised. 'Pyke,' they often told each other, 'has to be rude in order to protect himself – otherwise he would always be *put upon*.'

A more surprising thing was the way in which Major Bognor joined in after he had dealt with the last of the gasping oysters. He stood in his shirt-sleeves, laughing heartily and talking (for some reason best known to himself) about witchcraft. Speaking of witches, did Pyke know Miss Miriam Birdseye, the revue artist, a great friend of his? Pyke did not bat an eyelid. He regretted so much that he did *not*. He had also (it must be admitted) lied to Miriam when he had told her that Bognor knew she was in the hotel.

Bognor dried the dishes most industriously, remarking from time to time that the Cherry Pickers had taught him method and order, what? He stacked them neatly in their racks ready for supper. Celia, released from her hysteria, went to dispose the twins for their afternoon rest. 'If I were you, Mrs Robinson,' shouted the Major, as she left the room, 'I'd sack this Chef and her girl friend out of hand. They're even worse than the last two yer had.' He turned back to Pyke and began to explain about the Army chef and his little newly wedded wife who had been Connie's and Tommy's predecessors. The Major, when he was in the cavalry, had learnt to rough it, but really, what?

To his surprise Pyke began to like Major Bognor, although he was still surprised that Miriam could take him seriously. By the time they had dealt with the last great pile of dinner plates he was agreeably drawn to him. They had their womanly wrangles over the amount of 'chemicals' (in the Major's phrase) that should be used in the water, but on the whole parted delighted with their mellowing knowledge of each others personality. It was then three o'clock.

II

At ten minutes past three Tony Robinson, dazed with drink, returned to the hotel. He had forgotten everything. Until closing-time he had been in Bob's cubby-hole at the Warhaven Arms, roaring with laughter at some indecent drawings that Bob had had that morning from a traveller of the Warhaven Breweries. Tony walked up the steps into his office and there fell asleep in an armchair. He remained asleep, noisily, for two and a half hours. Celia looked in twice, once when she came downstairs from the twins – and once after her own rest. She did not attempt to disturb him.

III

At five o'clock everyone but Tony awoke from their siesta. Mrs Bognor's tea was taken up to her room by Celia on a tin tray. She then returned for her mother's. Miriam Birdseye woke, turned restlessly over, and prepared herself for another half-hour with the *other* eye shut. Tommy came out of her bedroom and said she was ever so sorry she had been so mean to Connie, and Connie said roughly, 'Skip it.' They then went into the kitchen together and promptly had another alarming quarrel about a football coupon.

Pyke told himself that he needed a breath of air. He left the Oranmore Hotel by the front door and walked briskly down towards the sea, past the Rialto, which repelled him. All the decadent Edwardian flowering of Brunton-on-Sea lay in front of him as he stood on the esplanade; from the monstrous West Pavilion (like an enormous warped Chinese hat) to the public lavatory in the East. The municipal street lamps, grasped by weird, dragon-like shapes of concrete, the waste-paper baskets with the arms of Brunton worked upon them in dark-green wire: all these things combined to give a flavour of evil that would have upset a less sensitive man than Pyke. Pyke was first amused, and then, as he contemplated the awful morbidity of the West Pavilion, terrified.

A thick navy-blue cloud drifted from the horizon, gathering others towards it as it came. The sea was cold and savage. A patter of rain began as the light failed. Pyke felt himself trembling on the brink of danger. All the devils inside him, usually so carefully controlled, were about to be challenged. He might even be *forced* to face up to life. Or so he felt. He was scared stiff. It began to rain quite heavily.

'That—' he said, shaking his shoulders as the rain fell on them, '*that* comes of all that washing-up.'

As he turned up towards the malignant shape of the Oranmore Hotel he was in time to see Tony Robinson plunge into the Rialto cocktail-bar for the first drink of the evening.

IV

Tony excused himself for his visit to the Rialto. He said that Mrs Bognor needed a white tablecloth for her party. There was nothing as simple as this in the Oranmore. All their table-napkins were of paper and all their tablecloths were covered with patterns and checks of a most disastrous kind. It was natural, surely, that Roderigo should lend him a tablecloth from the Rialto dining-room. Oddly enough, Roderigo *also* thought it natural. Tony came panting back from the Rialto through the first rainstorm, holding the tablecloth tightly inside his tweed coat. He felt much more lively than he had felt all day. That quick pink gin had cleared his brain nicely. He felt quite smooth and bright again.

Mrs Bognor was already in her sitting-room, gently bullying the Major. The furniture had been pushed to one side, the window was quite taken up with a kitchen table, and on this the oysters, the silver tankards, the bottles of stout and the bottles of champagne (for the Major had determined that he, at all events, should drink Black Velvet this evening) were spread out. Tony came in, opening the tablecloth, with a high-stepping action like a horse. He remarked at intervals that he was looking forward to handing round plates *no end*.

Mrs Greeb was the first guest to arrive. She was dressed to

the teeth in new and sparkling black; her vitality was quite renewed by her afternoon's rest. There was, too, a formidable speech of complaint against Tony rising inside her. She looked coldly through him as he handed her a plate of oysters. Mercifully, the scene in the dining-room had been expunged from his conscious mind. He simply remarked silently that his mother-in-law had a face like a thin, little, old miserable old *toad*, and left it at that.

Mrs Bognor was genuinely pleased to see Mrs Greeb. Her mild malicious mind was pleased by the tension and discomfiture of the various members of the Robinson *ménage*. She made room for Mrs Greeb beside her. They sat together on Mrs Bognor's wide green sofa and greedily ate their first dozen oysters, carefully lifting their veils to do so. For some time there was no sound in the room but the faint noises of people with moderately good manners eating bread-and-butter. Oysters, by their very nature, are consumed in silence.

Outside, the storm began to rise and the raindrops to rattle with violence on the windows. The Oranmore Hotel was stoutly built, but it shivered as the wind struck it from every side. The corner site received every gust from west, east and south-west. Mrs Greeb shivered as she heard the wind increase its violence. Mrs Bognor asked her politely was she cold.

'Someone walking on my grave,' said Mrs Greeb.

Pyke arrived next, alone, strolling up the room with the bland dignity of a Roman emperor. His dislike of Tony was almost as obvious as Mrs Greeb's. Tony, unaware of it, continued to flash about being an awfully good sort. He leapt forward and pressed a plate into Pyke's hand. He introduced him to Major Bognor. They both looked sick with boredom.

'But we know each other very *well*,' said the Major. 'We opened all the oysters together this afternoon, what?'

The unspoken words, 'When you were in a drunken torpor in your office, you coarse brute,' echoed in Pyke's mind. He started guiltily. He had almost spoken them.

'We like each other, in spite of everything,' said Pyke.

Tony, quite unembarrassed, said what awful rot, he had opened at *least* a dozen oysters himself before he went to sleep.

'Because of everything, my dear sir,' said the Major gaily. 'We like each other because of everything. And here is our charming lady hostess . . .'

And he stepped forward to meet Celia. She had arrived in time to hear Tony's defence of his laziness. She said she had seen him open the oysters. Tony promptly scowled and turned his back on her. She was wearing a very flowered afternoon dress and high-heeled court shoes that were rather worn down on the left heel. Tony carried another dozen oysters to his mother-in-law, who thanked him coldly and passed on the plate to Mrs Bognor.

'Thank you, my dear,' said Mrs Bognor. 'I *dearly* love a nice oyster.'

Mrs Greeb then stamped rudely forward to the table and helped herself. Tony, evidently unaware that he had been insulted for his obvious coldness towards Celia, helped himself and spoke enthusiastically through a mouthful of brown bread of the quality of the oysters.

It was at this moment in the party's flowering, when the Black Velvet had already sustained and soothed the guests to a receptive mood, that Miriam chose to make her entrance.

V

Miriam looked superb. Everyone else was dressed sadly in conventional post-war clothing. Even Pyke's iron-grey suit and hard white city collar seemed casual beside Miriam's magnificent oyster-eating costume of black velvet, cut low on the bosom with a tremendous train. Her long gloves, incongruous and delightful as the paws of a tight black cat, waved an inconsequent greeting to her *dear* Pyke. He bowed from the waist and set down his tray to serve her slightest whim.

Her smile for Tony was warmer than the African sun. The room, which had been cold with draughts, suddenly vibrated with all Miriam's personal electricity. Miriam often had this effect on a party. Tony, immune to the hostile glares of everybody else, blushed and stammered as he attempted further abortive introductions.

'Major Birdseye, Miss Bognor,' said Tony insanely.

'Not at all,' said the Major, making a little more sense. He had gone snow-white. His eyeglass had fallen, tinkling against his waistcoat buttons. He swallowed the oyster in his mouth with a gulp of pure misery. It would have been impossible to believe that until that moment he had been fairly happy.

'Oh, I know Major *Birdseye*,' said Miriam, staring loftily over his head. Tony, stuttering, attempted to unravel the coils caused by his slipping tongue.

'My mother is there on the sofa,' said the Major miserably.

He put down his tankard and advanced with Miriam towards Mrs Bognor and Mrs Greeb. They were (not unnaturally) transfixed in *bourgeois* attitudes of astonishment, with their mouths wide open, staring up at Miriam as though she was a visitor from another world.

'Mother!' said the Major. 'This is Miss Miriam Birdseye, whom I have often spoken to you about . . .'

'Any mother of Reginald is a friend of mine,' said Miriam, and bent forward dramatically and kissed Mrs Greeb on both cheeks.

VI

Miriam, in spite of her enviable entrance and the warm charm that she set to work upon the two old ladies (she sat between them on the sofa, and often called out to Pyke and Major Bognor when she saw that their plates were empty), said afterwards that from the first the party had the kiss of death upon it. To begin with, the room was as chill as the grave. Even the photographs of Reginald Bognor's papa, withering on the mantelpiece, seemed like decorations in a French mausoleum. The icy winds that fluttered the fans and the thin ferns, that made the mauve carpet rise along the floor beneath their feet – all these things touched Miriam's spine with an unholy *frisson*.

She was, therefore, not at all surprised when Pyke came thundering next morning to tell her that Mrs Bognor was dead. She had died in the night. It must have been the oysters.

'Exactly,' said Miriam, and smiled. 'Exactly what I have been expecting. She was poisoned, of course.'

BOOK TWO

———

HOW DO YOU AFTER YOUR OYSTERS?

Or a true and lamentable account of how One and Twenty Ingenious Gentlemen were set upon on Wednesday morning last, about One o'clock and LISTED as it is thought, for the service of the PRETENDER with many other remarkable discoveries . . .

Title of an anonymous pamphlet, dated
1721, in the British Museum.

CHAPTER NINE

Miriam of course, had no justification for her extraordinary remark. She had, in the past (once through no fault of her own* and twice by her own will†), become involved in dramas where sudden, unnatural deaths were a mere commonplace. No doubt, as a result of these experiences, she assumed (I admit morbidly) that all deaths were unnatural. Much of this was (possibly) consequent upon a sense of her own immortality. Miriam was a genius. Such people are, they say, quite unaware of the impermanence of natural life.

She greeted Pyke's news with her charming, left-handed smile. She wrapped herself in a heavy Jaegar dressing-gown and asked him to tell his story as quickly as possible. And, occasionally impeded by his stutter, Pyke did so.

II

It had been a wild night. Pyke had often woken. The rain returned in its fury at about two. Pyke had then become aware,

---

* *Death Goes on Skis.*
† *Poison for Teacher; Cinderella Goes to the Morgue.*

first of the small rustlings and crashings of the hotel, rocking in the storm like a ship at sea, and then (even more disturbing) of someone thumping about next door to him. Someone, moreover, who was being very ill.

Pyke's hatred of violence certainly dictated his negative behaviour at this point. He lay in bed and stuffed his fingers in his ears. He hoped that *he* would not succumb to the sickness. He thought anxiously about oysters. Pyke was very suggestible. Eventually, he fell asleep, worn out by concentration. He woke again to find Maggie Button, the chambermaid, in his room with a cup of morning tea. She talked incessantly as she drew the curtains. Beyond them was a grey and weeping sky. Maggie told him how difficult it was for dailies and how her mother, Mrs Button, said every morning, when she saw Maggie going for the bus, that she ought to live *in*. Maggie had then left the room, not obviously vexed by Pyke's monosyllabic replies. Maggie had gone immediately into Mrs Bognor's room.

Then Maggie Button had screamed.

III

Thereafter, to his annoyance, Pyke had been forced into action. Wrapped in his silk dressing-gown (a most inadequate protection against the February Brunton draughts, as he pointed out to Miriam, who merely drew her own voluptuous robe a little closer), he had padded into Mrs Bognor's bedroom. Maggie Button was by now hysterical. It was impossible to calm her.

Mrs Bognor's bedroom was all that Pyke had expected it to be. He wished that he had been able to examine it in happier circumstances. The room was furnished with Mrs Bognor's own furniture: the mahogany tallboy, the massive wardrobe, the cheval glass; they were all that was left of the furnishing of the dockyard house where she had lived with Admiral Bognor. Maggie, by now, had reached a plum-coloured and strangled silence.

There was the brass bedstead where the sheets were torn back to expose the old-fashioned stone hot-water bottle. And there was the bedside table with its poised and jointed lamp, the boxes of pills, the two Boots' library books. Pyke brought himself to consider the wash-hand basin (where the vast extravagant sponges were piled up and the denture lay in its plastic dish) and the small pathetic corpse. Mrs Bognor had an old lady's meticulous passion for neatness, order and sanity. There was no trace of her last, pitiful, retching agony. Poor darling. She had washed it all away.

At this point Pyke's warm heart (for he had liked Mrs Bognor and enjoyed her malice) was pierced. He began to waver in his stern resolve. Maggie Button suddenly recovered from her hysteria and became helpful. Surely the doctor should be called? Dr Stalag-Jones, Mrs Bognor's own lady doctor. *So* good with expectant mothers. Pyke ignored this irrelevance and asked where the telephone was. Maggie Button led him to Tony's office. The door was heavily labelled, as we might expect, in Gothic script.

Dr Stalag-Jones answered her own telephone in a high clear voice, evidently from her bed, and said that she would be along right away. In fact, as soon as her Austin had started. Pyke turned, shivering, from the telephone, surprised but gratified at the information about the make of the doctor's car. Behind him he found Celia Robinson, looking wildly unattractive in a pink flannel wrapper. She was very angry.

'And do you *know*,' said Pyke to Miriam, who had not

83

interrupted him at all during this narrative, 'the really curious thing about the whole business was the *scene* she made. About me using the telephone, I mean. She said I h-had no r-right. It wasn't m-my *authority* . . .'

Miriam still said nothing. Her expression showed unvarnished suspicion.

'I th-thought she was hysterical enough y-yesterday when B-Bognor and I did the w-washing-up . . .'

Miriam expressed surprise with one lifted eyebrow that Pyke had not mentioned the washing-up before.

'B-but it was nothing to the hysteria this morning. As g-good as told me I was a b-busybody. And didn't believe me.' Pyke wearily passed a hand through his hair. 'Mrs Bognor *wasn't* dead. That was her idea, and she was sticking to it.'

Miriam spoke at last.

'But,' she said, 'surely she only had to go and look, dear? I mean examine the body and all that, dear?'

Outside in the grey and hopeless morning a church bell began to ring in single, tiresome strokes. It was (as everyone had forgotten) Sunday.

'No,' said Pyke sulkily, 'she couldn't. I've locked the door. I've got the key in my pocket. I d-don't intend to let *anyone* in there until the doctor comes.'

Miriam sat upright. She was suddenly excited.

'Not even Mum?' said Miriam.

'*Not even Mum,*' said Pyke firmly.

He crossed to the window and stared down into all the wet length of Durbah Villas. Some shining mackintoshed figures with pathetic umbrellas raised against the storm crept through the rain to church. He thought he saw a motor approaching, but it turned out of Durbah Villas towards the sea. Pyke bit his lip, wishing that the doctor would come.

'I see what Celia Robinson *meant* about busybodies,' said Miriam coldly.

IV

Dr Stalag-Jones arrived in her Austin. She was tall and spare and striding, and somehow gave the impression that she was accompanied by a wire-haired fox terrier. Pyke, meeting her on the front steps, even looked behind her for the dog, snapping metaphorical fingers. There was, of course, no dog. Dr Stalag-Jones was most forthright.

'Where is Mrs Bognor?' she said immediately. Behind her the street was emptied. The last hurrying people had gone to church. Only one small boy on a bicycle delivering the *News of the World* to the hotels relieved the monotony of the shining seaside pavements.

'In her room,' said Pyke, and shut the front door. They left outside the wind and the sad rain and the paper-boy. And also, of course, the *News of the World*.

'And you are her son?' she said.

'N-no indeed.' In this difficult moment Pyke's stutter magnificently protected him. 'It was m-myself and the ch-chambermaid who f-found the body. I don't suppose – unless Mrs Robinson – I mean unless *she* has told Major Bognor, I have not ...'

Above them someone whispered and someone else cried out that something else was 'Monstrous!' A door slammed.

'Mrs Robinson?' Dr Stalag-Jones was very brisk indeed. '*That's* the little woman with those delicious twins?'

85

A door opened a little, someone peered out at them. The door was abruptly shut again. Pyke recollected the delicious twins that he had observed the day before in their play-pen. He nodded dumbly.

'I remember now,' Dr Stalag-Jones continued. 'She *did* say she lived here – at least, she said she lived in the Oranmore.'

'Sh-she is the p-proprietor's wife,' said Pyke.

'Naturally,' said Dr Stalag-Jones. 'No one would be allowed to have children in a hotel of this sort.'

'Unless they owned it,' said Pyke.

'Precisely,' said the doctor.

They were by now on the landing outside Mrs Bognor's door, panting slightly. Pyke took the key from his pocket and turned it in the lock.

'You locked it?' said the doctor. 'Now why?'

A cold draught crept along under the stair carpets and bit Pyke round the ankles.

'I wasn't satisfied,' said Pyke, and stood politely on one side.

'Now I wonder why,' said the doctor. She went into the room.

Pyke became aware of Major Bognor, at his elbow, in a thick checked rug-like dressing-gown. He was in a frightful rage. Pyke, surprised, shut the door behind Dr Stalag-Jones. He remained standing against it, holding the door-handle. His attitude (perhaps a little melodramatic) further maddened the Major.

'How dare you!'

The Major frothed alarmingly and little points in his eyes glowed red.

'I know *all* about *you*. In and out of my fiancée's bedroom at all hours. You're answerable to *me*, you and your nasty sneaking ways!'

'Oh, I say!' said Pyke. He did not let go of the door-handle.

'And not only that,' went on the Major, bimbling through his moustache, 'here's my mother, dead. My mother, blast your eyes! She's dead. Or so they say. Celia Robinson tells me. Everyone tells me. Oh, it's not fair. She *can't* be dead. You've been in and out of her room, too. Don't attempt to deny it. Everyone tells me. Celia Robinson tells me . . .'

The cold draught evidently bit the Major too, for he sprang in the air like an angry cat.

'*Certainly*, I telephoned for your mother's doctor,' began Pyke. He prayed that his stutter would not impede him at this moment. His prayer was answered. 'I had reason to believe that her death was not caused by natural causes.'

'*How dare you!*' The Major's voice rose and broke into a shriek. 'Oh, really, this is too much!'

He held himself up by the stair rails. They shook and creaked. They had not been built to support heavy weights.

'*I must see my mother!*' he cried. His face was now quite suffused. The vein in the middle of his forehead throbbed and throbbed. Dr Stalag-Jones reappeared in the doorway. She looked coldly at the Major. 'I should like to see my poor mother,' he said. His tone was more reasonable than before.

'I am afraid you cannot,' said Dr Stalag-Jones. She turned to Pyke. 'Perhaps *you* will show me where the telephone is? I *do* find myself unable to sign the certificate. Just as you thought. Frankly, I should like the police surgeon's opinion.'

Major Bognor, gasping, accompanied them downstairs. Every now and then he attempted a long and explosive speech about the rights of heirs-at-law. Dr Stalag-Jones paused in the doorway of Tony Robinson's office and looked at him with cold, cod eyes.

'Major,' she said, 'I am afraid that in the immediate future you are going to find it is far from an advantage to be your mother's heir.'

And she shut the door of the office in Major Bognor's face.

CHAPTER TEN

The atmosphere that pervaded the rest of the hotel while this was happening was quite enough to make Miriam Birdseye break her habit of late rising. First, she peered from the window to see if anything was happening in the office window. It was *not*, so she opened her bedroom door. The cold on the landing drove her in again, muttering about long winter underpants. Twenty minutes later she came downstairs, dressed for deep-sea fishing in a thick navy-blue sweater with a roll collar and navy-blue trousers. In spite of the fact that her normal rising-time was twelve noon, she seemed happy.

II

She first met Celia Robinson. Celia (as usual) seemed covered in various child-sized utensils. Miriam turned, shuddering, from motherhood in the raw. Downstairs in the hall Major Bognor could be seen (now dressed) seated outside the office door glowering. Miriam particularly wished to avoid him. Words like 'twenty minutes' and 'bloody cheek' and 'intolerable' rose towards her, somewhat muffled by rage and the Major's rampant moustache. Miriam stole downstairs and turned quickly to the right. She had suddenly recollected the extraordinary omniscience of Connie the Chef. If she wanted the latest intelligence she would certainly find it in the kitchen.

III

Connie Watson sat gloomily slouched at the kitchen table. There was a neat double gin at her elbow. She was laboriously writing a letter with a great many extraordinary flourishes. Every now and then she dipped the remnants of a fountain-pen into a clogged bottle of ink. She was breathing hard. She acknowledged Miriam by raising her heavy eyelids. To her own surprise, Miriam said she *would* like some breakfast, thank you very much. Presently she was sitting at the kitchen table eating large quantities of fried bread, bacon and tomatoes.

'Oysters didn't harm *you*, then?' said Connie. 'Pardon me enquiring.'

The kitchen seemed more friendly than it had seemed the day before. At least, it was warmer than the rest of the hotel.

'No,' said Miriam, with her mouth full. Nervously she eyed the gin at Connie's elbow. 'Oysters always kill or cure. They are the most easily assimilated of food . . .'

'Come again?' said Connie politely. She rested the fish-slice on top of the stove. She leant upon it as though she were a Field Marshal leaning on his baton. She hummed tunelessly and sipped her gin.

'One digests them easily.'

'Ah!'

There was a pause while Miriam began to eat toast and

marmalade and butter. (There were, of course, unlimited quantities of all these things in the Oranmore kitchen. In the dining-room things were very different.) After some time Connie spoke again.

'Little old Mrs Bognor didn't digest those little old oysters quite so easy as all that, seemingly? Doctor's up there now,' she added. She jerked her head sideways as though she were a soccer footballer heading the ball in the goal-mouth. 'I knew when the cat come in.'

Miriam looked surprised. What did Connie mean? Connie had (as the journalists say) a new *slant* on the story. For her it revolved round Mrs Bognor's black tom cat, Justin. He had been missing for a day or two (that being his habit and him not arranged, if Miss Birdseye took Connie's meaning), and he had come a-tapping on the window of the base-ment bedroom at about two in the morning with his little black nose.

'*There* he was, jus' like a great black shadow, on the window-ledge, askin' me to let his highness in. Didn't half give me a turn. Quite *relieved* I was when I saw what it was, worn out and all covered with mud. And all that good horse-meat *she* got down from London for him quite gone to waste. Though indeed, judgin' by the meat Tony buys for the *guests* to eat, there should be a horse butcher's in Brunton same like anywhere else. And as for that no-good son of *hers*—' And here, at this point of the strange disjointed narrative (that seemed to combine all the more obvious characteristics of the English spinster and the tough momma from the underworld of Soho), Miriam interrupted. She wished to know why Connie had *known* that all was not well with Mrs Bognor.

'By Justin. Oh, he was strugglin' and kickin' all right. See here ...'

And Connie rolled up a sleeve and showed Miriam her fine big mottled forearm, where a furrowed scratch ran downwards from her elbow. 'He knew well enough his mum was dead, didn't he then, poor beast. And not died natural, *neither* – he knew that too, you bet.'

Here Connie stroked a great black mat of fur that lay luxuriously across her lap. Miriam, surprised, half rose and saw an enormous tom cat with yellow eyes like lamps. He stirred and stretched his claws and yawned.

'Goodness,' said Miriam. 'What a *very* beautiful animal ...'

'Ah,' said Connie.

She went on stroking the cat. She seemed to have no further interest in Miriam. Miriam felt herself on the edge of important discoveries.

'You are writing, I see,' she said anxiously. 'I expect you are writing a book? I have written some books myself and I disliked it *very much*. It left me too much *alone* ...'

Connie seemed gratified at the thought that Miriam might think her a literary lady. And indeed, in her green and torn boiler-suit, with her heavily cropped head, she looked sinister enough for anything.

'No,' she said reluctantly, 'I'm not writin' a book. Though, mind *you*, I've always thought, on me old Cook's Tour like I am, there's material for a good one. I've got the title and all. *Adventures of a Hotel Proprietor*. Good, eh?'

'Yes indeed,' said Miriam. 'Catchy,' she added, as Connie did not seem altogether satisfied.

'I'm writing a letter. Sending some dough to the old bank

manager to pay for me funeral. Whortleberry Down where I went bankrupt. Broke me heart,' said Connie. 'Still had a heart to break. Thought I'd all the money in the world. So did my partner.' Connie Watson sighed. 'She was a Glory.' And Connie seemed to float away on a sad little tide of gin and memory.

'Sending some *dough*?' Miriam leapt on the only relevant remark. 'So Mr Robinson has *paid* you?'

'For a wonder,' said Connie. 'Talk of the devil.'

She swilled the gin round and round in her glass and stared at the door. She seemed to expect someone. Miriam, who had heard nothing, was surprised.

Sure enough, Tony hurried in almost immediately. He was white and shaking. He gave the impression that he was half dressed. His braces flapped behind him on the floor like black elastic snakes. His eyes looked like pale-blue poached eggs. He obviously had a terrible hangover.

He held himself up by the kitchen table.

'For God's sake, a drink . . .' he said. His teeth chattered.

Connie, unmoved, slowly swallowed all her gin.

'No spirits,' she said firmly. 'Bottle of sherry in the sideboard,' she added. 'You can have *that*, if you like.'

She jerked her head. Tony slammed back the sliding door and cried out as he put his head down. Inside, wrapped in a shroud of twisted paper, was a bottle labelled 'British Wine – Sherry Style'. Miriam was horrified. Tony drew the cork and addressed himself seriously to the consumption of British wine, sherry style. He drank it *all*. When the bottle was empty he went through into the scullery. They heard the tinkle as the bottle dropped in the dust-bin.

'My God!' said Miriam.

'Oh, that's nothing,' said Connie.

It did indeed seem to be nothing. Tony did not seem drunk. He actually appeared to have more vitality. He even ate some toast. He beamed round at Miriam.

'Telephoning for the police. Fun, isn't it?' he said gaily. 'Forgive me. Half dressed.'

He slipped his braces over his shoulders and groped behind him for his coat.

'*Perlice?*' said Connie, shaken from her immobility. 'What the hell for?'

'Old cow of a woman doctor won't sign a death certificate for old Mum Bognor.' Tony was quite unperturbed.

'Never did care for women doctors,' said Connie.

Miriam agreed, wagging her head, that they always seemed unnatural somehow.

'Old Glass Eye's in a terrible rage,' added Tony, with his mouth full of toast.

'*Hey!*' Connie was indignant. 'You forget this lady's by way of being *engaged* to old Glass Eye.'

'No,' said Miriam hastily. 'No. All off.'

'Sorry, I'm sure,' said Connie. 'Sker-washed.'

There was a long pause in the kitchen, while Tony mumbled his toast and said he didn't feel very well. Connie abruptly broke the silence.

'Now that *other* boy who's with you. Freddie Pyke. I've got very fond of *him*.'

Miriam made another (and less frightening) grimace. Tony had gone rather quiet. He was sitting drawing patterns on the top of the kitchen table with one long bendable finger.

'Celia's mother,' he said. 'It's all her fault. Bloody old woman.

94

I *said* to Celia we couldn't afford to have her *and* give her one of the best bedrooms. Now look what's happened . . . You mustn't think I can't be economical too . . .' He turned to Miriam.

'Don't be silly, dear,' said Miriam. 'I don't suppose your mother-in-law poisoned the oysters, do you?'

'*The oysters weren't poisoned!*' Tony sounded quite hysterical. He had half risen to his feet. 'The whole thing is a bloody awful mistake.'

Miriam leant back in her chair and smiled her most annoying, most provocative, smile.

'Now you've got some money, dear Tony (if I may call you so),' she said, 'you can take *me* out and buy me another drink.' Connie, for some reason, had also risen, and Justin, the beautiful black cat, sprang like a panther to the floor, hissing furiously, almost crackling with sparks. A cup was broken and a plate fell noisily to the ground. When the excitement had subsided Tony turned to Miriam.

'Damned awful cat of Mrs Bognor's,' he said. 'Women with cats like that are witches. Witches come to a bad end. What did you say? I've got some money? Where did you get that idea from? I'm as broke as I was yesterday. And I've an overdraft of a hundred and forty-two pounds.' He sighed spectacularly. 'Ah well,' he said. 'We mayn't have much money, but we do see *life*.'

Connie hurried out of the room. Miriam and Tony heard Connie kick open the door of the bedroom. Then it slammed shut. There was a low murmur of voices. Miriam scowled and turned to Tony.

'Everyone is lying,' she said. 'No one is to be trusted an inch.' Tony raised his eyebrows.

'Not even me?' he said gallantly.

'You least of all,' said Miriam.

'Oh, but why?'

'My dear boy.' Miriam stood up and brushed off her navy-blue trousers. They had collected (amongst other things) breadcrumbs and tom-cat hairs. 'A more *obvious* *wastrel* it would be harder to find.'

But she patted him on the top of the head when she went out of the room.

CHAPTER ELEVEN

Upstairs, also, the hotel was progressing slowly towards a state of turmoil. Celia Robinson ran up and down, carrying various disagreeable pink and blue objects painted with black cats and yellow elephants that were obviously a part of the furnishings of April's and May's bedroom. She was moving them, she said. She could no longer allow them to remain on *that* landing, poor darlings. She did not explain how April and May (who had never shown signs of human intelligence) would be able to discern between Mrs Bognor Living and Mrs Bognor Dead. Mrs Greeb, answering to the courtesy title of 'Granny', was helping her with a steady running commentary.

Granny, for example, thought it odd (if it *were* the oysters) that *she* had not had sickness in the night. Granny's stomach had always been Ever so Tender and susceptible to that kind of thing. She added other (more unpleasant) details. Pyke, whose room was on this floor, went away from Mrs Bognor. He was found later, by Miriam, leaning his forehead against the cool glass, looking sadly out of his window. It faced north, away from the sea.

'What's the matter *now?*' said Miriam unsympathetically.

'W-we are w-waiting for the police,' said Pyke coldly. 'You w-wouldn't understand.'

He went on looking out of the window.

Miriam was extremely angry. Few people, she said excitedly, in the last few years had had more opportunity of acquiring an understanding of police procedure. Particularly in cases of violent death. She began a rapid *résumé* (that might have been entitled *Murders I Have Been Mixed Up In*), making her points by waving Pyke's comb. Pyke went on suffering.

'L-look, dear,' said Pyke eventually, 'I'm v-very fond of you. As an actress. B-but to be f-frank, I *dislike* amateur d-detectives. The law, after all, was once my business. Th-they b-bore me s-stiff in fiction. In life they are merely sordid. P-pray let the police attend to their own business and continue to b-be yourself. Whatever you have done in the past, Miriam, I *implore* you to leave this business to th-those c-competent—'

Miriam's large pale-blue eyes acquired a vague, cynical expression.

'You're jealous,' she said briefly.

'L-leave b-blood and thunder to those whom it becomes,' said Pyke.

'But there's no blood and you're stealing my thunder,' said Miriam.

II

Outside they could hear a car that stopped and clashed its gears. The engine was turned off. Miriam opened the door to the landing and peered out. Maggie Button, her large flat face mauve with effort, was approaching up the stairs two at a time.

'It's the police,' said Maggie, very excited.

'And they want me?' said Miriam, rather too casually.

'They want *him*,' said Maggie Button, and disappeared down-stairs again.

III

In the hall there was a little sandy man. A bristly toothbrush moustache stood out at right angles in the middle of a pink, agile face. He was holding a green pork-pie hat in his hand.

'Tomkins is the name,' he said. 'Detective-Inspector Tomkins. Sussex CID. Something *up* here. Or so I understand. A good lady dead, I believe, who shouldn't be?'

Celia Robinson leant nervously forward over the banisters. 'That's right, Inspector,' she said, coming down one step at a time. 'That's right. Perhaps you'll come into my office? It's much cosier there. My name's Robinson. Celia Robinson. The hotel belongs to my husband.'

Celia stopped hovering and came into the hall. She was wearing a yellow jersey and a brown skirt. Her legs were bare and very vulnerable. Tomkins allowed himself to be led into the office.

'Ah ...' he said. 'It was Dr Jones who rang me up, surely? I was expecting to find *her* here ...'

He looked round him, twinkling and sniffing. His face con-tracted into a rubber ball. The office was pleasant enough. It faced south, and therefore had all the sun that ever shone on Brunton-on-Sea. For this reason it became stuffy rather quickly. This morning it was somewhat over-furnished with play-pens, corals, bells, little fur animals and all the other hideous impedimenta of golden childhood. Pyke, wrinkling his fine big nose, stopped in the doorway and disappeared inside his stiff white city collar.

'Oh, come in, come in, Mr – er ...' said Tomkins affably. He had put his hat and his brief-case down on a chair that was already full of gramophone records and a Kiddie Picture Book called *Mogsie the Mechanical Mouse*.

'Mr *Pyke*,' said Celia Robinson, and bit her lip as though she wished she had said nothing. 'I'm sorry the room's in such an awful mess.'

'Not at all, miss,' said Tomkins kindly. 'Mr Pyke's a guest in the hotel, I take it? Now, the room where the good lady passed over? It's locked, I hope?'

There was something endearing in Tomkins' unruffled cockiness. Pyke, inclining his head, implied that he might take anything he pleased.

'Oh indeed, yes,' said Celia in a rush. 'Mr Pyke found poor Mrs Bognor. Dr Stalag-Jones has the key. I'm terribly sorry. She's just gone up to examine April and May, my twin daughters. April seems to have the beginnings of a rash, and I always say you can't be too careful ...'

Pyke, who had picked up *Mogsie the Mechanical Mouse* and was reading it, shuddered and hastily put it down.

'Nothing infectious I'm *sure*, Mr Pyke,' said Celia, and looked at him with open hatred.

'I wasn't exactly *enthralled*,' said Pyke coldly.

Tomkins coughed.

'I'm a family man myself,' said Tomkins. 'But ...'

He looked towards the door and twitched his sandy eyebrows.

'Yes, yes,' said Celia nervously. 'Of course. I quite agree. I'll go and get the doctor immediately.'

She rushed out of the room. Tomkins sauntered to the window and looked out on Durbah Villas. For a moment it had stopped raining. The fitful sun had emerged. The raindrops along the length of the green, wooden balcony winked and glistened like glass beads. Tomkins waved a hand. He turned back to Pyke.

'This just about ought to put the kibosh on this place, eh?' he said cheerfully.

'I'm sorry.' Pyke was hesitant.

'The Oranmore,' explained Tomkins. 'Last owner's wife committed suey the pud,' he went on cheerfully. 'Dived off the cliffs on to the shingle after the owner shot 'imself. *This* owner . . .' He raised a significant right elbow and winked his right eye. 'Or so I've heard. Goes on payin' five bob in the pound or thereabouts, I suppose?'

Pyke said slowly that he didn't know. His nose, in spite of himself, twitched disdainfully, announcing that *he* couldn't see the point of all this gossip. Tomkins shrugged his narrow shoulders and plunged his hands deep in the pockets of his tight grey flannel trousers. Apparently he possessed unusual intuitive feminine perceptions, for he turned on Pyke as though he sensed the atmosphere, and said accusingly:

'*You're a writer.*'

'I – er – er . . .' Pyke's stammer returned. 'Y-yes, I am,' he said eventually, mildly astonished.

'You writers are all alike.' Tomkins sounded very cross about it. 'Life's a nice, smooth, intellectual problem to *you*. One, two, three, four, maybe five suspects – at the most *six*. Bob's your uncle. Then who dun it? That's what your sort think life's like. I tell you, the police 'ave *got* to gossip. To find anything out at all. *We* can't be strong an' silent – like in the detective stories.'

'Oh . . . b-but I *h-hate* d-detective stories,' said Pyke anxiously. 'R-really I do.'

'Well, it *isn't* all neat an' tidy, see?' Tomkins stared truculently up at Pyke, who winced but stood his ground and stared back. 'Life's a mess,' said Tomkins, 'that's what it is. People don' even die tidily. I ought to know. Writers. They don' know the first thing. Hear them talk. Read their books. Cor'! Cordin' to them, a case goes straight from "So Miriam heaved a tumultuous sigh. "Ow brilliant you are, Mr Carfax,' says she, failin' forward on 'is manly bosom," to the Old Bailey. *Writers!*' said Tomkins.

He annihilated all writers and students of criminology with a brisk and rather dirty thumb, pressed with a rotary movement into the palm of his other hand.

'What's all that about *Miriam*?' came a familiar voice behind them. 'And who, might I ask, is brilliant Mr Carfax?'

IV

Detective-Inspector Tomkins turned slowly round from the bow window.

'I know that voice,' he said. His whole face lit up. He advanced on Miriam with broad, pink hands outstretched. 'It's Miss *Birdseye!*' he said. 'It is Miss Birdseye, isn't it?' He turned to Pyke. 'Everything will be all right now,' he said.

'*Tomkins!*' cried Miriam. To Pyke's somewhat jaundiced eye she appeared much too pleased.

Tomkins shook her by both hands. He was obviously transported with pleasure. He flung explanations and greetings in all directions.

'I always look on Miss Birdseye as my little old mascot,' he began. 'Was as a result of our association in that screwy girls'-school case I got my promo.* Been longing to tell you, Miss Birdseye. Gave you a tinkle several times when I was in Town, but no reply. Yes indeed, miss. I'm detective-inspector now.' Tears of pure delight seemed to stand in his eyes. 'All thanks to you, miss.' And he shook her hand again.

'*Mascot* I like,' said Miriam. 'And *little* I like. But old I am not so keen on. Tell me,' she went on; her voice changed a little and became very slightly patronizing. 'How is *Mrs* Tomkins?'

'Passed over, poor dear,' said Tomkins briskly. 'That's why I was able to be took on in this new appointment. Takes me further afield, as you might say. County Special investigation. Chief Constable's *delighted*.' Tomkins laughed and dug his elbow near Miriam's ribs. Miriam stood it remarkably well. ''Aven't 'ad to call in the Yard *once* since I seen you,' he said.

'You've had *many murders* in the county since the Radcliff Hall Case, then?' said Miriam curiously.

'To be honest,' Tomkins cast down his eyes, 'no. This is the first.'

Pyke showed his surprise at this premature Police Diagnosis of the death of Mrs Bognor with a faint cough. Miriam scowled at him and he instantly regretted it.

'Not like the old days in Kensington, eh?' Tomkins continued enthusiastically. 'Then we'd always something on. If it

---

* *Poison for Teacher.*

wasn't child murder an' rape, it would be grievous bodily 'arm linked up with forgery. And every week, too.'

'Very nice,' said Pyke primly.

'You've met Mr Pyke?' said Miriam, as though she hoped to regularize the position.

'Oh yes,' said Tomkins smoothly. 'Been tellin' me how he writes his books. Though, mind, I don't care for detective stories as a rule, really ...'

Pyke slowly became purple. He began to stammer all over again that he was a poet. Miriam smiled evilly. Then Dr Stalag-Jones (shepherded by Celia Robinson) reappeared in the doorway.

'If you're *quite* ready, *Sergeant?*' said Dr Stalag-Jones, in a very high-class voice. 'We can go and view the body.'

V

No doubt, if, at the beginning of his association with Dr Stalag-Jones, *Inspector* Tomkins had not been quite so wounded, he might not have invited Miriam to accompany them. As it was, a very pretty clash of wills took place on the staircase. Dr Stalag-Jones raised her eyebrows while Inspector Tomkins pointed out in the nicest possible way that he was (*a*) an inspector and (*b*) in charge of the case from now on. Pyke (still rather too purple for real charm) was left at the bottom of the stairs.

'I'll take your evidence later on, sir,' said Tomkins, maddeningly turning back to put him in his place. 'After you, Miss Birdseye.'

And Pyke and Celia Robinson sourly watched the three figures disappear upstairs to the next landing.

VI

'Now, Madam,' said Tomkins rapidly, a quarter of an hour later, 'we will certainly order a post-mortem. *Our* Dr Fawcett-Smith will be up this afternoon to make all arrangements. The organs will be opened. You will make your statement and appear at the inquest?'

'Quite,' said Dr Stalag-Jones. 'Well' – she was vexed – 'until Dr *Smith* decides whether or not there is any poisonous matter (as I suspect) that might have caused such immediate and sudden death in my patient—'

'Such as arsenic,' said Miriam suddenly.

She was over by the window, making an abortive attempt to appear inconspicuous.

'Such as arsenic,' said Dr Stalag-Jones. She stared at Miriam as though she were hardly human. It seemed to Miriam she was much less than a sheet of looking-glass where Dr Stalag-Jones occasionally adjusted her hat. 'You will not need me until then.' The doctor's manner was quite final. She snapped shut her little leather case.

'Well, no,' said Tomkins regretfully. 'But quite between ourselves, madam, what gave you the idea? I mean, why wouldn't you sign the certificate?'

'Natural caution,' snapped Dr Stalag-Jones.

She stood up, cracking her fingers savagely.

'No, but between ourselves,' said Tomkins. He looked directly into the doctor's eyes. He turned on *Powerful Personal Magnetism, Grade I*. Miriam wondered if he had been taught it at Police College.

'Between ourselves,' began Dr Stalag-Jones, responding

nicely. 'Mrs Bognor was a very healthy woman for her age. With an excellent digestion. Although her heart was subject to palpitation on occasion (and whose is not?) ...'

'And whose is not?' repeated Miriam in (she felt) a tone of appropriate enthusiasm. She was rewarded with a blank, unfriendly stare.

'There was no organic weakness. It is also more than strange that the lady should die after eating *oysters*. Her favourite food.' Dr Stalag-Jones' very faintly watering lips suggested that she, too, was not altogether indifferent to oysters. 'At a party where everyone else in the hotel *also* ate oysters, or so Mrs Robinson tells me—'

'And we took no harm, and anyone who ate them if they were funny,' said Miriam rapidly, 'wouldn't die in the night, or would we?'

'As a matter of fact you wouldn't,' said Dr Stalag-Jones, with sudden warmth. 'But I am very surprised that you should know that.'

'Well, forgive me,' continued the doctor. 'I've the findings from my medical board to write up. Call me up, Sergeant, will you?'

And so, with (it must be admitted) the last word, Dr Stalag-Jones swept out of the room.

CHAPTER TWELVE

Tomkins did not proceed to an immediate examination of Mrs Bognor's bedroom. He stood and looked at Miriam, his moustache quivering as delicately as the antennae of a butterfly. Miriam wondered if it had some extra-sensory significance.

'You know, I always admired you, Miss Birdseye,' he was saying. 'And that Russian friend of yours, Miss Natasha, I always admired her, too. But if you'll pardon me, I've always wanted to meet *you* again, so to say—'

'How very kind,' said Miriam.

'This gentleman downstairs now, Mr Pyke. Is he a friend of yours?' Tomkins' tone changed abruptly and his blue eyes were suddenly fixed and (Miriam thought) glazed.

'Oh yes,' said Miriam. 'He's a very good friend of mine.' But it would be inconvenient if Tomkins really 'took against' Pyke. 'It's the other one I was supposed to be engaged to,' she added hastily. 'Pyke is just a friend.'

Her tone was vague. To Tomkins she seemed genuinely uninterested. Her unfocused stare drifted lazily over the lawn, the garden-seat, the cacti below her.

'Ah!' Tomkins suddenly smiled. 'Kind of tame cat, eh?' Tomkins' face changed again. He came closer to her.

'"The other one"? What d'you mean "the other one"?' he said suspiciously. 'Are you still engaged to him?'

'Oh no.' Miriam was at her most inconsequent. 'Bognor. Reggie Bognor. *Her* son.'

She indicated poor dead Mrs Bognor, somewhere behind her, with a jerk of the head. She felt ashamed of herself.

'Her son!' Tomkins sprang on tiptoe with excitement. 'What's he like?'

'Oh, well ...' Miriam was reluctant. 'Honestly, dear, you'll see for yourself. And I'm not really engaged to *him*, either. The last of the stage-door Johnnies, perhaps? Carlton Club and all that sort of thing. I never agreed to marry him, either. I came down here to stop him telling lies about it. Spent stacks of money always. Lately, I think, it was Mum's money. Mum was hanging on a bit tightly.'

'Mum's money.' Tomkins considered it pensively. 'Champagne parties after the show?' he went on wistfully. 'That kind of thing?'

'Well, actually, *yes*,' said Miriam.

'And what made you think Mum was closing up her purse?'

'Fewer parties. Less flowers. Less presents. More letters. More avowals of enthusiastic unwavering devotion.' Miriam turned to Tomkins as though she were earnestly seeking information. 'Have you ever noticed how gentlemen are suddenly definitely in love with ladies when the gentlemen have no money?'

'No. Do they?' said Tomkins.

'Oh yes,' said Miriam. 'Rich gentlemen don't declare themselves.'

'Oh. Don't they?' said Tomkins.

But he became extremely quiet and he allowed the small change in his trouser pocket to fall slowly from a height with a spectacular series of little rattles.

II

After this, the inventory of Mrs Bognor's possessions, and the examination of her room, proceeded without interruption. Tomkins had looked at the contents of the wardrobe and the underclothing drawers before he came upon Mrs Bognor's plastic handbag. It had been stuffed down behind the chest of drawers and the wall. It was quite empty.

III

'And another thing,' said Miriam, a few moments later. 'I should have that work-box forced if I were you. Women always keep lovers' letters in work-boxes.'

'At *her* age?'

'Oh well, other things, important things, you never know ...'

'She ought to have keys for it herself.'

'Whoever swiped the bag swiped the keys.' Miriam was testy. 'I'm almost sure,' she added, 'that Mrs Bognor had sables ...'

'I see what you mean,' said Tomkins. 'Wasn't that a sable in the wardrobe? There *was* a fur coat ...' He was on all fours beside the bed.

'It was a musquash,' said Miriam coldly. 'And incidentally, it was common knowledge that Mrs Bognor had two hundred pounds yesterday in that bag ...' Miriam spoke slowly, but excitement mounted in her voice.

'Oh, my God, no!' Tomkins sat back on his heels. 'Any way of checking?'

'Reggie might know the bank they came from,' said Miriam slowly. 'He's bound to know his mother's affairs. I *suppose* he's the heir. It would be definitely in his interests to disclose everything he knows.'

'Yes,' said Tomkins, 'even if ...'

'Even if what?' said Miriam. 'Don't vex me. You know I can't concentrate for more than half an hour at a time ...'

'Even if he murdered his mother,' said Tomkins.

IV

'Well, there we are,' said Tomkins ten minutes later, brushing chalk from his knees. 'I'll let my photographer come up now. The ambulance should be here, too.'

'I'll go into her sitting-room and see,' said Miriam. 'You can see the road from there.'

She returned in two minutes, frowning. She had nearly broken her leg over Maggie Button, who was on all fours outside the door, 'doing' the carpets with a duster. This was an unusual proceeding.

'It is there,' said Miriam, and she heard a scuttling of feet behind her and went on: 'It's collecting quite a crowd. Extraordinary, on a Sunday morning. The street was quite empty five minutes ago.'

The quick clatter of feet on the stairs suggested Maggie Button rushing for a dress-circle seat.

'Oh yes, they love ambulances,' said Tomkins. 'They'll come

out from under stones to see an ambulance. Very morbid they are.'

He straightened his back.

V

The late Mrs Bognor left the Oranmore Hotel without incident, unless we may count Maggie Button, who decided to faint in the hall.

Tomkins, carrying his brief-case, locked his photographer in Mrs Bognor's bedroom and moved his headquarters to Mrs Bognor's sitting-room.

'This is where you had the oyster party, miss?' he said to Miriam, enviously sniffing the air. He put his brief-case down and began to clear a light bamboo table that carried a tablecloth and an unflowering green bush in the window. The stale, Edwardian room showed no signs of the party. Someone had tidied it most efficiently. Miriam commented on this. It was a macabre background for the inspector's neat sparrow-like intelligence. The faint thumping of the photographers next door came, slightly muffled, through the wall. Sometimes a heavier footfall also rather maddeningly shook the floor.

'That's Lake,' said Tomkins, and grinned. 'Very heavy on his feet is Lake.'

He went primly round the sitting-room. On the mantelpiece, among the yellowing photographs and the Japanese fans and the dust that collected on all these things, were two invitations: 'Mrs Stalag-Jones At Home. Cocktails 6.30–8.00. RSVP. The Plot, Mitre Road, Brunton-on-Sea,' read Tomkins slowly. 'Twenty-eighth

February. Colonel Rucksack, Cherry Pickings, Pondicherry Parade. Tea and Bridge 4–7.00 *p.m. Twenty-fourth February.*' The last invitation had 'Mind you Come – Charlie-Arlie' written across it in a wavering hand.

'Twenty-fourth February. That's this afternoon,' said Miriam.

'The doctor we know,' said Tomkins. 'But we haven't been introduced to Colonel Rucksack. Someone will have to RSVP and say "Miss Otis regrets" to Charlie-Arlie . . .'

'Reggie will know,' said Miriam.

'Reggie had better know everything we want him to,' said Tomkins unkindly. 'About time I saw the heir-at-law.' He propped up the invitation from Dr Stalag-Jones against the mantelpiece. 'I often wondered if it would be Mr Stalag she married, or Mr Jones.'

'I'm sure she was a Miss Stalag,' said Miriam. 'She looks like a Stalag.'

Tomkins turned the invitation from Colonel Rucksack over and over in his short, blunt hands. He suddenly slid it into his pocket.

'Got an idea,' he said. 'We won't tell Reggie about *this* one.'

'No?' said Miriam.

'You and me are going out to play bridge,' said Tomkins. 'With this Colonel Rucksack. This afternoon.'

Miriam, who had never played any card game except poker, opened her eyes very wide indeed. But she did not seem annoyed.

VI

When Reggie Bognor finally came he was clothed and bathed and still very angry. Then he realized that Miriam would remain in the room while Inspector Tomkins interviewed him. His control abruptly snapped.

'Highly irregular,' he began hysterically. 'Shall say nothing at all. Damned impertinence. Shall see the Chief Constable – break you ...'

His voice trailed away, spluttering helplessly.

'Just as you please, of course, sir,' said Tomkins amiably. 'It would save *time* if you were to see me instead.'

'As a matter of fact, Mum is a very old friend of the Chief Constable herself,' said Miriam slowly.

'You honestly won't do yourself any good by making complaints, Major Bognor,' said Tomkins.

'Shall get m'lawyer to write ...' Reggie was still spluttering. 'Monstrous behaviour—'

'Or lack of it,' said Miriam warmly. She suddenly smiled. 'Now do stop being silly, dear, and tell the sergeant (I beg your pardon, ducks. *Inspector*) all. You've been righteously indignant quite long enough, dear. Getting boring.'

And to Tomkins' great astonishment, Major Bognor threw back his head and roared with laughter, clucking like an old hen, showing his two neat plates of false teeth and most of his epiglottis. Miriam found this sudden surrender endearing.

'Very well, then,' said the Major when he had finished this sad exhibition. 'What do you want to know?'

Tomkins unscrewed a silver pencil and flipped open a reporter's note-book.

'Well, what was your mother's bank, for one thing?' he said. 'And is this her handbag?'

He held out the black plastic bag. The Major took it from him. He turned it over in his firm, spatulate fingers. Then he opened it.

'Nothing in it, nothing in it, but the binding round it,' he said. 'Yes, it's Mother's all right.'

'We saw that about it being empty, dear,' said Miriam. 'Was there anything in it *yesterday*?'

'Oh, indeed yes,' said the Major. 'Two hundred pounds, for one thing. Intended for me. And the usual woman's rubbish, I suppose. Mother took the two hundred out of the bank for me. That's one of the reasons I was getting in such a tizzy. You can't blame me?'

He looked apologetically at Tomkins, who coughed non-committedly.

'What bank would she have drawn these pounds out of?' said Miriam.

There was an appreciable pause before the Major replied. Tomkins had time to look up, startled, and his pencil (with which he had been making rapid and illegible notes) went squeaking senselessly sideways across his pad.

'The Westminster,' said the Major. And passed his hands over his head, where his sparse brown hair was carefully arranged to hide a bald patch.

CHAPTER THIRTEEN

Pyke stood in the hall of the Oranmore Hotel. It had been upon him that Maggie Button had fainted. He had escorted her to the kitchen and Connie Watson, and cups of strong, sweet tea. He had accomplished his task, and had even succeeded in softening Maggie to a semblance of old-world charm. Hiccuping noisily, the wretched girl now sat in the kitchen, while Connie Watson told her she had only wanted the limelight again. 'Should 'ave thought,' she said darkly, stirring away at her own unpleasant tea, 'that findin' a corpse would have been *enough* for one day. Think of the newspapers. They'll be bound to interview you. Think of the publicity.'

This remark soothed Maggie. Her general health seemed all at once to improve. She toyed with her gilt and clammy hair and every now and then rubbed a thumb along the contours of her chin. Pyke fled.

Now he stood in the hall and decided, rain or no rain, that the Oranmore was no place for him. Brunton-on-Sea lay in front of him. He set out briskly for the front.

II

Brunton-on-Sea is one of those seaside resorts where char-à-banc tours are rigorously controlled by a decaying Anglo-Indian population, well versed in the *mystique* of public administration. But in spite of the letters of 'Disgusted' and 'Ex-Indian Judge' and 'Administrator', a little proletarian gaiety often surges along the sea front on Sundays. There is an Ice Cream Parlour that also sells weak, tepid coffee with milk in it. There are newspaper and tobacconists' shops. There is a Twopenny Library with (by way of window dressing) any number of terrifying, vacant book jackets scattered across a wooden framework. They represent the extreme violence of human behaviour, so much deplored by Pyke. Now Pyke stopped and looked at them gloomily.

Here a young lady in an evening dress with a 'plunge' neckline brandished a smoking revolver in a sexual manner. Here a young gentleman in thigh boots and riding-breeches, his hands lashed behind his back, picked cleverly at his bonds with a heavy blood-stained knife. The same young lady, in the same neckline, crouched in front of him, making an equal gesture with the same sort of revolver. Pyke sighed. He wondered if one of the books could be the sequel of the other. That would be soothing. But no, the authors were quite different. The titles were very odd. One was called *The Luck of the Kicking Kay*, the other *Screaming Midnight*. Pyke walked on, quite sure that the girl in the neckline was called Kay, and no doubt kicked a very great deal.

At this point, aware that his legs were cold and the small of his back shivery, he came to the Ice Cream Parlour. It was heavily labelled 'Strong's Sarsaparilla'. It was obviously very much hotter than the sea front. A fog of warm steam had already formed on the inside of the windows. There was a false Tutti Frutti, with cotton-wool cream and a tin cherry, and cardboard globes of pink-and-white ice cream that announced Strong's other wares in the window. A card remarked simply, 'This style 2/6.' Pyke was in a new world. The door shut cosily behind him and excluded the draughty sea front and the sobbing hiss of the English Channel on the shingle.

III

There was a marble-topped bar. Behind some shining urns and a dubious machine with a label on the top that said 'Milk Shaker', and four terrifying taps called 'Raspberry', 'Strawberry', 'Vanilla' and 'Chocolate', there was a young Italian in a white coat called George. He was extremely good-tempered, with short, curling black side-whiskers. In the middle distance there were enormous green glazed china urns of no functional purpose whatever.

Pyke joined a short queue leading to the bar counter. It consisted of two middle-aged ladies and a little old gentleman with a sharply strung purple neck like a cassowary. Pyke listened carefully to their orders to make certain of the 'form'. The ladies asked competently for Strawberry Special and coffee, Vanilla Surprise and coffee. The old gentleman asked for coffee. He spoke to the barman and wished him good morning in the touching, eager tones of a lonely man. In this way Pyke found out the barman's name. Or perhaps the old gentleman habitually called servants 'George' ...

The coffee looked perfectly beastly. The little old gentleman spun round in a senile fashion and his sharp little elbow crashed into Pyke's ribs. The cool beige liquid flowed helplessly over Pyke's trousers. The old gentleman was very distressed. He apologized and dabbed at Pyke's trousers and tutted. George was deft and helpful, producing dusters and damp cloths, and by the time that Pyke's trousers had been dried, Pyke and the old gentleman and George were fast friends.

The old gentleman now bought more cups of coffee and included Pyke graciously in his order. They sat down together at a round, marble-topped table near the door. The old gentleman had gone very blue in the face, and Pyke was sorry for him. He wheezed and sighed a lot and joined his hands (purplish and, like his face and neck, covered with large dark-brown freckles) together in his lap. He pressed them painfully, as though he were trying to make himself relax.

'Rucksack is my name, sir,' he began. 'Colonel Charles Rucksack. Ask anyone in Brunton. They all know *me*. Think we should make ourselves known to each other, don't you?' He laughed suddenly, looking at a table near them. 'By Jove! Lady looks as though she's suppin' with the devil, eh?' Pyke turned and observed the middle-aged lady digging down into her Strawberry Special.

'It is a v-very l-long sp-spoon,' agreed Pyke gravely.

'Been here long? Stranger, aren't yer?' Colonel Rucksack drank some of his coffee. 'Filthy stuff. Always come here on a Sunday morning. Something to do.' He banged his cup back in the saucer and looked at Pyke. The Colonel's gaze travelled down from the tip of his large nose to his shining, well-made shoes. 'Been sent out. Kept out of the way while they cook m'Sunday dinner. Curious to be takin' a holiday in *February*. Where are yer stayin'?'

Pyke agreed that it was indeed curious, but in fact he was not on holiday. He had come to Brunton to *work*. He was silent, biting his full lips, thinking of his play, unregarded, lying pathetically in his bedroom in its brief-case. Damn Miriam! She really was impossible. *Policemen* indeed!

He admitted he was staying at the Oranmore Hotel.

'Really?' Colonel Rucksack was excited. It seemed that his dear, his very dear, his *favourite*, sister lived there. A permanent guest. A Mrs Eithne Bognor with a scamp of a son. But probably Pyke had already met them?

A demon of caution whispered in the back of Pyke's mind. This and a choking and monstrous jealousy that had risen in him ever since he had observed Miriam gaily admitted to the confidence of Inspector Tomkins. In such an intimate fashion, too ... Certainly here was a heaven-sent opportunity to get even with her. It would take *them* some time (for poor Pyke already saw Miriam and Tomkins in not altogether innocent attitudes) to work through Mrs Bognor's acquaintances to find her dear, her *very* dear, her favourite, brother.

'N-no,' said Pyke, as firmly as his stammer would allow. 'Wh-what does she l-look like?'

The Colonel beamed, obviously delighted to be allowed to talk about his sister.

'Oh, a most striking woman. Most strikin'. Thorough-goin' gentlewoman. Walks with an ebony cane. Excellent business head, though, oddly enough. Plays a dash' good game of bridge, too. Excellent sense of humour. *Our* father (Eithne's and my father, y'know) always used to say to me, "Charles," he used to say, "Eithne has all the brains in this house, Charles," he'd say. "You're only fit for the Army." Oh, you won't be able to miss Eithne ...'

Pyke said very gravely that he was quite sure he wouldn't be able to miss her.

'*Actually*,' said Colonel Rucksack, suddenly very intimate indeed, leaning forward, 'she's been very much happier since Bognor died. Funny thing, Minnie (that was my dear wife), she died within a week of Edgar (that was Rear Admiral Bognor, Eithne's husband), of typhoid. That was in '46. Terrible blow to Eithne and me. But we were able to console each other, up to a point. That's why we both live down here ...'

He searched among several woollen waistcoats with trembling purple hands and produced a note-case.

'M'card,' he said faintly. The effort had obviously taxed his strength. He sat back feebly and continued to sip his coffee.

'What a good name for a house, the Cherry Pickings,' said Pyke politely, handing back the card. It was very correct indeed, engraved in copper-plate handwriting.

'Yes, isn't it? From m'old regiment, of course. We got Reginald – that's Eithne's son, you'll meet him ... an awful bounder, like Edgar his father – we got *him* into the Cherry Pickers. Failed to make good, y'know. Terrible disgrace. Eithne felt it keenly at the time ...'

The old man was obviously delighted that Reginald Bognor had disgraced himself. Pyke began to feel rather sorry for Major Bognor. Surely he couldn't have disgraced himself so much if he had become a major? Pyke reflected that he had never quite understood the Army. He had, after all, only been in it for five years.

'Any son of Edgar Bognor would be bound to come a cropper in a decent regiment. Afterwards he did quite well in the Infantry. But there, Engineers are all alike, aren't they?'

Pyke, who had always found Engineers most intelligent and delightful people, was startled. Evidently he had raised his eyebrows too high, for the old gentleman went plunging off into a difficult explanation about the exact status of executive and specialized grades in the Royal Navy.

'And of course we have the same thing in the Army – not to the same extent. The Royal Army Service Corps, for example. Excellent chaps.' The Colonel lowered his voice. '*But not Gentlemen.*'

Pyke was more than doubtful about all this.

'But damn it,' said the old voice, singing like a mosquito in his right ear, 'one gets that sort of thing in every profession. What's yours?'

'A-a-another coffee,' said Pyke unhappily, rising to his feet. He felt big and awkward beside this fragile little old man.

'No, no. I mean what's your *profession?*'

'I'm a writer,' said Pyke unhappily. He did not dare say he was a poet.

'Oh, I see,' said Colonel Rucksack grimly. 'Even so, *taint tells.* I mean, doesn't it? Take those splendid things by Kipling. "The dawn with silver-sandalled feet crept like a frightened girl" – eh? You can tell the feller was a Gentleman, can't you? Just by the *feel . . .*'

Pyke was very upset. He thought, however, that Oscar Wilde would have been the first to keep Colonel Rucksack in ignorance about the author of this verse. He went hastily to the bar counter and came back presently with two more cups of coffee.

'Nice to talk to yer,' said Colonel Rucksack. 'We speak the same language, eh?'

IV

'Do tell me,' said Pyke seriously, 's-some m-more about your family. Are you and your sister the only children?'

Colonel Rucksack was obviously flattered. He drew a silk handkerchief from his sleeve and remarked: 'Old Army habit. Can't break misself of it.' Then he began a long explanation of the Rucksacks.

'It's a German name, o' course,' he began gaily. 'But we've been British a long time now. Since the nineteenth century, in fact. No. There are the three of us.' He checked names on his fingers. 'Eithne, myself, and my brother Bob.' He paused confidentially and leant forward. 'Bob's a dear chap. While m'mother was alive he was the apple of her eye. Absolutely. But not quite . . .' He paused and darted an anxious glance at Pyke. 'Not quite like us. Well. He was a seven-month child *and* my mother had him at the age of forty-five.'

Pyke nodded enthusiastically.

'And h-how old would he be now?' he asked guardedly. Colonel Rucksack seemed surprisingly anxious to talk about his brother and sister.

'Bob? Must be about forty. Forty-odd. Let's see. I'm sixty-five and Eithne . . . Eithne would be seventy-one yesterday. Hope she got m'birthday present. Must toddle along and see some time. Sad thing about Bob. Forty, but with a mind like a child. Nice child, but child of twelve. You know the sort of thing. Embarrassing.'

Colonel Rucksack broke off and traced rings on the marble table-top with his little finger. Pyke observed (with distaste) a signet ring with a little heraldic beast. A rucksack, no doubt. The Colonel seemed singularly unembarrassed.

'When Mother died we got a very nice married couple there, the Parsons, to look after Bob. Been with them ever since.'

'Where would *there* be?' said Pyke.

'What d'you mean, "there"?' said the Colonel, puzzled. 'I see. There. I mean *here*. Brunton. They have a little semi-detached villa out on the old Brunton Road. Not a bad house in its way. Garden and all that. I fancy Bob does himself rather well. Certainly gets better food than *I* do!'

And the Colonel laughed. Pyke watched him curiously. A great many questions rose to his mind. Why hadn't Colonel Rucksack come to Mrs Bognor's birthday party? And the brother, too. Pyke could see why *he* might not have been invited. Or perhaps they *had* both been invited. Then why hadn't they come? His puzzled expression drew a sharp enquiry from Colonel Rucksack.

'Coffee disagreed with yer already, eh? Really is filthy stuff, isn't it?'

The lady beside them finished her Strawberry Special, sighed heavily, and went away.

'Indeed it is,' said Pyke. He searched desperately for a form of words that would not give him away. Once Colonel Rucksack discovered that he had known Mrs Bognor well enough to attend a birthday party to which the Colonel had (possibly) not been invited, that would be the end of all confidences. 'I expect your sister had a birthday party,' he said slowly. 'At the hotel?'

'At seventy-one?' The Colonel laughed uproariously, throwing back his head again. 'I can see you don't know very many women, Mr——?'

'Pyke,' said Pyke, and stared at the ceiling.

'Thank you. They don't want it to be remembered, y'know.

Anything over fifty – and the whole thing's hushed up. Hushed absolutely right up. Idiotic, really, because everyone else is a year older, *and* knows it.' There was a pause while the Colonel gnawed his lip. 'Pyke,' he repeated softly under his breath. 'Pyke. Any relation to Archie Pyke? Archie Pyke of the Inniskillings? We were at The Shop together ...'

During the war Pyke had abandoned all attempts to understand the Greek claptrap that one regular service officer spoke to another. So he nodded and admitted that Archie Pyke was his uncle (which was true), and did not try to remember whether The Shop was Sandhurst or Woolwich, which he did not know. Never mind. No doubt Colonel Rucksack knew perfectly well himself ...

But at this moment a frenzied, hatless woman burst into the Ice Cream Parlour. She was elderly, with an overcoat carelessly thrown over a cotton dress or overall. Pyke could see there was a smear of gravy on her cheek. She had obviously come straight from her Sunday joint. Once again he deplored the violence of human behaviour. Then he realized with horror that she was approaching their table with unwavering steps. Moreover, she was calling upon his companion by name.

'Colonel Rucksack! Colonel Rucksack!' she was crying. 'You must come at once. At once. Master Bobby. Poor Master Bobby'

'Eh? What? Pull yourself together, Mrs Parsons,' said Colonel Rucksack. He sat fast, but went a little blue round the gills. 'What's the matter with Bob?'

'He's dead,' said Mrs Parsons, and she collapsed into the empty wickerwork chair at their table. And she burst into tears and put her head on the marble table-top to do so.

CHAPTER FOURTEEN

The door eventually shut behind Reginald Bognor, but not before he had given Tomkins a full account of his movements of the night before.

He had been restless apparently after the oyster party and had gone for a walk, as a matter of fact. With any particular object in mind? Well, yes, actually, he *had* had an object in mind. He had gone up to the old Brunton Road, to Mrs Parsons – where his Uncle Bob—

'That would be your father's brother?' suggested Miriam, breaking in excitedly.

'Indeed not.' For some reason the Major was outraged at the suggestion. 'Robert is my *mother's* brother. My mother's younger brother. We are the same age, which is curious. We were brought up together almost. Alas.'

'What d'you mean, "alas"?' said Tomkins suspiciously. He leant back in his chair and bit his silver pencil.

'I am very fond of my Uncle Robert,' said the Major. There was a very faint pause. 'Poor chap! He has the brain of a child of four. Quite undeveloped. So sad. No value of money or anything. Thinks fourpence is *quite* wonderful. The lawyer gives him his pocket-money every week. Two and sixpence, if you please! For a man who owns an estate worth about seventy-five thousand . . .'

'Good heavens!' said Miriam. 'Is your uncle as rich as that? Was your mother as rich as that?'

'Seventy-five thousand is not riches today, madam,' said the Major coldly. 'And my mother was much, much richer. She had opportunity, in her lifetime, for wise, sound investment. I am glad to think she took those opportunities. She had, I believe, doubled the initial value of her estate.'

'Which was seventy-five thousand also?' said Tomkins, with some interest.

'I believe so,' said the Major.

'And you are the heir?'

'Yes and no,' said the Major.

Everyone sighed and looked at their feet.

The expression in his hard brown eyes was (Tomkins was perfectly certain) sheer, unadulterated hatred.

II

'You say you went up the old Brunton Road to your Uncle Bob's?' said Tomkins.

The Major bowed.

'Did you see anyone?'

'Oh yes. I saw my uncle. He will tell you. If he is able to, poor dear.'

'What d'you mean, "able to"?'

'Well,' said the Major, 'he is not very clever. But he is extremely fond of oysters. I was taking him some of the leftovers from the party.'

Tomkins coughed and appeared to refer to his notes.

'It was a very wild night,' he said. His tone implied 'and what the hell were you doing, going for walks in it?'

'So I believe. Later. I got back before the rain.'

'You didn't get wet, dear?' Miriam's tone was as soft and maternal as the gentle dove.

'No.' The Major looked demurely at the floor. He did not seem to want to catch Miriam's eye. 'I did not get wet.'

'And did your uncle enjoy his oysters, dear?' Miriam's tone was suddenly waspish, and Tomkins was quite delighted.

'He ate them with every appearance of enjoyment,' said the Major, screwing in his eyeglass, staring at Miriam. There was a pause. 'His table manners are not of the best,' added the Major, and the eyeglass fell with a tinkle among his waistcoat buttons.

'Ah . . .' Tomkins made some rapid notes. 'Well now, sir, at what time would you think you arrived back at the hotel?'

'Oh, I can't say. Perhaps half past eleven.'

'See anyone?'

The Major considered carefully.

'Yes,' he said eventually. 'I saw Tony Robinson and he saw me.'

It was at this point that Tomkins said that would be all and could the Major ask *Mister* Robinson to come up, please?

III

Tony Robinson came into the room gaily. He showed no signs of the way he must feel. Miriam, recollecting the 'British Wine – Sherry Style' inside him, was astonished by his healthy appearance. Presently he began to rub his forehead and nose continually with the palm of his right hand, and in both hands she noticed faint, imperceptible tremors. Otherwise he seemed perfectly well and fairly sensible.

'This is a bad business,' he remarked. He sat down firmly in the nearest chair. Tomkins eyed him and said he supposed it would affect the hotel.

'Which way, though?' said Robinson. 'That's the thing. Badly or not, that is the question? Why, people might even want to come here and have a look. Stay a Week. See the Hotel of Death.'

He seemed (Miriam thought) pathologically optimistic. Perhaps it was only bravado.

'Meanwhile, of course,' said Tomkins, tracing patterns in his note-book, 'you've lost what my old mother would have called "a very good let".'

'Suppose we have,' said Tony. He shrugged his shoulders. 'The Lord will provide,' he said, 'as my old *father*, the Vicar, would have said.'

And he smiled politely at Tomkins and Miriam, as though he hadn't a care in the world. Indeed, it really seemed as though he had not.

'Well ...' said Tomkins, 'suppose you describe what happened last night in your own words?'

Tony Robinson frowned sadly.

'There were the oysters to be opened,' he said slowly. 'I helped with some of them. Celia *says* she saw me. Major Bognor and your nice friend' – he smiled broadly at Miriam in approval of Pyke. Tomkins suddenly looked savage and sadistic – 'opened the remainder. There were rather a lot of them.'

He suddenly looked sick and passed his hand over his head for the twentieth time. He looked up with a frank, boyish grin.

'Sorry,' he said. 'I get these dizzy spells. Gunfire, y'know. Haven't been feeling so well since the war. Some things are still a bit much for me ...'

Tomkins' sniff suggested that he had little patience with chronic alcoholics and that he didn't believe in the gunfire that had caused it.

'Where were the oysters opened?' he said.

'Oh!' Tony was rather hurt. 'Downstairs in the pantry. The housemaid's pantry. I'll show you, if you like.'

Tony half rose out of his chair. Tomkins waved him back.

'And then there was the party?' he suggested.

'Yes. Yes. Then there was the party.'

A heavy lethargy, obviously compounded of alcohol and nervous exhaustion, now crept over Tony. He yawned. His head felt like lead. His eyes prickled and burned. His arms and legs were impossibly heavy. He couldn't move them. What on earth was the little man saying?

'How many oysters did Mrs Bognor eat?'

'How the hell do I know? I can tell you how many *I* had. I had three dozen. And my ma-in-law. *She* had four dozen. Greedy old beast ...'

His head fell forward on to his hands. He went through his monotonous routine again of polishing his forehead and chin.

'Shock?' suggested Tomkins to Miriam, with raised eyebrows. Miriam pursed her lips and shook her head very slowly from side to side. Tomkins went on with his questioning. Had Robinson by any chance seen what *Major* Bognor had eaten at the party? Robinson had not. Had he seen what his wife, Mrs Robinson, had eaten?

'Oh, hell!' said Tony. He moved restlessly in his chair. 'We're all fond of oysters here. I expect we all ate about three dozen, except old Greedy. She certainly ate four dozen,' he repeated sullenly.

'Your mother-in-law, Mrs Greeb,' said Tomkins primly, and wrote it down.

Had Mr Robinson noticed if there were any oysters left over? Well, it wasn't Tony's party (he wasn't host, you know), but actually there were about two dozen oysters left.

What had become of them? Could the inspector see them? Tony slowly shook his head.

'They were opened, you see. Someone had to eat them or they'd have gone bad. *Bognor* said he would take them along to his dotty uncle.'

'And did he?'

'Oh yes. I went part of the way with him. Felt I wanted a walk. Oysters and Black Velvet. You know. They pep a feller up. Couldn't have slept after *that*—'

Tomkins scowled.

'And what did you do then?'

Tony moved uneasily in his chair.

'Went to see a friend,' he said.

'Who?'

'Rather not say. Is it necessary?'

'No, I don't suppose so. But it would help us check movements and get an accurate picture of what went on last night. It would be co-operative.'

'Oh, well ...' There was a pause. 'I went along to the

Warhaven Arms to see old Bob, the hall-porter-barman chap.'
Tony paused and looked consciously ingenuous. 'I owed him
five quid.'

'I see.' Tomkins looked down at his notes. 'What time were
you back in the hotel?'

'Oh, I dunno. About eleven.'

'See anyone?'

'Well, yes, I did. I saw Bognor. Major Bognor. Didn't seem
to walk very steady either, I can tell you.' Tony laughed gaily
at his reminiscence. Then his lethargy seemed to creep over
him again. His head sank forward on to his chest. His eyes
suddenly shut.

'*Tony!*' Miriam spoke for the first time, like a whip cracking.
'*Where did you get the money to pay back your friend?*'

'Eh?' Tony's eyes came slowly unglued. His face showed a rem-
nant of intelligence. He shook his head as though he were trying
to shake off a clinging fog. 'Eh? Oh. No.' He smiled cunningly. 'I
didn't, you know, I didn't. See? *I didn't pay back my friend.*'

There was a pause.

'May I go now?' said Tony, in the artificially naive tones of
a schoolboy.

'If you like,' said Tomkins, and Tony bolted towards the door.
'But ask *Mrs* Robinson to come, if you please.'

Tony halted abruptly and stood on one leg. He said could he
be present while she was being questioned, please? She was so
very nervous, you see.

'I'm afraid *not*,' said Tomkins coldly.

'But *legally*,' said Tony. 'I'm sure you're out of order. Wives and
husbands and evidence, and all that—'

'Legally,' Tomkins reminded him very gently, 'to the best

of my knowledge and belief, no crime has yet been committed here.'

Tony held on to the door-handle and swayed slightly.

'I see what you mean,' he said doubtfully.

'So just be a good chap and ask Mrs Robinson to come up here, will you?' said Tomkins. He brushed Tony's objections aside as though they were very small flies. Tony went slowly out of the room.

IV

However, instead of young Mrs Celia Robinson, her bare legs and her wild, uncontrolled movements, Mrs Greeb presently burst in through the door in what the inspector afterwards described as 'a rare old state'. She seemed very angry. Miriam and Tomkins were too surprised to say anything.

'I've been robbed!' she cried explosively. '*I've been robbed!* It's that good-for-nothing cook and her friend the kitchen maid, I'm positive—'

'Now, madam, what is all this?' said Tomkins. 'Just relax. Sit down here and tell me all about it.'

His little face was all sympathy. But behind his hand he murmured something about not letting Tony get anywhere near Celia. Meanwhile, Mrs Greeb sank into a chair, splayed her legs wide apart and remarked: 'It's gone, that's all! And I saved it so carefully, too. I'd meant it for Celia, poor Celia. She's been nothing but a fool. That awful man . . .'

Here, to Miriam's consternation, Mrs Greeb began to sob and cry in noisy, intermittent sniffs. She occasionally dabbed her eyes with a little rolled-up ball of handkerchief, while

Miriam remarked tartly that she thought Tony would have some difficulty in finding Celia in any case.

'And I'm so *tired*,' went on Mrs Greeb, whining rather. 'So tired all the time. And such a terrible headache. It's this dreadful place. The air's too strong for me. I *never* feel like this in Harrogate. And I have all my own friends there too. And Celia with no one to turn to. But someone must do the shopping this morning. Everything will fall on Mother, as usual, I suppose. And Tony drunk all the time. That impossible man. I must go and do the shopping . . .'

She was half-way to the door before Tomkins got her by the elbow and pulled her back. Her elbow seemed very dry and hot. Perhaps she was running a temperature?

'Now, madam.' Tomkins was severe. 'You said you'd been robbed. Of something you'd saved up very carefully. What is this, please? Where did you keep it?'

'My Post Office savings book, of course,' said Mrs Greeb angrily. 'There was two hundred pounds in it. All for Celia. That woman. That Awful Drunken Cook. She's stolen it. She and her friend. I'm quite positive. It was in my bedroom, of course, where else? What other reason would That Awful Cook have for coming up into the Upper Parts of the Hotel?' Mrs Greeb's tone contained a hint of nameless obscenities. 'But forgive me,' she said, and sprang up again. 'I must go now I've reported its loss. As long as I get my property back I don't wish to prosecute.'

And before Tomkins or Miriam could stretch out a hand to stop her, Mrs Greeb had nipped across the room and out at the door. It slammed behind her. And almost immediately Celia came tapping nervously on the door.

'May I come in?' she said coyly. 'Tony said you wanted me.'

Tomkins sighed as Celia poked her nose round the door about two feet below the door-handle.

V

'Is your mother feeling queer this morning?' asked Tomkins; 'or does she always go on like that?'

Celia blushed and said, 'Pardon?' If the inspector would forgive her, she was listening for April and May. They might cry at any minute.

'Your mother?' said Miriam. 'She is very excited.'

'Oh, *Mother*!' Celia was vexed and evidently inclined for confidences. 'She's always angry. She says Tony'll drag me down to *his* level. And she doesn't like Chef.' Celia tossed her head. 'Don't know what she thinks of me, I'm sure. Or where we can get another chef.'

Tomkins coughed.

'Your mother seemed more upset about her Post Office savings book. She says it's gone.' Tomkins spoke severely. Celia frowned.

'Oh, indeed. I didn't know she *had* a Post Office savings book. I'm sure.' Celia tossed her head again.

'Oh, well.' Tomkins dropped the whole subject wearily. 'I'm trying to get some sort of picture in my mind about what went on last night.' He pointed to the various items with his silver pencil as he mentioned them. 'The oysters were opened. You had the party. Who opened the oysters, by the by?'

'Mr Pyke and Major Bognor,' said Celia quickly.

'Mr Robinson helped?' Tomkins suggested.

134

'Well, he didn't. He had no opportunity at *all* of doing any-ting funny to the oysters.' Celia spoke in passionately defensive tones.

'But,' said Miriam gently, 'you told my friend Mr Pyke last night that—'

'I don't care *what* I said last night. Tony was nowhere near the oysters. He was asleep in his office.'

Tomkins made a note and raised his eyebrows.

'I see. Then there was the party. I wonder if you can remember how many oysters you ate?'

'A dozen,' said Celia instantly. 'I don't care for oysters. Well, not like the others do.'

'And I wonder if you know how many poor Mrs Bognor had?'

'I don't, I'm afraid.' For the first time that morning Celia was not on the defensive. She wrinkled her forehead and obviously tried to remember what had happened. 'She sat by Mother on the sofa. They ate at about the same speed. So I suppose they ate about the same amount. Mother had about a dozen, anyway—'

Tomkins considered all this with his head on one side. 'Thank you,' he said; 'and after the party?'

'I went to bed.'

'And Mr Robinson?'

'He went to bed too, of course.' The angry, defensive tone had returned, redoubled, in Celia's voice. She glared at Tomkins with overt hostility.

'He didn't go for a walk, by any chance?'

'Certainly *not*.' Celia was savage.

'I see.' Tomkins was slow and reflective. 'And you fell asleep immediately?'

'Oh yes. I always do.'

'But you woke up later?'

'Yes. I woke about three.'

'And you always do that too?'

Celia frowned nervously.

'Well, yes. I often wake in the middle of the night, I'm afraid.'

'And where was Mr Robinson, then?'

Celia was genuinely astonished.

'Why, he was in bed asleep, of course.'

'He could sleep through anything, I suppose?'

Celia suddenly smiled.

'Oh yes. He could sleep through the Last Judgment. He snores too. I always say that if the world came to an end, Tony wouldn't know anything about it until the next morning.'

'Wonderful gift,' said Tomkins. 'Lucky fellow. I'm a light sleeper myself.'

'Oh, so am I.' Celia seemed to have come to an understanding about Tomkins, for they smiled at one another. Tomkins lifted his head and stared at her.

'Now look here, Mrs Robinson,' he said. 'Why did you say Mr Robinson didn't go for a walk? We know quite well he did.'

'But he didn't,' said Celia, and appeared genuinely astonished. 'I'm quite *sure* he didn't. We went to bed at half past ten, I know we did. Oh dear, oh dear! I even saw the clock ... before I fell asleep ...'

Tears appeared in Celia's eyes, about to spill over on to her cheeks.

'Well, then, you must find Mr Robinson and ask him why he told *us* he went for a walk. Will you do that, please, Mrs Robinson?'

Celia twisted her hands nervously in her lap.

'Oh dear, oh dear, must I? Tony's acting so strangely since all this happened. He never speaks to me at all, you know.'

'It would help us.'

'I'd much rather not.'

'Why would you rather not?'

'Tony gets so angry if I ask him any questions about what he's doing. And then, if he says he's done one thing he's actually—'

'Done another?'

Celia looked fearfully over her shoulder before she nodded her head up and down, which she did a very great number of times.

'Particularly about where he's been and when,' she said.

'And of course you don't ever tell lies yourself?'

Celia suddenly relaxed.

'Oh, but I do, of course I do. Who doesn't? But I only tell them when I'm frightened.'

Tomkins smiled.

'You're not frightened of me any longer?'

'Oh no, thank you very much.'

Celia Robinson left the room and Tomkins turned to Miriam. 'What the hell?' he said. He shrugged his narrow shoulders 'What can you do?'

'I don't understand,' said Miriam. 'What's the fuss?'

'Well, which is lying? You're a better psychologist than I am—'

'Oh, my dear Tomkins, take those words out of your mouth. You don't know where they've been. These Robinsons both tell lies as fast as they can. They don't like the truth at all—'

'Well, the truth is an uncomfortable bedfellow.'

'No wonder, dear, lives at the bottom of a well, they say.'

Tomkins muttered that it was a hell of a silly business and he wished it was all over. The Chief Constable had been on about the expense of maintaining a full Inspector CID. Frankly, he wished he could get back to London. What did Miss Birdseye think? Perhaps everyone was wasting their time and it was an accident, after all?

It was at this moment that Maggie Button interrupted. The inspector was wanted on the telephone and she thought it was police headquarters. Miriam, watching Tomkins rushing from the room, was no longer in two minds. She reflected that Tomkins (unless curbed) might be very tiresome. She wished she had not run up a situation out of the whole thing. Pyke was jealous enough of everybody already – now he would be furious about Tomkins. And she could see his point. Damn! She picked restlessly round the room and wondered what had become of Pyke. She hadn't seen him since he stood on the stairs, his aristocratic face quite obviously hurt – damn again. Tomkins was gone about a quarter of an hour. When he reappeared he was grim and determined.

'Well,' he said, 'we're for it all right.'

'What *can* you mean?' said Miriam.

Tomkins spoke in a low, anxious tone. He seemed almost to be talking to himself.

'I've got to get this one,' he said. 'It might even get me a job at the Yard.'

He walked round the room, pacing up and down like a lunatic. Miriam watched him for a moment before she said, 'Don't understand, don't understand, don't understand.' Tomkins then stopped pacing and addressed her quite rationally.

'It was old Fawcett-Smith, the police surgeon. Mrs Thing was absolutely bung-up with arsenic. Even this coroner down here will see they bring in a charge of murder. I simply *must* make an arrest so that the charge won't be Person or Persons Unknown.' There was a frantic pause while Tomkins' certainty and cockiness crumbled away and showed itself to be a fragile façade. 'Oh, Miss Birdseye,' he said earnestly, 'you *must* help me. You've always been lucky to me. Do please help me. I must make the arrest. I must pull this one off—'

'My dear Tomkins,' said Miriam, 'much as I appreciate your very flattering remarks, I am afraid you must pull yourself together. You are being *most* unscientific. How d'you know I didn't do it myself?'

CHAPTER FIFTEEN

Pyke was alarmed as he followed Mrs Parsons and Colonel Rucksack out of Strong's Sarsaparilla. He had lost all sense of initiative. It was raining again. He was suddenly apprehensive and wished to withdraw from the whole adventure. He looked nervously at his two companions. Colonel Rucksack had turned up his coat collar. Mrs Parsons (who was behaving more like a fluttering bird than anything else) darted on ahead of them, and occasionally turned her head to suggest that they should hurry, hurry . . .

'Have you sent for the doctor?' said Colonel Rucksack. The pace was telling on him. He was already bluish in the face. Between his gasps and wheezings he ejaculated monosyllables such as 'tut' and 'dear' and 'm' word'.

'Yes, yes. Hurry, do!' cried Mrs Parsons. 'She will be there already, I expect—'

'Dr Stalag-Jones?' said Pyke. He stopped dead, halted by the impossibility of continuing to penetrate this weird episode. Colonel Rucksack was grateful for the pause. He stood, wheezing, on the steep slope of Old Brunton Road (which seemed to run away, glistening, uphill for ever) and held one claw-like hand to his side.

'My dear chap. Excellent woman. You know her? Believe she couldn't be better over children and child-bearing. So forth.' The Colonel slowly regained his breath. 'Very nice woman. Don't have her professionally myself. Only know her socially.'

'Oh, do please hurry, Colonel!' cried Mrs Parsons, in her agony of despair. Her large, dry hands twisted together, rasping slightly. 'Poor Master Bobby—'

'H-how far *is* it?' asked Pyke, gently rebuking her. 'W-we have come as fast as we c-could, after all—'

'Only a few yards now,' snapped Mrs Parsons. She seemed to Pyke a non-existent and nightmare figure, something like the Red Queen in *Through the Looking Glass*. She represented nothing but urgency. 'Faster, faster,' breathed Colonel Rucksack, as though he agreed with Pyke.

'L-look,' said Pyke, 'm-my people' – he made his first effort of will, a little impeded by his stammer – 'back at the Oranmore, w-will be w-wondering wh-where I *am* . . .'

'Now, my dear chap,' said Colonel Rucksack, in his old word of command. He had quite recovered his breath. 'You can perfectly well ring up from the Parsons'. Can't he, Mrs Parsons?' Mrs Parsons did not reply, because she had hurried on ahead of them, scowling. 'You really mustn't go now. It's most important to me to have an impartial observer . . .'

These words suddenly seemed to possess an entangling significance.

'Oh, b-but . . .' began Pyke, stammering fearfully in his indecision.

Colonel Rucksack seized his elbow in a light grip and hustled him forward. His fingers, through Pyke's winter overcoat, felt as brittle and clutching as barbed wire.

'Yer can't leave me now, yer know,' said Colonel Rucksack. And Pyke found, reluctantly, that this was indeed so.

II

The Parsons lived in a small, hideous by-pass house called Bobandoris. There was an Austin outside the gate and Pyke's heart sank lower as he saw it. He knew the car well by now. He had seen it once that morning already.

Bobandoris stood back from the Old Brunton Road at the end of a strip of garden that had been combed neatly back on either side of a straight, concrete parting. Some beige clay figurines, representing gnomes and dwarfs and elephants, peeped out among the tangled undergrowth of hedges. The footscraper was a blank iron representation of the type of dog known (colloquially) as a Scottie. As they came up the three shallow concrete steps to the front door they found Dr Stalag-Jones, scraping the clay from her neat laced shoes on its ears and tail. Her bright, bird-like eyes flashed quickly past Colonel Rucksack and Mrs Parsons (already embarked on a sentence beginning, 'We 'urried as fast as we ever, Doctor') to alight on Pyke. An almost human emotion began to struggle among her bleak features. Pyke hoped, vainly, that it might not be recognition.

'Well,' said Dr Stalag-Jones, 'in at the death again I see, Mr Pyke?'

III

Dr Stalag-Jones' remark went more or less unnoticed. At this moment the dark-green front door opened. The brass door-knocker (shaped like the Lincoln imp) flapped suddenly and made a clacking noise in the wind. Pyke looked in at the man who opened the door. He was above medium height with a long, sad, grey, suffering face. He was dressed in navy-blue serge uniform trousers with a silver stripe down them and a waistcoat with a strip of medal ribbons that peeped out under a rough brown tweed jacket.

'So *here* you are at last,' he said coldly. 'Mother's little boy, Robert Parsons, 'as got to go down the hill on duty. I can't leave me job down jus' because the lodger dies. Oh, beg pardon, Colonel. Didn't see *you* were there . . .'

He stiffened and came to attention. His thumbs were suddenly rigid alongside the silver stripes of his trousers.

'Good morning, Parsons,' said Colonel Rucksack coldly.

''Morning, sir,' said Parsons. 'You do understand? Duty calls?'

'Quite right, Parsons, quite right.' Colonel Rucksack was slightly condescending. 'I'm sure the doctor fully appreciates the position. In any case, your responsibility ends *here* . . .'

Colonel Rucksack's sudden pomposity was almost beautiful. Parsons (as though he had uttered the command, 'By the right, dismiss!') turned sharply on his heel, clapped a very old felt hat on the top of his head and marched away, through the front door, and down the desolate and shining cement path to the Old Warhaven Road. Consumed with curiosity about him, for he had seemed a mildly sinister figure, Pyke turned to Mrs Parsons. She was at his elbow. She, too, was looking after her husband with more concentration than he (surely) deserved.

'Wh-where does Mr P-Parsons work, then, on a Sunday?' he asked finally.

'Him?' Mrs Parsons was reluctant. 'Oh, he's hall-porter-barman at the Warhaven Arms.'

CHAPTER SIXTEEN

Connie Watson, the sinister cook, changed into a navy-blue linen 'bib and brace' and a checked shirt that was fairly clean, was truculent all through her interview with Tomkins. She had been employed by the Robinsons (*she* called them Tony and Celia) for about three months. The employment bureau (from whom, she was quick to tell Miriam and Tomkins, she had so often hired staff in the past, when she was on top and the world was fine and Mavis was a Glory, ironical, eh?) had sent her and Tommy in reply to an urgent summons from Tony. Mind, Connie liked Tony and he had the right ideas. But ... Well, he was going the same way as *she* had gone, back in 1946 at Whortleberry. Her and her partner. Ah, but Mavis was a Glory.

At this point Tomkins broke crisply into the narrative to ask if Connie had succeeded in paying off her creditors. Connie looked at him through heavy, snake-lidded eyes. She said slowly that she had paid three shillings in the pound.

'So, as an undischarged bankrupt, you haven't a bank account?'

Connie moved in her seat and said fretfully that she didn't see the point.

'The point, dear,' said Miriam, 'is that you told *me* that you were sending some money to your bank manager to pay for your funeral, dear.'

Connie scowled.

'And the other thing, dear,' continued Miriam mercilessly, 'since we're on it, dear, is that you actually *had* some money to send to the bank (or whatever it was), isn't it? And Tony is quite sure he *didn't* give it to you.'

There was a long pause while Connie Watson registered annoyance, incredulity and finally indignation.

'Did he say that? The bloody liar! My God! They don't know what truth is, the swine! My oath!'

And a stream of accusations, obscenities, anger and unrighteous indignation poured out at Miriam and Tomkins. But whether it was genuine or not was quite another matter.

II

By the time that Connie Watson had wound her peroration to its thunderous close and had left, banging the door behind her, and Tomkins was quietly muttering 'Deadlock' to himself, Miriam felt that her mind had been sucked dry of all vitality. She was able, however, to remark, soundly enough, that if Connie had been sending away some money the letter would surely have been registered and should be fairly easy to trace at the post office. Tomkins, observing the lines that had appeared one by one under Miriam's eyes, and the shadows that suddenly made her long nose pinched and beaky, leant forward. His blunt, friendly hand was suddenly warm on her long, cold fingers.

'Look,' said Tomkins, 'you're tired, Miss Birdseye. And I don't honestly think you can add very much to Mrs Thompson's and Miss Button's stories, do you?'

Miriam shook her head vaguely.

'Thompson?' she said. 'Button?'

'The kitchenmaid and the parlourmaid.'

'Oh, Tommy and *Maggie*,' said Miriam. 'Oh yes. Well, you can always tell me, can't you?'

Tomkins shuffled his papers.

'You get some air. Miss Birdseye. I'll be needing your brain later. You go and give it a good airing.'

Miriam rose gratefully to her feet, saying that was a suggestion that verged on the indecent. Tomkins looked gratified and preened himself.

'Leave me the old routines,' said Tomkins. 'And give me the brilliant inspirations later on, when I need 'em ...'

'I do not suppose,' said Miriam, in her deepest tones, halted by the door, 'that Maggie Button or Tommy Thompson would really enjoy being described as "old routines"!'

She was rudely disturbed by Tommy Thompson, who came pushing past her in a frightful rage. Who the hell was going to do the veg for lunch, she would like to know, if she was all the time being sent for by this one and that one?

Miriam faded quietly away to the hall, where the comparatively clean, fresh air that blew from the sea across Durbah Villas filtered in through the open door.

III

She was not at all surprised to bump into the Major at the bottom of the stairs. He seemed to be straining against his collar. His face was (somehow) swollen.

'See here, Miriam,' he began nastily, 'this savage silence is no *good*. I can't marry you and you know it.'

Miriam's involuntary laughter annoyed him very much indeed. He seized her arm in a furious grip. His right eye, behind his eyeglass, glowed with a strange, dangerous flame.

'Now, darling,' said Miriam cosily, 'it's quite all right. No one wants to marry anyone. The thing is to stop *you* getting yourself hanged, you old fool.'

'Thanks very much,' said the Major.

'That is, of course,' said Miriam, at her most viciously inconsequent, 'unless you *want* to be hanged? That's quite different, of course ...'

The Major's eyeglass fell with its usual tinkle against his waistcoat buttons.

'Very well. You win. Tell me what you want to know. But no marriages now, hm, ha, what?'

Miriam had long given up hope of understanding the Major's wilder interjections. And this had been her conclusion in the days when she thought him a nice quiet stage-door Johnny. Now she knew he was a terrible old madman who raged and stormed and screamed at a moment's notice, she merely shrugged her shoulders. Now she laid her hand lightly on his arm, caught sight of the opal ring on her finger and was transfixed, admiring it, with her head on one side.

'Come somewhere, then,' she said gently. 'I want you to explain about your expectations under your mother's will.'

The Major withdrew his arm and began to splutter a lot of confusing stuff about 'marriage portions' and 'settlements'.

'No, Reggie,' said Miriam severely. 'Come into that awful drawing-room where that piano is, and tell me ... Come on.' Miriam rolled her large pale-blue eyes and looked very like a charming pantomime horse. 'I shall then be able to protect you from poor dear Tomkins and his zeal.' She steered the Major skilfully through the door marked 'Lounge' and pushed him down on a sofa upholstered in brownish carpet. 'Sit there,' she said, 'and relax.'

The Major promptly bounded from the sofa and kicked the fire.

'So restless,' said Miriam faintly, and shut her eyes.

'All very well for *you*,' snarled the Major. 'All dressed up for deep-sea trawling. Shots all round the wicket, what?'

Miriam opened her eyes and concentrated.

'Now then,' she said firmly, 'don't a. about, dear. Who are the trustees of your mother's will?'

'Me and Uncle Charles,' said the Major gloomily. 'And Bere, the solicitor.'

'Senior partner,' said Miriam dreamily, 'of Fox and Fox.'

'*How the hell do you know that?*' said the Major, genuinely astonished. 'Such a provincial little firm – I wouldn't have thought—'

'Natasha DuVivien met him in that Brunton-on-Sea Case. The Radcliff Hall School business.* Mum's got a Kim's Game memory, dear, that's all. Don't be cross with Mum ...'

---

* *Poison for Teacher.*

The Major struggled with his unwilling admiration.

'You always were a clever devil, Miriam,' he said reluctantly.

'Oh yes,' said Miriam sadly. 'I am a clever devil.' She cast down her eyes and appeared very depressed. Then she suddenly brightened. 'Well, as her trustee, you probably know what your mother *had*, as they say? And where her investments were and so forth?'

'I suppose so.' The Major was still sulky. He stood by the smoking fire and glared down into it, his shoulders hunched like an angry cat.

'Well, then, come to the point, dear. Explain. There's no use kicking the fire, dear. You'll put it out. *Much* better to sit down and keep still and tell Mum all about it.'

The Major settled unwillingly beside her.

'There were the three of them,' he began slowly. 'Charles and Mother and my dotty Uncle Bob. There was an estate of about £300,000 which passed on to them at my grandmother's death. It was mostly from Rucksack's Rubber Belting and the oyster-beds and so on, and after duties had been paid and so forth, I suppose they had about £75,000 each—'

'When did you become your mother's trustee?'

'When Father died.'

'Oh! I'm sorry.'

'I wasn't.'

'Oh, then I'm *glad*. When was that?'

'That was in 1946.' The Major's little red eyes seemed to turn back in his head as he recollected the event. He grinned with pleasure. 'Mother's will, in which she had left everything to *him*, was revoked and she made a new one, leaving it to *me*. But . . .'

He emerged from the past and stared wildly round at the piano, the smoking fire, the hideous mantelpiece and the sofa with its carpet upholstering.

'But?'

'But the terms of my grandmother's will are a bit tricky. She was an arbitrary old girl.' He pronounced 'old girl' to rhyme with 'real'. 'It lays down that in the event of any one of the three children pre-deceasing the others, *that* the estate then goes to the others in equal shares – all without commas, too – most disconcerting.'

'So your mother's premature death wasn't a blessing at all for you? It simply means that all the money goes to your two uncles? Legally?'

'Yes.' There was an unhappy little pause. 'Funnily enough . . .' The Major paused again. Miriam prompted him and he hurried on with his explanation, without very much more encouragement. 'Uncle Charles's wife died within a day of my father, they were all on holiday together – um – he made a new will, too, he's childless, you see—'

'And you're trustee of that one, too?'

'No.' The Major scowled most frightfully and looked at his two shining feet that lay like fish on the rug below him. 'No. He said he didn't trust me. Bloody cheek! He always suspected me, y'know, of embezzling mess funds in his old Cherry Pickers—'

'And did you?' asked Miriam.

The Major laughed disarmingly.

'As a matter of fact I did,' he said. 'But it was never proved.'

'Oh God,' thought Miriam, 'he *is* border-line.'

'Well, then,' she said, 'he was quite right not to trust you, wasn't he?' The Major scowled again. 'There's no need to come the injured innocent over me, my dear Reginald,' she added.

'Perhaps,' said the Major blandly. 'Oh,' he went on, with heavy sarcasm, 'I'm a swine. You're well out of me, Miss Birdseye, that's certain.'

Miriam said she knew that, thank you, and the Major promptly looked hurt.

'Where did your aunt and your father die?' asked Miriam, as though she were changing the subject. 'It must have been a great tragedy.'

'Oh, it was,' said the Major gaily. 'A great tragedy. Food-poisoning. At a little place in Devon with a funny name. Wait a minute. It's on the tip of my tongue. Just a second . . .'

He snatched at the air in front of him as though he were catching flies. Miriam then had one of those blinding revelations that are given to human beings every two hundred years or so.

'Don't tell me,' she said, watching him. 'I'll tell you. It was at Whortleberry, wasn't it? Whortleberry Down?'

The Major looked up startled.

'My God!' he said. 'You're damn' right! How the hell did you know?'

Interlude

'H'r'm!'

Mr Justice Mayhem brought his fine hands finger-tip to finger-tip, and leant back in his chair. His eyes half closed as he glanced down at the pile of notes that lay on the desk in front of him.

'By now, Members of the Jury, you will have begun to realize the facts of this case, as they appear, one by one.'

Each word that he spoke was thin and dry. They crumbled from his mouth, as brittle as biscuits.

'You will find yourselves considering this somewhat inefficiently controlled private hotel and its occupants. Radiating from it (almost like the spokes of a wheel) are influences that touch upon a wider, if more private, circle. I mean, of course, the inter-relative effections of a large and comparatively wealthy family. The Rucksacks.'

His Lordship here lowered his hands and seemed to poise on them, above his notes.

'The Rucksacks were, one by one, whether by accident or design, almost exterminated. I do not care for sensational adjectives. However, I must use one here and I think I might be justified. If, indeed, a premeditated and far-reaching design began to reach its conclusion on the night of 23rd February, in the death of Mrs Eithne

Bognor (with whose unlawful killing the prisoner stands charged), I can only speak of such a design as anti-social . . .'

A titter ran round the court-room and was instantly suppressed. His Lordship frowned.

'Once upon a time oysters were the food of the poor. Now, no doubt they are linked in your minds with champagne, actresses, and what are sometimes called the idle rich. For this reason you may have gained the impression that they are anti-digestive, injurious, positively lethal. You would be mistaken. The oyster is the most easily digested of food. And the birthday party at the Oranmore Hotel was not synonymous with dissipation. One of the largest oyster-beds in the country was the property of the Rucksacks. And I understand it was Mrs Bognor's practice to have oysters sent to her from time to time, on her birthday, and in September, when, as you are aware, the R returns to the month. It was Mrs Bognor's pleasure on these occasions to invite a few friends to share in them . . .'

Here Mr Justice Mayhem paused and passed his tongue rapidly over his lips. And he did not seem indifferent to the thought of oysters. He glanced up at the clock that ticked away the inexorable minutes above the prisoner at the bar.

'. . . And in the past she had often done this.

'Indeed, it was in September 1946, when she was staying in the little Devonshire village of Whortleberry Down, that some oysters – I think I am right in speaking of a cran or half a cran – from the Rucksack Beds (for in this way they are spoken of in Whitstable) were sent by rail to Portarlington, the nearest station to Whortleberry, by (as it then was) the Great Western Railway. They were, most unfortunately, delayed in transit, and when Rear Admiral Bognor and his sister-in-law, Mrs Charles Rucksack, died, as they did ten days later from typhoid fever, it was assumed (and with justification you may feel) that it had been from "oyster-poisoning" that they had died.

'Now, oyster-poisoning is the hardest thing in the world to prove. You have seen the specimens referred to as "A" and "B" exhibited in Court. And you have heard Sir Godfrey Pawson-Hailsam and Dr Fawcett-Smith give it as their opinion that arsenic and the resultant sickness arising from it, and nothing else, was the cause of death of Mrs Eithne Bognor. Nevertheless, you may well ask yourselves if this may not have had some connection with the fact that oysters were served at this evening party: and whether, in fact, one oyster or more may not have contained a fatal dosage of arsenic.

'The common oyster, or ostrea edulis . . .' continued Mr Justice Mayhem, in a voice that very faintly droned.

BOOK THREE

FOUR OTHER OYSTERS FOLLOWED THEM

Four other oysters followed them,
*   And yet another four,*
And thick and fast they came at last
*   And more and more and more . . .*
All hopping through the frothing waves
*   And scrambling to the shore.*

LEWIS CARROLL: *The Walrus and the Carpenter.*

CHAPTER SEVENTEEN

'The common oyster,' said Inspector Tomkins, under his breath, 'is a rum little beast.'

He stood by the glass-fronted bookcase in Mrs Bognor's sitting-room and idly stared in at the backs of the books. Tomkins (though not a great reader) was an addict of girls' school stories. He read every one that he could find. When he was left alone in a strange house he looked around for them. And once he had been rewarded by a most important clue folded into a book that he had enjoyed very much, on its own merits, called *Mamzell of the Remove*. However, there were no early imperfect Angela Brazils in Mrs Bognor's bookcase. Instead, there was a small neat book called *The Oysters and Dredgers of Whitstable*, by A. O. Collard (1902). Tomkins removed it, recollecting (somewhat late in the day) that he had been born and brought up in Whitstable himself.

It was nicely illustrated with photographs of small boys in Edwardian knickerbockers, and oyster trawlermen in waterproof hats and boots. At the bottom of the page his eye suddenly caught an arresting phrase.

'"It may not be generally known,"' he read slowly aloud,

'"that the Roman empresses frequently employed the bivalve as an agreeable method of administering poison to their lords – to say nothing of their lovers."'

'Oh, I say!' said Tomkins. He shut the book with a little snap and tucked it into his jacket pocket. He crossed to the window and looked down on Durbah Villas. He suddenly felt hungry. There was no *reason*, of course, why arsenic in white powder or in solution should *not* be introduced into an oyster. But how the hell would it get there? Humming a tune from *Oklahoma!* called 'Many a New Day', Tomkins trotted gently downstairs. He wanted a search-warrant. And then he would like to find a hypodermic syringe in someone's bedroom.

The telephone shrilled as he reached the hall. He was convinced the call was for him. As usual, he was right. An unimpressed voice from police headquarters told him that a character giving his name as 'Pyke – Frederick Pyke' wanted him to proceed immediately to Bobandoris, Old Brunton Road.

II

The big, shiny Wolseley arrived in the Brunton Road, driven rather too fast by Police Constable Beatty, and Tomkins was ruffled. A second death of oyster-poisoning – in one day, and that day a Sunday when Tomkins normally put his feet on his desk and read *The Fourth Form Invaders*; and it was not even as though the news might be wrong. It was supported by the unemphatic testimony of Dr Stalag-Jones, still vexed, still anxious to get away to the findings of her medical board. It was almost more than he could bear.

He came up the sweating path to the front door of

Bobandoris, slapping his brief-case against his legs and occasionally taking off his hat to ease the top of his head. If anyone had asked him *why* the top of his head felt as though it were about to burst he would have said: 'Oh, I dunno – hangover, I suppose. Should take more water with it.' The plain truth, however, was that his nerves were strung to breaking-point, and when Pyke opened the door and stammered out that he was g-glad that the i-inspector had been able to c-come so quickly, Tomkins nearly screamed. He glared ferociously at Pyke, who interpreted his stare as one of purest suspicion. He waved him nervously into the dining-room.

'Th-this is Colonel Rucksack,' said Pyke. 'H-he is M-Mrs B-Bognor's b-brother.' He took a deep breath and decided to make the best of a bad job. 'He d-doesn't kn-know . . .'

'Know what?' snapped Tomkins. He took off his hat and laid it alongside his brief-case. He took the invitation from his pocket and held it out to Colonel Rucksack. '*You*,' he said brutally, 'would be Charlie-Arlie.'

'Wha'? For God's sake. I've had a shock.' Colonel Rucksack seemed to give at the knees. 'What d'y' mean? For *heaven's* sake, how did y' get this?' Colonel Rucksack went blue to the lips. He took the card from Tomkins and backed away.

The dining-room looked through opaque, roguey-poguey lat-ticed windows on to a fairly large lawn where some untidy boxes with wire netting runways suggested whippet-kennels. There was a massive mock-Tudor table in heavily stained black oak and some chairs to match it. It was neatly laid for one person, with a paper table-napkin in a tumbler. Colonel Rucksack leant against it now and went extremely white.

'You got this invitation?' he said in flat, slow, dead tones, 'from the Oranmore Hotel? You're a policeman? Something's happened to Eithne. *What* has happened to Eithne?'

Tomkins pursed his lips until his moustache seemed like a dandelion clock. He looked at Pyke.

'He doesn't know?' he asked.

Pyke shook his head.

'Mrs Bognor passed over early this morning,' said Tomkins carefully. 'She 'ad oysters for supper last night ... Here, steady on, sir ...'

For Colonel Rucksack's old knees had buckled under him. Tomkins helped him into one of the incredible, vulgar chairs. He sat still, his head sunk on his breast.

'Oysters ...' he said slowly. 'Oysters will be the death of all the Rucksacks. Y'know ...' And his sudden, confiding change of tone as he looked up into Tomkins' eyes with a wide blue stare was that of a child. 'Y'know, I'm the only Rucksack who has never touched an oyster.'

III

'Now what's all this about?' said Tomkins kindly. He sat down beside Colonel Rucksack. He sent the tumbler and its little paper napkin spinning with his elbow, caught it and replaced it, saying, 'Pardon me,' all in one breath. 'What Rucksacks have already died from eating oysters?'

Colonel Rucksack smiled a wintry little smile and rubbed his small purple beak of a nose with his forefinger.

'Well, perhaps I'm speaking prematurely,' he said, with some gaiety. He seemed to be recovering from his shock. His face slowly became a fairly normal colour, although the blue tinge round his nose and chin was still in evidence.

'It was the Rucksack *spouses*, so to speak, whom oysters originally killed, if y'follow me? M'wife Minnie and Eithne's husband, they both died within a day or two of each other. As I was tellin' this gentleman this morning.' Colonel Rucksack here glanced up at Pyke and frowned and looked away. Tomkins' note-book came out and flapped slowly open.

'I think I should warn you,' he said, 'that anything you say may be used in evidence.'

'Oh, please yerself, please yerself,' said Colonel Rucksack sharply. 'I've some idea of discipline, I hope.' He looked up once more at Pyke, this time somewhat wistfully. Pyke stood with his arms folded and glowered out at the garden. It had begun to rain again and the dark clouds were slowly gathering over the horizon. '*That* young man,' he said, and his voice, suddenly sharp, broke up the gloom of the room as a pickaxe breaks up a dark pavement, 'that young man knew about Eithne this morning?'

'Eh?' Tomkins looked quickly towards him. 'Yes. Yes. I suppose he did. He says he found her body.'

Colonel Rucksack drew in his breath with a hiss. Pyke, twirling on the spot to defend himself, saw Colonel Rucksack turn his head aside, looking exactly like a turkey cock, ready to peck at him. He flinched.

'No,' said Colonel Rucksack coldly. 'Don't attempt to explain y'self. Thoroughly ungentlemanly, that's all. Very ill-bred way to behave. Extractin' confidences under false pretences ...' Pyke winced, for he was well aware that his reticence *had* been prompted more by impertinent curiosity than by *laissez-aller* or inability; he began to stammer a form of apology. 'Don't say another word,' snapped Colonel Rucksack. 'Yer should be ashamed of yerself.' There was a small pause. And then, *'I don't believe y'are Archie Pyke's nephew at all!'* he cried in a terrible voice.

IV

Deflected from his rage against Pyke, and reminded of that sad business at Whortleberry Down, Colonel Rucksack made a statement. (Pyke, trembling, was far too upset at the accusation of ungentlemanly behaviour to ask Colonel Rucksack to describe the owner of Whortleberry.) Colonel Rucksack was well informed about *the wills*, and spoke clearly of his charge as a trustee. He made a good impression on Tomkins, who liked candid old military gentlemen.

'And so I suggest,' concluded Colonel Rucksack, in his severest tones, 'that you accompany me to Andrew Cathcart's house.'

Tomkins looked surprised.

'You know who I mean?' Colonel Rucksack seemed angry. 'Andrew Cathcart. The manager of the Sussex and Provincial. Very decent chap. Was coming to play bridge with me this afternoon.' He stopped and bit his lip. 'No,' he went on quickly, gnawing at the ragged ends of his moustache, 'of course. I must put it off.' For a moment the love of his Sunday afternoon's amusement wrestled fiercely with his sense of duty. 'Well, then, I must call and tell him so. Yes, indeed,' and he nodded his head at each point in the sentence to confirm himself in his decision. 'To be sure. That's what I'll do. I'll call on Andrew and take you along with me. Andrew'll bear me out in all I say.'

It was at this moment that Tomkins very gently suggested that surely Mrs Bognor had banked with the *Westminster* Bank?

'Who the hell told you that poppycock?' exploded the Colonel. 'Everybody knows Eithne's always banked with the Sussex and Provincial!'

He glared at poor Pyke. This was merely another example of his impertinent and under-bred behaviour. He implied, flashing his eyes under ragged eyebrows (that looked, thought Pyke, very like the untrimmed hawthorn bushes that ope in the month of May), that the whole thing was Pyke's fault from beginning to end. Pyke sighed.

'But what about your dinner?' said Tomkins, sniffing at this point. He tapped on his front teeth with his pencil. He was strongly aware of the smell of mutton that now penetrated the dining-room from the kitchen.

'Dinner?' snapped the Colonel. 'Oh, you mean me *luncheon*.' He was outraged. 'What d'y' take me for, eh? One of Napoleon's bloody soldiers marchin' round Europe on me stomach?'

V

They set off for Mr Andrew Cathcart's house, but not before Mrs Parsons had shed many tears over poor Master Bob. The police ambulance had swirled away from Bobandoris far too fast, because the driver was anxious about his luncheon. Mrs Parsons (whose name was, of course, Doris) dried her eyes and bobbed and suggested that as poor Master Bob wouldn't be needing his, she had one cut off the Sunday joint to spare, if any of the gentlemen fancied it, particularly the Colonel.

The Colonel's outraged snort could have been heard in Charing Cross. Tomkins perfunctorily examined Bob Rucksack's bed-sitting-room and locked the door. It was scrupulously neat; remarkable in that there were so many piles and piles of old theatre programmes in the underclothing drawers. Tomkins said good-bye to Mrs Parsons and said he would come back later that afternoon.

They went out into a warmish, dampish south-west wind that left a faint crust of salt on their faces.

Colonel Rucksack strode nervously ahead of them; he was evidently compelled by some strong tension. Tomkins made several half-humorous observations about the weather and bank managers. Pyke did not reply. Colonel Rucksack snorted savagely that this wasn't a music-hall joke.

And so they came to another villa, called *West Hartlepool* (for Andrew Cathcart had become engaged to be married in that place), set back from the road behind a carefully arranged rose garden. Little wooden labels, thrust into the reddish soil, indicated where Hugh McCreedy, Betty Uprichard and Kersten, Karen and Elsie Poulsen would presently, in four months, lift then-lovely heads. But meanwhile, naked flower beds and twigs of rose trees (like exhausted middle-aged spinsters) did nothing to relieve the appearance of the red-brick villa. It was one of old Jo Mabberly's best. Andrew Cathcart had foreclosed on the former owner (a Mr DeSarum, who had been associated with Captain Fortescue-Sykes in the pepper crash). An over-toppling arrangement of salt- and mustard-pots hovered uncertainly above the stained-glass door, where the pattern was of fleur-de-lis, hopelessly entwined. A tessellated pavement in the porch (scarlet Grecian urn) and a yellow glass door-knob (engraved Grecian nymphs) were obviously intended to reassure callers about the affluence of the Cathcarts, as they had once attempted to reassure callers about Mr DeSarum.

166

Pyke was uneasy. With bright and fascinated eyes he watched the Colonel tug away at a heavily encrusted old baronial bell. He no longer fussed about whether the Colonel liked or disliked him. No picturesque old retainer shuffled to the door in list slippers to answer the baronial bell. Andrew Cathcart came himself, wiping his mouth. He asked them to pardon his serviette.

'Come along in, Colonel, come along in,' he said genially. 'This is Liberty Hall. Any friend of yours is a friend of mine. Come one, come all. Perhaps Mother can find you a bite of something? I don't feel inclined to leave the roast myself. It's done to a T. Mother's surpassed herself . . .'

And so, for the second time that day, Pyke found himself walking fearfully forward into a very strong smell of roast mutton.

VI

Pyke never quite recovered from the horror of the next fifteen minutes, when Andrew Cathcart pressed Colonel Rucksack and Inspector Tomkins to join him and 'Mother' in Sunday luncheon. He and Inspector Tomkins had to take their lead from the Colonel, who (with a very over-sensitized idea of gentlemanly behaviour) turned shuddering from the food as though mutton had never passed his lips. So the three of them sat rigidly upright against the wall on Andrew Cathcart's red-velvet-seated Jacobin chairs and were forced to observe Mr and Mrs Andrew Cathcart eating themselves silly, and taking (or so it appeared) helping after helping of roast leg of mutton.

Tomkins, by this time extremely hungry, could hardly

restrain himself. Pyke was weak at the knees and faint for food. And their condition was not improved by Mrs Andrew Cathcart, who thought they must be 'daft to refuse a good roast like this'. It was Mrs Cathcart who had originally been a native of West Hartlepool.

Eventually the plates were cleared away and Andrew Cathcart, with every congested vein sprung bright in view on his nose and chin, led them to his 'den'. Here he collapsed in an armchair, belched, and lit an enormous pipe. The window was closely shut. It, also, was of stained glass. The light that fell on the brown-and-orange furnishings was filtered through scarlet, blue and yellow lozenges. It gave a strange effect.

'Now,' said Andrew Cathcart, kicking out his legs sideways, 'what is all this, Colonel? Don't curdle me blood.'

And Pyke was hereafter rigid with disgust and dismay.

CHAPTER EIGHTEEN

In the Oranmore Hotel, after a good deal of fuss, luncheon was served. And (oddly enough) it was roast mutton.

There were many deserted little tables in the underground dining-room, but they could hardly be seen in the twilight that always hangs belowstairs. Mrs Greeb, Miriam Birdseye and Reginald Bognor, each of them sitting alone, were waiting for their helpings. Miriam, who was expecting Pyke to come in at any minute now, carried on a brisk, nervous conversation with Reginald. This made very little sense. By and by, Celia Robinson hurried into the room with two slopping plates of soup for herself and her mother. She was followed (gloomily) by Maggie Button with apple tart and bright yellow custard for the others. Mrs Greeb hardly acknowledged her daughter. She took a brief sip of her soup and pushed her plate away.

'Not hungry, Mum?' said Celia cheerfully. 'OK I'll eat it.' She spun round in her chair like a teetotum, and (apparently) spoke to the Major and Miriam, who seemed shocked. 'Sorry, all. Tony'll be late, as ever. Everything's at sixes and sevens, but ...'

'Er – have you seen the pier yet?' said the Major to Miriam.

'Very remarkable piece of decadent Edwardian baroque – hideous, what?'

'I am quite off my food,' whined Mrs Greeb.

'Oh?' Celia was very unfeeling. 'But you never did fancy oxtail, though, did you, Mum?'

Miriam said she thought she might stroll down to the pier after luncheon. That was, of course, if the inspector didn't want her. She could hardly have been more annoying or more inconsequent. The Major looked vexed and continued to eat his apple tart with intense concentration. The expression on his face suggested that it was more than indecent to mention the doom (or, as Mr Michael Sadleir once put it, 'the amber threat') that overhung the hotel. This did not affect Celia Robinson. After several more unfeeling remarks about her mother's perennial pickiness, she swung round in her chair and addressed Miriam.

'D'you think the inspector actually suspects anyone yet?' she asked ingenuously. 'I mean – it is awful, isn't it?'

Miriam gravely agreed that it was (indeed) awful, and added that she did not know where the inspector *was*, let alone whom he suspected.

'Oh,' said Celia gaily, 'he went off after your boy friend. Oh, I beg your pardon; Mr Pyke rang up. Mr Pyke said he wanted him (the inspector, I mean). He had *further developments*, he said. Sorry I didn't mention it sooner.'

And it was Miriam's turn (like Mrs Greeb) to go a pale and jealous green.

II

After luncheon Miriam escaped up one side of the hotel and down the other and found Connie Watson brooding in the scullery among the washing-up. She seemed surprised when Miriam banged on the scullery window. She tapped her nose with one thick forefinger and looked like Noah Claypole in the Cruikshank illustration to *Oliver Twist*. She rubbed Justin (the big black tom cat) along his back with her foot. She opened the scullery window.

'What d'ye want?' she said.

'I want to speak to you *alone*,' said Miriam.

Connie was obviously gratified.

'Well, you haven't a hope of seeing me alone *here*,' she said. 'But I do get from two until nine tonight off. Suppose I meet you somewhere in the town, eh?'

'If you like,' said Miriam, depressed at the thought of Connie in her 'going-ashore' togs.

'D'yer know the Pier Tea Rooms?'

Miriam said she could find them.

'See you there at 'alf pars' two, then,' said Connie, and dismissed Miriam with a jerk of her head. And Miriam regretted her suggestion.

III

However, at half past two she waited in the Pier Tea Rooms, opposite the glistening *chinoiserie* of the pier itself. Miriam could see the Major quite plainly; he was pacing up and down, carrying two deck chairs. She smiled wolfishly and sank down lower into her pale-blue wickerwork chair. A young lady, dressed entirely in pale blue, with 'Joan' worked on her left breast in red, approached and suggested that Miriam should have tea.

'If you like,' said Miriam absently, and Joan went disconsolately away.

Connie Watson presently lurched in through the door. A cardboard notice (that said 'Closed' on one side and 'Open' on the other) twirled out on a piece of string when Connie opened the door. Miriam had been quite right to be afraid of her 'going-ashore' togs. Connie was dressed in a pair of white flannel trousers cut very wide, a striped waistcoat, a man's brown-and-white-checked sports coat and co-respondent shoes. Round her neck there hung a single lorgnette. Miriam cowered, but Connie had her taped.

'I didn't suppose it was my bright eyes,' she said truculently.

She sat down firmly and put both hands square upon her knees.

'Well,' said Miriam quickly, 'it's about Whortleberry ...'

'Ah,' said Connie. 'Mavis ...' and went abruptly into a day-dream.

'No, not Mavis. Those people who stayed there in 1946 and died two days later.'

A look of angry stupidity appeared in Connie's eyes. She rubbed her nose.

'But look,' she said; 'that wasn't my fault. Or Mavis's. See? They died when they got home, pal. And it was their own oysters as killed 'um. See? Nothing to do with me or Mavis whatsoever, chum.'

'That may well be,' said Miriam. 'But who were these people?'

Connie became more confidential. She hitched one leg over the other and drew out a packet of American cigarettes. She took one and lit it and blew a cloud of blue smoke all over the Pier Tea Rooms. Miriam began to feel that she was dealing with an American gangster from a Humphrey Bogart picture.

'Look,' said Connie eventually, 'I'll be frank with you. It was in '46 that Mavis lef' me.' Tears rose slowly in Connie's eyes. 'I said to her, "Mavis," I said, "don't let me go in there to them and let them see the hurt in my eyes . . ."'

'I'm quite sure you did, dear,' said Miriam. 'But who were "they" who you didn't want to show the hurt in your eyes to?'

'Why, these people you were asking me about.' Connie snapped her fingers angrily. 'Old man What's-'is-name, the Admiral and wife, and Colonel What-have-you, Bizzazus and Bizook and wife. *And* the dotty brother . . .'

'Can't you remember their names?'

'Look, lady, I'm tellin' ya, aren't I?' Connie's secondary (or Humphrey Bogart) personality suddenly crystallized. She began to punctuate her remarks with the butt end of her glowing cigarette.

'Excuse *me*,' said Joan, standing still and looking at Connie with horror. She plonked down Miriam's tea.

'Oh, sorry,' said Connie, quickly cowed, moving restlessly in her seat. 'Well, I'm tellin' ya, aren't I? Mavis *went*. I cried for four whole days. They tell me as I didn' eat anythin' at all. And when I came to . . .'

'Mavis had gone,' said Miriam wearily.

'Ya, ya. How did ya know?'

Miriam got a good grip on herself. She did not bother to tell Connie how she knew Mavis had gone.

'What about the Admiral, the Colonel and their wives?' said Miriam. 'Oh, and the dotty brother?'

'"The Admiral, the Col-o-nel,"' sang Connie maddeningly. 'I dare say I have their names, though, ya know.' She was suddenly anxious to please. 'I took the hotel register when I come away. For a keepsake. Mavis ...'

Miriam felt a sudden spurt of hope. She hardly flinched when Connie began to sing, 'She'd leave me something to remember her by.'

'I tell you *what*,' said Miriam, cutting across the melody. 'If *you* go and get me that hotel register *now*, I'll give you a pound.'

'Ya will?' Connie was astonished. 'Well, what d'ya know?' She rushed madly from the Pier Tea Rooms. The door swung in and out behind her in the wind of her going.

'Get all sorts, don't you?' said Joan, looking down at Miriam. 'That tea-cake's very nasty, isn't it, dear?'

IV

Connie returned within ten minutes, completely out of breath and gasping. She slammed down a big pale-blue morocco-bound visitors' book amongst the debris of Miriam's nasty tea-cake. Miriam examined it. Whortleberry Down Guest House did not seem to have done very good business in September 1946. Miriam had no trouble in finding among the entries, 'Edgar Bognor and Party, Charles Rucksack and Party, and Robert Rucksack'. The last entry was inscribed with the sinister scribble of a child of six. Miriam pointed out the entries to Connie. Connie looked portentously solemn. She remarked, 'What a coincidence!'

'And there's another thing,' she said, peering forward over Miriam's shoulder. '*That* old b——, I mean. I remember *he* was an inhabitant of this god-forsaken hole, too. The Brunton Bizazzuses and Bizooks, they wouldn't have anything to do with him, and, boy, was he sore? Boy! are the English class-conscious?'

And her stubby finger ran down the page and stopped before the entry, 'Mr and Mrs Andrew Cathcart, West Hartlepool, Brunton-on-Sea'.

CHAPTER NINETEEN

When Colonel Rucksack and Tomkins had both finished speaking, Andrew Cathcart rose to his feet. His armchair (a tasteful little number, strongly upholstered in bright brown rexine) went spinning back across the tomato-coloured carpet. He replaced his pipe in a fine fretwork pipe-rack inscribed 'Tak' a Pipey an' Have a Draw', with a Scotsman's head sketched upon it in poker work.

'Well,' he said, 'afternoon nap or *not*, I think we'll go down and open up the bank. What d'ye say. Rucksack?'

Colonel Rucksack began to put on his little boy's woollen gloves.

'I was hopin' you were goin' to say that,' he said.

'Well, then,' Andrew Cathcart turned expansively to Tomkins and Pyke, 'if it is the Colonel's wish that I do this, as he is Senior Trustee, so to say, I don't suppose that Major *Bognor* ...'

'What's *he* got to do with this will?' Tomkins was suddenly all attention again. His hunger was forgotten, his eyes were bright with terrier intelligence.

'Bognor? M'nephew?' Colonel Rucksack sounded thoroughly

disapproving, and (Pyke could see) was still bitterly regretting his morning indiscretion. 'Well, he's co-trustee. But it would be to his interest – advantage, I mean – to agree to our lookin' into his mother's affairs. Don't you agree, Cathcart?'

Colonel Rucksack was standing up now, and he suddenly turned to Pyke, who jumped and stammered that indeed he would agree. Pyke stood up too, and wished he did not feel so ineffectual.

'That's settled, then,' said Andrew Cathcart. He buttoned up his waistcoat, which had (of course) been unbuttoned after lunch. 'I'll just pop up and let Mother know I've got to go out. Won't be a jiff after I've got my hat.'

He went from the room and left Tomkins and Pyke and Colonel Rucksack nervous of each other and very irritable indeed.

II

As they went down the curving carriage sweep of *West Hartlepool* Colonel Rucksack began a long and irrelevant speech about the importance of trustees managing people's estates in a proper fashion. Where would it all end, he asked himself, if any irregularities were to begin in the *middle classes*? The backbone of the Empire was inherited wealth. It was the saviour of polite society. Once one allowed one's motto to be 'Easy Come, Easy Go', then one would end up socialist MPs with expense accounts to beat the band, just to evade the income tax, eh? It was downright immoral, eh? Andrew Cathcart said he quite agreed. He would go further than that, actually . . .

Tomkins and Pyke said nothing. They trudged down the hill towards Brunton and the Sussex and Provincial Bank. Tomkins' head was low, his eyes were on the ground and his hands were thrust savagely into his pockets. Pyke had the impression that he was sulking. In fact he was trying to stop his thoughts running madly away in vain pursuit of dreams of cheese sandwiches. As they came in sight of the corner where Mr Twiggs' Greengrocery faced the Warhaven Arms and the Warhaven Arms faced the Bank, they saw Tony Robinson galloping up the steps into the hotel. He had a thirsty look.

'There goes "young Tony",' said Cathcart gloomily. 'Drink will be the finish of *him*. I wonder his poor young wife can stand it.' Colonel Rucksack said he believed that Padre Robinson, Tony's father, had been a very fine type of man, and it was all very sad.

'Oh, definitely. The good old man, ye know, never owed a penny in his life. Every bill paid on the nail. Don't know where "young Tony" gets it *from*, I'm sure.'

Mr Cathcart withdrew a number of complicated keys on a long chain from the bottom of his right-hand trouser pocket. He hauled them up so slowly and so cautiously that Pyke was irresistibly reminded of *mackerel fishing*. He unlocked the door in three different ways.

'Funny thing,' he said. 'We only had Mrs Bognor in here on Saturday morning, I remember. Makes you think doesn't it?'

Colonel Rucksack said that he couldn't realize it, shock he supposed, and so they came into the dim, shrouded coolness of the Sussex and Provincial Bank. The big mahogany counter was polished. The desks were laid out with blotting-paper and new, clean pens. The ink-pots had been filled by a junior clerk before he went home on Saturday. A tiny blue-black pearl of ink lay staining the shining mahogany. Cathcart clicked his tongue.

'No, no. The place does y' great credit, Andrew,' said Colonel Rucksack, wheezing slightly. 'Positively regimental.'

'Thank you, Charles,' said Cathcart humbly. He knew the Colonel had no greater adjectives of praise to offer. He led the way to his office. 'Take a chair,' he remarked, waving a hand. 'I'll go and get the pass-books, etcetera.'

III

A quarter of an hour later (when Pyke, slowly reading the notices on the walls to himself, had learned that the Sussex and Provincial Bank had agents in *all* parts of the world and fourteen and a half million assets) Andrew Cathcart returned. He looked whitish under his veins. He carried an old-fashioned pass-book (bound in fawn leatherette), some peculiarly typed accounts (some of which were in red) and an enormous ledger. He put them all down on the desk, pulled up his chair and began, very nervously:

'Look here, there's something wrong. Very wrong.' He was no longer the pompous, slightly bombastic, greedy little man who had greeted them at *West Hartlepool*, monarch of all he surveyed.

'What d'y' mean? Wrong? How can *anything* be wrong?' Colonel Rucksack sprang half out of his chair. He was furious.

'Terribly sorry,' said Andrew Cathcart. 'If I'd had any inkling ... if I'd dealt with all this myself ... or if any member of the family had approached me *before* ... or any of those things ...'

'Dammit man, *come to the point!*' Colonel Rucksack was now very angry indeed. His little hands thumped on the table in front of Cathcart.

Inspector Tomkins spoke very quietly.

'Yes, please, sir. What is the cause of your anxiety? What precisely 'as gone *wrong?*'

IV

Andrew Cathcart coughed.

'Mrs Eithne Bognor was a very rich woman indeed,' he began; 'with (if I may make so bold) a very good business head.' Here he bowed to Colonel Rucksack, who said peevishly:

'Yes, indeed, m'father always said so, but come to the point, please.'

'She had four accounts. Her private, current account for immediate personal expenditure; her Number Two account for payment of income tax; her Number Three account where she deposited all dividends as received, and her main Number Four account where the bulk of her estate was deposited and upon which we paid her an interest of half per cent. She often drew on this fund to make investments.'

'Quite, quite, I'm well aware of all this,' said the Colonel.

'But *we* are n-not,' said Pyke, suddenly asserting himself. 'It's f-fascinating.'

Andrew Cathcart smiled suddenly, for Colonel Rucksack had snarled like an angry dog. Then he became grave again.

'To continue,' he said. 'We sent Mrs Bognor a note every six months, suggesting that we should pay a certain sum into her current account. The sum naturally varied, according to the amounts that she was overdrawn (or not, as the case might be).'

'Oh, quite!' cried the Colonel in an agony of exasperation.

'F-fancy *ever* n-not b-being overdrawn!' said Pyke.

'Hall-mark of respectability,' said the bank manager. He showed his teeth. 'Well, the point is *this*; Mrs Bognor's current account, by virtue of the cheque which she cashed on Saturday for two hundred pounds, was overdrawn by one hundred and ninety-two pounds. Now, that was unusual. Not that we should have *minded*, you know.' Mr Cathcart was deprecating and looked anxiously at Colonel Rucksack. 'But Mrs Bognor was too clever a woman not to know what she was doing. She would probably have called in at my offices and signed the note transferring the necessary funds to cover the over-expenditure. Also, you know, she was too wealthy a woman *not* to know exactly what she had. It is the rich, you know,' said Mr Cathcart, turning, for some reason, to Pyke, 'who are always well aware of how much, or how *little*, they have in the way of funds.'

Pyke said he couldn't agree more, and Mr Cathcart went plunging on:

'So I have just been examining our records of Mrs Bognor's current account, dating back over the last six months. And what do I find?'

'How the hell do we know what you find, you silly fellow?' snapped Colonel Rucksack. 'That's for you to tell *us*.'

'I find that the account has been steadily "milked" by Bearer cheques for various sums, ever since Christmas – for two months, in fact.' Mr Cathcart glared around him at the company and gripped the desk very hard. 'In some cases Mrs Bognor wrote a note and said that she did not feel well, or was unable to come herself and that we were to give "Bearer" the money. Now I am *perfectly certain*, if I know Eithne Bognor (and if Colonel Rucksack has the same opinion of his sister that I have), that Mrs Bognor was unaware of these notes and extravagant Bearer cheques. That they were, in fact—'

'Forgeries,' said Colonel Rucksack, and went very white indeed.

CHAPTER TWENTY

Mrs Greeb leant her aching head against the play-pen. April and May were (as we might expect) unsympathetic. They beat on the floor and the play-pen with indiscriminating fists and feet and bricks. Poor Mrs Greeb had seldom felt worse. She wondered if she were getting influenza.

'Less noise,' she said wearily, 'hush up, do. Granny's feeling her age. Got a bone in her leg.'

She wondered if the room would feel less unhealthily hot if she opened another window.

"Anny, 'anny, 'anny," screamed April monotonously.

'Age! Age! Age!' cried May, and thumped in between each word with a tin spoon.

'Oh, hush up, *do*,' said Mrs Greeb again. But the twins only screamed the louder. Presently the door opened and Celia's tousled head peered cautiously round it. Mrs Greeb recollected that she had even had this peculiarly irritating trick as a child.

'Oh, there you are, Mother,' she said, and progressed further into the room. She appeared relieved to see her mother there. 'It's perfectly terrible,' she went on, 'but we're out of milk, and I've no one else to ask.'

Mrs Greeb got slowly to her feet and disengaged one sticky little hand from her skirts.

'Where is it?' she asked.

'The Dairy?' Celia was brisk, as though she were giving directions to her subordinate typists in the Ministry of Industrial Warfare. 'You can't miss it, Mother. Straight along Durbah Villas till you come to Station Road. Then *up* Station Road beyond Twiggs and the Warhaven Arms. You'll see it on the left-hand side of the road: *Brunton and Old Town Dairy*. Go round at the back to the yard . . .'

The directions poured on, in a maddening stream. Mrs Greeb was to ask for Harold and say who sent her and to insist on a *pint*, anyway.

'What's Twiggs?' said Mrs Greeb dully. She pressed one hand against her forehead.

'Wiggs, wiggs, wiggs,' screamed April and jumped up and down on the spot.

'There's a clever,' said Celia automatically. 'The greengrocer's, of course. *You're* not looking very grand,' she went on, accusingly, peering closely into her mother's face. 'Quite sure you're all right?' Her tone suggested that Mrs Greeb had better be. Mrs Greeb nodded.

'G'and, g'and, g'and!' shouted May at their feet. Then she sat down abruptly and produced the ear-shattering and desolate wail that spells immediate domestic crisis all the world over.

'Oh, go along, *do*, I'll attend to her.'

And so Mrs Greeb went despairingly along, pausing only in her bedroom to wonder where her Post Office savings book might have got to. She pulled her grey felt cloche hat down about her ears and asked herself why she felt so sick. She noticed, in spite of her aching temples, her nausea, and her throbbing feet, that (as she came out of the front door of the Oranmore Hotel) it had begun to rain again. She debated whether she should go back for her umbrella. She decided against it, poor dear, because she felt too rotten to climb upstairs. By the time she reached the corner of Durbah Villas and Station Road her feet and shoulders were quite wet through; and by the time she had penetrated the Yard of the *Brunton and Old Town Dairy*, and had interviewed Harold (a sad little man in rubber boots) about the Oranmore milk, she had a temperature veering steeply about 100 and 102. She was (although of course she did not realize it) already in the grip of typhoid fever.

II

Graham Micah, the only chemist in Brunton-on-Sea, remained open on Sundays between 2 and 3 p.m. for the convenience of the querulous and hypochondriac inhabitants of Brunton-on-Sea who required urgent prescriptions and obvious medicine. He could not, and (more important) *would* not, sell hot-water bottles, or Icky Bicky Pegs, or any other things considered inessentials. Graham Micah was a small, neat man, who was quite humourless. He was also a passionate amateur photographer. When Major Bognor came bumbling into the shop in his most unpleasant humour (for he had, as they say, '*been stood up*' by Miriam Birdseye in the Pavilion, and while he waited there for her it had rained quite hard on him), Mr Micah did not bother to look up from his work. He was fixing some prints for his wife. This needed extreme delicacy and extreme concentration.

'Too busy to serve me, are yer, what?' growled the Major. His unrolled umbrella flapped wetly against his legs. He added under his breath irrelevantly, 'I'll *murder* them.'

Graham Micah's sad, square brown face (for those who live in Brunton-on-Sea are, in spite of themselves, healthy) lit up. He looked at the Major through his heavy, horn-rimmed glasses. He was quite unafraid of his petulance.

'Oh, it's you, is it, Major Bognor,' he said amiably. 'What is it you want, exactly?'

The dispensary was a small, tidy room, cool and dark, at the back of the shop. The Major advanced into it cautiously, making wet marks with his feet on the floor.

'Only a repeat of my sleeping pills. I know where they are,' said the Major. 'Can I help myself?' He drew a pattern in the wet with the ferrule of his umbrella. To Graham Micah, the unimaginative, the mark seemed to have the shape of an oyster.

'Are you *due* for a repeat?' said Graham Micah suspiciously.

The Major held out his prescription, at arm's length and flapped it up and down.

'It's only got *one* of your bloody stamps on it,' he said peevishly. 'I thought I was allowed to have it renewed three times – what?'

The rain came down steadily on the ground-glass roof at the back of the dispensary. It was a restless, maddening sound, like the flickering of finger-tips on the skin of a drum.

'Not within a certain date,' said Micah. He laid down his prints and his fixative with a sigh. He covered them and held out his hand. The Major put the prescription in it. 'I'll see—' said Micah maddeningly.

'Oh, but look here, your good lady let me help misself last

time. I don't want to interrupt you. *I* know how absorbin' hobbies are, what? Used to train polo ponies misself, once. I know how you feel ...'

'Very kind of you, I'm sure, Major,' said Graham Micah solidly. 'But it's no trouble, no trouble at all.'

He took the prescription and held it up to the light that filtered through the dim, rough glass. He muttered, 'Seems quite in order.' He crossed to the prescription book and entered it with his back turned. The Major fidgeted about the dispensary, opening and shutting drawers marked *Tinct* and *Bism* and *Sodm*, and generally got upon Graham Micah's nerves. Eventually Micah finished the laborious entry. He turned back several pages.

Yes, the other entry was there – in his wife's beautiful handwriting. He bit his lip. Never mind. There *was* something funny going on somewhere ...

He turned slowly round, to find the Major peering over his shoulder in a froth of exasperation. Deliberately, Graham Micah shook the little red capsules into their bottle.

'Forty?' he asked with his back turned.

'Eh, wha's 'at? Can't hear you with all this damn' rain,' said the Major savagely.

'I said *do you want forty, sir*?' said Graham Micah with maddening patience. 'Is that what you usually have?'

'Eh? Oh yes. I expect so.'

'I'll give you forty-one for luck, then,' said Graham Micah kindly. He made an exquisite little package of white paper and sealing-wax. 'Terrible thing, insomnia, isn't it, sir? Quite a lot of people down here, you know, say this is the best air ever for sleeping. On your mother's account, as usual, is it, sir?'

The Major hesitated for a second. Then he said 'Yes' once or twice, and 'Why not?' and 'Very kind of you, I'm sure,' and stamped out of the shop with his little package, putting up his umbrella as he went. Graham Micah sighed and entered '40 Secconol taken Major Bognor' under 'Mrs Eithne Bognor, the Oranmore Hotel'. Then he carefully tied a knot in his handkerchief. Then he went back to his beloved prints and fixatives.

III

Mrs Graham Micah (a young and beautiful woman with golden hair) returned at about five o'clock, when she prepared high tea in their flat above the shop for her husband. She had been to an orchestral concert in Hastings and had enjoyed it immensely. She had a *New Statesman* under one arm. It had been Beethoven, Beethoven and Grieg, and Mrs Micah had been (she said) transported to another world. Mr Micah said 'good'. He thought his wife very, very cultured and admired her for it. Sometimes they shared the pleasures of the mind, wagging their heads up and down together in the concert hall, the theatre or the cinema. They did not care for fantasies, which they felt to be out of touch with reality.

'How did you come on with those snaps of Dora and me?' said Mrs Micah when she had finished humming the slow movement of the Beethoven to her husband and he had said it was jolly.

'All right,' said Mr Micah. He took out his handkerchief and looked at the knot. 'I had that old nut Bognor *in*,' he began conversationally.

'Oo, haven't you heard?' began Mrs Graham Micah in a great rush, culture quite forgotten, her eyes very wide indeed.

'It's all over the town – I meant to tell you. Old Mrs Bognor, his mother's dead, they say, *and* her brother, too, the poor fellow who wears a beret who's not quite right – Rucksack, isn't it? Mr Robert Rucksack, who lives with the Parsons, you know. He's dead, too, they say. And they say it's *not natural* . . .'

Mr Micah went rather white and pushed his plate away.

'What's the matter, Graham?' Young Mrs Micah was (as she would have said) ever so upset. 'Isn't your kipper nice?'

'Look here, my girl,' began Graham Micah. 'That old Bognor says you let him help himself to Secconol on the 15th inst. I looked up the date and the entry's in the book, whatever you say.' Mr Micah paused and then flushed angrily as another, deeper thought struck him. 'And that old b— had me make the entry to his mother, when he must have known she was dead. Really, some people!'

'Oo, he never!' cried Mrs Micah. 'He *never*! The big liar . . .'

'Whatcha mean?' Graham Micah put on his horn-rimmed glasses and stared fixedly at his lovely young wife. Direct contradiction was not at all what he had expected.

'Major Bognor hasn't been in himself for *weeks*,' said Mrs Micah indignantly. 'It was Tony Robinson came in last for him. Tony said he was too ill to leave the hotel. And the prescription was perfectly OK, I remember. I stamped it myself. Graham, don't *look* at me like that . . .'

'Well then, what *is* all this?' Graham Micah was very annoyed. He drew his plate towards him again. 'What's all this about people helping themselves? *That's* what I don't like . . .'

'I expect *Tony* helped himself,' said Mrs Micah idly, pouring out another cup of tea. 'After all, he usually does. He's quite one of the family, is Tony.'

Young Mrs Graham Micah and Tony Robinson were members of the same lawn tennis club.

An hour later, after profound wrangling with Mrs Micah (who said it was jolly mean and unfair and disgusting to Tony Robinson), Mr Micah put on his black Anthony Eden hat and his neatly brushed winter overcoat; and Mrs Micah put on her best hat; and they set off together up the hill to the police station. It so happened, therefore, that when Celia Robinson, perturbed by her mother's leaden appearance and ice-cold hands and feet, telephoned for a *Quick Cold Cure* after closing hours, there was no reply from Micah's flat.

CHAPTER TWENTY-ONE

Mrs Greeb died in the Cottage Hospital on Tuesday morning. Dr Stalag-Jones, a white-faced probationer, and a very experienced Scottish Sister indeed, attended her at the last. It was perfectly certain if *anyone's* life at that stage could have been saved it would have been Mrs Greeb's.

Dr Stalag-Jones had made her decision to operate *immediately*, but she was already too late. Mrs Greeb died on the way to the theatre. Dr Stalag-Jones turned sadly from the bed. Sister said she was indeed surprised and also alarmed at the speed with which the patient had sunk. Who would have expected the crisis so soon? Delirious, too, and *on* all that time about the oysters, and yet she had only eaten the oysters on Saturday, she had said ...

'Was she only delirious about the oysters?' said Dr Stalag-Jones. She stopped suddenly half-way down the ward.

'I couldn't say, Doctor,' said Sister. 'Perhaps Nurse here knows. Nurse, you have been with Mrs Greeb since she came in, haven't you? Tell the Doctor, now, and don't be frightened.'

'Can you remember anything she said?' said Dr Stalag-Jones. She surveyed the young and scarlet-faced probationer with cold, kind, grey eyes.

'No, no, she didn't say anything,' said Nurse, and shifted nervously from foot to foot. 'Except of course about her Post Office savings book. About how it had been stolen and so forth.'

Dr Stalag-Jones now surprised Sister and the probationer nurse very much indeed. She went straight to the telephone at the end of the ward, amongst the sluice, and rang up Inspector Tomkins.

II

Tomkins answered at once when the telephone rang. He was sitting in his office, gloomily surveying Mrs Bognor's sables. They had been found in Mrs Greeb's wardrobe by Celia Robinson on Monday evening when (panic-stricken) she had packed her mother off to the Cottage Hospital.

Tomkins agreed with Dr Stalag-Jones that the police surgeon should perform an autopsy at once in case some other cause of death besides typhoid fever had aggravated the latest victim from the Oranmore Hotel. Tomkins also wondered gloomily how long it would be before the Press got hold of it, and Dr Stalag-Jones laughed grimly and said she would do her best to get 'her people' to remain silent. Then they rang off.

Tomkins then put on his commonplace little green pork-pie hat and (clutching *Oysters and Dredgers of Whitstable, 1902*) walked round to the Oranmore Hotel. He hoped that the sea air and the fresh evening wind might clear his wearying brain. The first thing he found on his arrival was Celia Robinson, white-faced, with a twin under one arm. He thought she must just have been told of her mother's death. In her other hand she held a buff envelope, typed. It was addressed to Mrs Greeb, c/o the

Oranmore Hotel, Brunton-on-Sea. The capital letters were very slightly out of alignment. Inside was a Post Office savings book.

III

The last entry showed date 23rd February, and, under Withdrawals, £3. The stamp showed the office mark as Brunton-on-Sea and the same date. Celia limply held it out to Tomkins, remarking that she expected he would like to see it.

'So *this* is what she was making such a fuss about before she passed over,' said Tomkins gloomily. 'We 'ave a pretty average competent bunch of forgers around here, eh, miss? Do you have a typewriter in the hotel?'

'Pardon?' said Celia. She seemed very calm about her mother's death. Perhaps it was delayed shock? Tomkins fingered the envelope and (mysteriously) April was silent, sucking her thumb, entranced at the lovely gentleman. 'Yes, there's one in the office, if you want to use it. What *I'm* surprised about Inspector, is how quick the Post Office have been about returning Mother's book. And surely they oughtn't to have taken the book away, just for three pounds?'

Tomkins marched purposefully into the office, remarking that he would give Celia a receipt for the book, as the police would need it for a little. He was now astonished at Celia's lack of feeling. Celia produced paper and carbon paper from a very untidy drawer.

'Ah, well, miss,' he explained kindly, pecking away at the machine with one finger, 'there's been rather a lot of these forgeries goin' on. And to safeguard against them there's been this police order, see?'

Celia stood on one leg and blushed scarlet and evidently wrestled with her secret thoughts. Finally, she decided to confide in the inspector.

'Look!' she said. 'Inspector Tomkins, do you *have* to have the book? I mean, I'm rather hard up just now ... I know Mother would have *wanted* me to have the money.'

Tomkins said he was terribly sorry, but murder was murder and he would let her have it back again as soon as possible. And so, with compassion in his piggy little blood-shot eyes, he signed the receipt for 'Post Office Savings Book, Property of the Late Mrs Ada Greeb' and handed it to Celia. The type face of the machine was identical with that of the Post Office envelope. And the capital letters were very slightly out of alignment.

IV

On his way back to the post office Tomkins saw Miriam Birdseye and Pyke, their heads close together, striding towards the pier, furiously quarrelling. Tomkins decided not to catch them up.

He looked at Mrs Greeb's book as he walked. The total now stood at £197. He looked at the date-stamp and Mrs Greeb's signature. Obviously the book had been stolen by someone with access to the hotel typewriter. But who?

The signature 'Ada Greeb' was one that might easily be copied by a quick and clever writer. The writing was characterless and curiously unformed. Tomkins was surprised, for Mrs Greeb had seemed an old lady of character. But surely February 23rd had been a Sunday? Surely the post office didn't transact business on a Sunday? And what was that other thing Miss

Birdseye had told him? *Someone* had been sending off money in a registered envelope to Whortleberry Down. Of course, Connie Watson, the old 'Les Chef', or whatever she called herself. Mrs Greeb had suspected her, anyway.

Tomkins grimaced as he came into the post office. Inside there was the usual queue of halt, maimed and blind Brunton population, buying stamps and drawing old age pensions.

Tomkins passed straight through them, sniffing and asking for the postmaster. When he produced his warrant the postmaster clicked his tongue. He was grieved indeed that Brunton-on-Sea should have been marked out by this gang of forgers . . . Tomkins interrupted him.

'I don't think *this* has anything to do with the big-scale London forgeries,' he said quickly. 'I think it's a private little affair. All right? Can I see the clerk who was on duty on Sunday? But by the way, *are* you open for business on Sunday? Isn't that rather unusual?'

'We're open from nine until ten on Sunday. It's for the convenience of the visitors.' The postmaster appeared rather proud of this. He opened a door and spoke sharply to someone outside. Eventually he returned. 'Ah,' he said, rubbing his hands palm to palm, 'we are indeed fortunate. The young lady on duty last Sunday was Miss Cathcart, daughter of Andrew Cathcart, manager of the Sussex and Provincial.'

V

Young Miss Cathcart was very much her father's daughter. She had blonde hair, rigidly controlled in plastic waves, and round pale blue eyes. She gave the impression that she was one of those difficult persons who are never in the wrong.

'Good morning, Miss Cathcart,' said Tomkins. 'I believe you were on duty on Sunday?'

Miss Cathcart looked at the postmaster, who sat with his legs complacently crossed and fingered his row of fountain-pens. He fairly twinkled with confidence in Miss Cathcart.

'It's quite all right,' he said. 'Tell the inspector everything he wants to know.'

'Yes, I was on duty Sunday,' said Miss Cathcart suspiciously.

'Was there anyone on duty with you from nine until ten?'

'No, it's not necessary. We have very little trade then.' Miss Cathcart looked at the postmaster, who nodded and smiled encouragingly. Miss Cathcart was certainly Postmaster's Pet.

'So you would be in charge of Post Office savings *and* registrations?'

Miss Cathcart agreed that this was indeed so.

'Perhaps I could see the records that you kept of these transactions, miss?'

After some mutterings and fuss the sheet that showed Sunday's Post Office savings withdrawals and a separate book of rather frighteningly illegible counterfoils for 'registered letters accepted' were produced from the outer office and handed to the inspector.

There were five entries on the Savings Bank sheet. The first of them boldly stated that Mrs Ada Greeb, of Duchy Road, Harrogate, had withdrawn £3. This suggested the very first customer that Miss Cathcart had served that morning. And among the faint, distressing carbon marks that kept the record of registrations, Tomkins found that a letter had been sent to

Miss Vibart, of Whortleberry Down, Devonshire. So he was not at all surprised when Miss Cathcart told him how her first customer had looked.

CHAPTER TWENTY-TWO

At the end of the pier, the grey sea slapped and chuckled, and the cold waves (sometimes sunlit to green) poured endlessly through the piles. They stirred the seaweed that grew here like hair, waving on the iron scaffolding; they broke heavily over beige, crinkled shellfish and surged through the pier, pouring in swamping sheets of water that were torn apart, dripping, by sharp black iron. It was always wet and mysterious underneath the pier. Even when the sun shone out the water wiggled mysteriously, reflected and shimmering in another dimension.

Above, on the warm wood of the pier itself, it was gay, even on the deck chairs where Miriam and Pyke sat quarrelling. Around them, all the slot machines and fortune-telling devices that are so popular with the aristocracy and proletariat and (as advertised) consulted by theatrical celebrities and the crowned heads of Europe, twinkled and flashed. A mechanical musical-box, continuously fed by Miriam with pennies, filled the bright air monotonously and metallically with a tune called 'La Vie En Rose'. Every person of Pyke's acquaintance seemed to go soft-eyed when they heard this played, saying, 'Ah, *our* time.' As Pyke's own musical preference was for Purcell and the early and more obscure of the madrigalists, we may well imagine his exasperation.

'Look here, Miriam,' he was saying explosively, with only a suspicion of his stammer (it often disappeared under the influence of rage), 'we c-came to Brunton to write a *play*. And what happens? I sit around and make an a-absolute a-ass of myself, while you chase up and down with these policemen . . .'

Miriam said nothing.

'These murders and these Robinsons and Rucksacks are none of my business. I'm s-sick and tired of them. Unless you c-co-operate a little and do *some* work I'm going straight back to London by the next train.'

Miriam did not reply.

'It's r-really t-too bad of you, Miriam. After all, it's for you I'm supposed to be writing the play. *I* haven't got money to b-burn, playing up and down the South Coast, chasing m-mur-derers, even if you have . . .'

The juke-box, clattering, came to the end of 'La Vie En Rose' and Miriam silently held out a hand for another penny. Pyke gave her one and continued to rage about the waste of everyone's time, money and energy. Particularly creative energy. What would Linnit and Dunfee say, he would like to know? Miriam reset the pointer opposite a little label that announced 'La Vie En Rose', turned a handle, put in her penny and sat down in her chair again. Instantly, the infernal tune whined all around them like a sad sea-gull, multiplied a hundred times by the sea and sky and the sounding board of the wooden pier.

'Dear Pyke,' said Miriam, and laid a warm hand on his

knee. He started convulsively. 'I shall always think of this as Our Tune.' Then she suddenly became brisk, leaning forward in her chair as she remarked: 'Dear, surely that's Tony Robinson, walking along there by the Shooting Gallery? What's *he* doing out at this time of day? Oughtn't he to be drunk by now, dear?'

II

That morning Tony Robinson had got up early. He flung himself (much to Celia's surprise) at the postman as he arrived with the first post. He stood, blear-eyed and blinking, in his old Jaegar dressing-gown, an unpleasant sight in the weeping eyes of dawn.

'Expectin' something?' said the postman. He handed over the usual thick wad of typewritten envelopes that suggested unpaid accounts and final demands.

'S'right,' said Tony, flipping through them. 'Ma-in-law's expectin' something.'

'Would that be Mrs Greeb now?' said the postman. He was a friendly and interested soul. 'There are three for Mrs Greeb, two of 'em re-addressed . . .'

Tony scowled.

'Nothing much misses you fellows, does it?' said Tony Robinson. His smile was *not* friendly as he slid his own letters into the pocket of his dressing-gown. He went sourly back into the warmth of the Oranmore Hotel. The postman plodded on down the road, muttering to himself about 'some folks'.

III

At lunch-time Celia Robinson came into the office and found Tony lashing round, opening drawers and slamming them shut, riffling papers, and generally upsetting April and May. They clucked and screamed and dribbled in time to Tony's furious, controlled swearing.

'Do you *want* something, dear?' Celia stood in the doorway and pushed her hair up in a crest. 'Really, I'm so worried and overworked I hardly . . .'

Tony stared at her.

'Why can't you let those two lazy bods do something for a change?' he said. 'Of course I want something, you silly little fool. You don't suppose I'm looking through the drawers for fun, do you?'

Celia winced.

'And Mother's lying there—' she began in a whimper, her chin trembling.

'Oh, shut up, Celia, do! *You* know I'm sorry about the old girl. *But* you know as well as I do that money of hers in the Post Office savings book is damn' useful. The warrant's come, and now I need the book to draw the one hundred and ninety-seven pounds. Where did you put it when you came back from the post office, eh?'

Large tears rose in Celia's eyes and spilled over on to her cheeks.

'Put it? The Post Office book, you mean?' She was frightened. She was playing for time.

'*Of course that's what I mean* . . .' Tony whirled to face her. April and May were suddenly silent. They heard the savage, controlled fury in his voice.

'Why, the Post Office have to return it, Tony. You know that. That's why we typewrote the envelope . . .'

Celia showed her terror. She backed away to the door, one hand to her mouth, where she bit it, hard, so hard that she should not scream. Tony was coming towards her. Oh God! The last time he seemed as angry as this he hadn't hit her, but he would hit her, one day, she knew, sooner or later.

'Please don't hit me, Tony, please don't hit me . . .'

'You silly little fool! You're hiding something from me, I know you are. You silly little fool! We'll swing together if you aren't careful. The book's come back. Is that it?'

Celia nodded. She was dumb, frozen to the ground, her shoulder-blades crawled with horror. Swing together. Funny how the words had scared her. Yet 'swing together' was a jolly idea, really.

Then Celia was surprised to hear her own voice speaking, faltering:

'We'll all swing together, our bodies between our knees . . .'

It was at this moment that Tony hit her.

IV

'Yes, Tony, yes, the book came back from the Post Office. Yes – oh, please don't hit me again. Yes, it did – I swear it did. I don't *know* where I put it . . .'

Now Tony was no longer angry.

'Look, old girl.' He was suddenly kind. He put his arms round her and she cowered again. She expected another attack. 'Look, this is serious, darling. I'm sorry I was angry just now, dearest, but you don't *know* how serious this is. Where did you put the book, dear? No, Tony's not cross now, darling. *But just where is that book?'*

His voice changed. It was again as intense and terrifying as the whistle of a bomb falling from a great height. It penetrated her nerves until she sat still, shivering, on his knees. Even so, she hid her head on his shoulder for comfort. When she spoke her voice was only a whisper of unhappiness and horror.

'I gave it to the inspector, Tony. I thought he ought to have it. I didn't know you'd sent for a warrant for the one hundred and ninety-seven pounds, darling.'

Tony sat and patted his wife's shoulder. He seemed to reassure her, kindly. She sobbed and hiccuped against his chest. But his blue eyes stared beyond her, through the clouded windows of the Oranmore Hotel that hemmed them both in, beyond them both to the sea.

'Oh dear, oh dear, oh dear,' said Celia.

V

Tony walked down the pier, placing his feet firmly, as though he had never felt a sense of his own inferiority. Under his heavy tread the wooden planks seemed to swing and shake and ring. He did not see Miriam and Pyke, tucked behind the fortune-telling machines. He went on walking until he was far beyond them, right at the very tip of the pier. Here the wind was fresh and cold and the spray sometimes sprang up from the waves. He stood for five minutes, quite motionless, staring out to sea.

The horizon was as clear and bright as summer. No one would think it was February. Soon it would be March; spring again, blowing away the dead horror of the clinging winter months. The wind whipped in Tony's face and stung him, but it whipped away the dank misery of the Oranmore Hotel and his wife, Celia.

He had been a fool ever to buy the place. It had been madness. There was something *wrong* with it. He couldn't hope to break a hoodoo – not he. He was only flesh and blood. He might have realized as soon as he set foot in the place, when the Army came out of it, and he surveyed its peeling chocolate-and-brown paint; and its gloomy sweating depths of basement and kitchen: he might have realized there was something here stronger than his will. Something stronger than life. As strong as death.

Tony stuck his hands in his trouser pockets and scowled at the waves that tossed below him. Soon the Corporation would shut the pier, against the winds of March, and say it was dangerous. Plenty of other things in Brunton were dangerous, too. Keeping hotels for example.

'Hello, stranger.' It was a girl's voice in his ear. Tony spun round as someone took him by the elbow. 'Thinking of jumping over?' she said. 'You looked quite suicidal from the land.'

'Did I?' Tony was self-conscious. He coughed. He had not seen Rosemary since ... when? He turned on his most charming and gentlemanly manner. 'Well, Rosemary, how *are* you?' he said.

Rosemary scowled, but she continued to hold his arm.

'You may well ask,' she said. 'You've been avoiding me.'

'You're an old ass to say that.' Tony's voice held exactly the right amount of banter. 'You know quite well I haven't. That damned place absolutely absorbs me. And you know what

Celia *is*. Why, when you and I were both missing so long at the Harvest Festival Hop, behind the orchestra pit, she was absolutely *certain* about us . . .'

The wind blew his charm from his mouth and tossed it, contemptuously, three miles above their heads.

'It's easy to make excuses, Tony Robinson. I *know* you've been avoiding me.' She shook her head and her pale sculptured curls were wrenched away by the wind.

'But, anyway,' said Tony – he looked mysteriously in her eyes and fluttered his thick eyelashes at her – 'what are *you* doing on the pier at this hour? Oughtn't you to be in the post office, no? Aren't you on duty this morning?'

Miss Rosemary Cathcart (for this was indeed she) flung her curls back again. *Some* people appreciated her, even if that ne'er-do-weel Tony Robinson didn't.

'I was given the morning off.' A faint touch of self-satisfaction crept into her voice. 'We had the police in. Something about a stolen Post Office savings book or other. Old Tomkins had me up in the police station signing things.' She looked up at Tony, candidly, and smiled a carefully practised smile. 'As a matter of fact,' she said, 'I identified the person who brought the book in on Sunday *quite* easily . . .'

VI

'How rum they look, dear, don't they?' said Miriam to Pyke.

'Who do?' said Pyke grumpily.

'Tony Robinson, dear, and that girl he's talking to on the other end of the pier, there. And, do you know—' Miriam was suddenly all attention and excitement, almost leaping from her deck chair. 'I do believe he's going to push her over!' Her voice changed. 'Oh, what a pity!' she concluded sadly. 'He isn't.'

CHAPTER TWENTY-THREE

At about four o'clock that afternoon Miriam and Pyke began to walk back from the pier. The best of the day had gone; the winter had returned in all its gloom, as the sun swam, a crimson and sinister oyster shape, behind the mists on Beachy Head. Miriam shivered and put her hand in Pyke's arm to reassure herself. Ahead of them, along the esplanade, the lights suddenly came on, each one a mysterious star, unsuccessfully pin-pointing the advancing dusk. The rising tide sighed sadly along the shingle. The waves creamed in towards the beach in a series of ripples like tearing silk. Some emphatic, gallant old figures went spanking away, walking the dog, towards the East Cliffs. Trusty and Faithful, mis-shapen white bolsters of fox terrier misery, accompanied their masters on miserable, swollen legs.

'Surely those are the famous contortionists, Rucksack and Bognor,' said Miriam suddenly. She pointed with a witch's fore-finger at two of these figures, walking away from them into the gathering dusk. She was quite right. It was Reginald Bognor and his uncle, Charles Rucksack. They seemed distorted, incredibly malignant. The street lamps flung their shadows, now warped to dwarf size, now grown monstrous and over-towering, in front of them on the silent esplanade.

'And that's another thing.' Pyke was angry, glowering at Miriam down his big nose. 'Why don't you take things seriously? It may be a game to *you* – but it's damnably serious for Robinson and his pathetic little wife.'

'Looks as though she was pulled through a hedge backwards,' murmured Miriam. She was glad of the ringing of Pyke's heels on the pavement and (even if he was cross with her) the solid comfort of his arm.

'*That* is the sort of remark I m-mean.' Pyke turned on her, dropping her arm, obviously very much moved. 'Empty, devoid of feeling. Not even w-witty. It's only when I s-see you faced with some t-truly significant, f-fundamental t-truth that I see your sh-shallowness . . .'

'Oh, I say,' said Miriam. 'You are cross. Who is it you are jealous of? Tomkins?'

There was a pause before either of them spoke. Then Miriam (to Pyke's disgust) said:

'I wonder what Reggie and the Colonel are talking about. Shall we follow them?'

II

Tomkins, unaware of the differences that engaged Miriam and Pyke, sat in his office, gloomily marshalling facts. His thoughts were disjointed and meaningless. They made a jig-saw puzzle that might one day be fitted together. At the moment some of the pieces were missing.

So far as he could judge, Bognor and Rucksack had almost

equal reasons for murdering Mrs Bognor. Obviously on Rucksack's death Bognor would become sole inheritor of the Rucksack estate.

Certainly they were both quite unmoved by Mrs Bognor's death. And they were both astonished: Rucksack that his sister, living, should have allowed herself to be stolen from; Bognor that she should be dead at all.

Tomkins groaned and put his head in his hands.

He wished he had a copy of the Rucksack Bequest Trust, or whatever it was called. He tried to remember what Miriam had told him of it. Anyone wishing to scoff the lot (she had said) would begin by eliminating the in-laws. And after that one would move on to the dotty brother. Tomkins sat upright. For Bognor had visited the dotty brother that night and Bognor admitted it. That was something.

But suppose (for the sake of argument) that Bognor *had* done all these things. The last thing he would want would be to kill his mother so soon. He would keep *her* alive until the last, so that his claim on the estate would be absolute.

Here was another fact. Mrs Greeb had died of typhoid fever. Could this have anything to do with the Rucksacks? Was it chance that had led Mrs Greeb to Brunton-on-Sea and her daughter's shambles of a hotel, just at the moment when everything was being wound up for the Rucksacks? Poor interfering old bag.

Tomkins pulled at his moustache. If this went on much longer he would have it out by the roots.

There was one positive fact, anyway, contributed by Tomkins for the benefit of Tomkins. He would never eat another oyster again as long as he lived.

It was at this moment that Constable Beatty tapped on the door and announced 'Mr Robert Parsons, Inspector, hall-porter at the Warhaven Arms, who says he has some evidence for you in this Rucksack business.'

III

'That's right, Inspector.' Parsons sat opposite him, his grey face long and lugubrious as a horse's. 'There's *this* which Mrs Parsons 'as 'ad in 'er keeping for some time.'

Parsons produced an envelope. It was somewhat dirty and addressed in the pathetic childish scrawl that Tomkins had lately seen in the hotel register of Whortleberry Down. It was addressed to Mr and Mrs Parsons. Inside (on lined paper) was a tiny letter. It began, *Dear Aunt Doris and Uncle Bob.*

I do not know if the lawyers will give you anything when I die. But in case I do I should like you to have it.

(Signed) *Robt. Rucksack.*

Bob Parsons coughed and crossed his legs.

'Poor little chap wrote that when he come back from Devon that time he was so sick from eating them there oysters. He thought he was going to die then, but he didn't. We could see it wasn't legal, poor little chap. Not but what we *want* anything,' added Parsons hastily. 'He was fond of us, poor little chap. We were fond of him, too.' Tomkins was surprised at the feeling in his voice. He looked up suddenly to see Parsons' eyes suddenly angry and glittering, and he realized that *this* was the way that Reginald Bognor and Charles Rucksack (yes, and Celia

Robinson) should look. 'Mrs Parsons 'as no children, as you know. There's a rumour, as you know,' he wiped something from his eyes. 'In fact the 'ole place is aboil. They say he didn't die natural. Well, if there's any truth in it—'

He paused and looked at Tomkins. His eyes were hard and sharp in his long, sad face. Tomkins suddenly recollected Parsons' war wound. It was supposed to make him act a little oddly.

'Yes, there's a whole lot of truth in it,' Tomkins said firmly. 'Very well then.' Parsons came to a decision. He put his hat on the desk and leant back in his chair. He fumbled for something in the inside pocket of his coat. 'You must 'ave this. Mrs Parsons and me we talked it out, and we decided that you must 'ave it. Look, I'll wait while you read it, and see if you think it's legal.' And Bob Parsons now slammed down on the desk a pile of quarto sheets that had evidently been torn from a lined exercise book.

IV

Mr Robert Rucksack has been resident in our house for ten years, and although not right in the head he is a proper gentleman, and we have got downright fond of him and we would not like anyone to get away with anything, so we, Doris and Robert Parsons, have written this out.

As near as we can judge by memory, it was September 1946, after spending a week away with his sister, Mrs Eithne, and her family, and his brother Chas. (Col. Rucksack) he was very ill indeed after eating oysters. Since when he decided he would never touch them again, no matter what.

So the other night, towards midnight, Colonel Chas. Rucksack comes along to see him with a plate of oysters he says is his sister's (Mrs Eithne's) left-overs from her birthday party. He goes up to Mr Bob's play-room where he keeps his kites and so on, he being very fond of kite flying, and remains there with Mr Bob until about 1 a.m. when we believe (Mrs Parsons and I) that they both (Col. Rucksack and he) ate the oysters.

(Signed) *Robt. Parsons.*
Fan Parsons.
In full possession of faculties. Feb. 25th, 195–.

Tomkins lifted his sandy head, his eyes wide with astonishment.

'You're sure of this?'

'Sure of what, Inspector?'

Parsons seemed to come to attention in his chair. He reached for his hat as though he were about to bolt from the office.

'That it was *Colonel* Rucksack who called with the oysters that night and *not* Major Bognor?'

'Oh, perfectly sure, sir – that is Inspector. I let the Colonel in myself. He was late, you know – about 11 p.m. Would you know the cause of death yet, at all? It *would* be the oysters, sir, now wouldn't it?' Parsons' voice was frightening, low and persuasive.

And, to Tomkins' dismay, Bob Parsons tilted out of a brown-paper bag on to Tomkins' desk, a dozen tinkling, rustling, faintly smelling oyster shells. They lay in a great pile, phosphorescently shining, giving out a mild and evil glow of their own.

CHAPTER TWENTY-FOUR

On the cliffs beyond the town the twilight was frightening. Far below, the shadows of the breakwater ran out towards the rising tide through the sliding shingle. Even the shingle was now drained of colour, and the moon, rising vague and watery, did nothing to reassure the nervous. It intensified the pits in the ground, in the ditches, and in the mysterious horrors of barbed wire and broken fencing that cluttered the lip of the cliff.

Colonel Rucksack and Major Bognor came up the last stiff slope, wheezing and panting.

'Nothin' like a walk each day in the fresh air, m'boy,' gasped the Colonel, holding one claw-like hand to his side, 'to keep you in trim. Sorry to drag you along here, but at my age I have to keep to m'programme, y'know. In fact, I'm late today. Should have done this at tea-time.'

'I know, Uncle Charles,' said Bognor. He was subdued. His face seemed milky and his dark moustache was like a scar. He showed his teeth for a second in a gleam of compassion.

'There's a bench up here somewhere,' grunted the Colonel in little jerks and snatches. 'Often rest on it a bit, y'know, before I set out back again.'

'Can be pretty stiff, the return journey,' said Major Bognor kindly. He swung with his umbrella at a loose stone, and it skipped into the air, clicked against a post and was gone, leaping and bounding, to the beach, ninety feet below them. 'Particularly if there's a head wind, what?'

'Oh, exactly,' said Colonel Rucksack. He sank thankfully on to the wooden bench and stuck out his brittle old legs ahead of him. 'Now look here, Reggie, what's all this about "I must get married" eh? At your age. Seems a little unnecessary – yer mother—'

'*You keep my mother out of this*,' said Major Bognor, in exactly the same furious tones that Tony Robinson had used to the bank manager, Andrew Cathcart.

'And you keep a civil tongue in your head, m'boy,' retorted the Colonel. 'Who *is* this young woman, anyhow?'

II

Pyke was even angrier with Miriam when she said that she wanted to follow Rucksack and Bognor along to the cliff. He had already meddled enough, he said, and h-had n-nothing to sh-show for it. *He* would go quietly back to the Oranmore Hotel and have tea.

'Very frightening, the Oranmore Hotel, isn't it?' said Miriam chattily. 'As soon as I set foot there I was sure of it. Kind of haunted. I'm sure the atmosphere drives everyone to *hideous* social indiscretions.'

'Such as suicide,' said Pyke sulkily. 'And murder.'

There was a pause, while Pyke remarked that *this* wouldn't help him to write a sequel to *Rouge on Parnassus*.

'No, but honestly, dear, those oyster shells over the front

door alone, they're quite enough to give *me* the creeps. Don't you think so, dear?'

Pyke said coldly that Brunton-on-Sea gave him the creeps altogether and he wanted to go home.

'Oh, we can't do *that*,' said Miriam, in a spoilt child's wail; 'until we've found out who's doing all these *things* . . .'

Pyke abandoned all attempt to get his own way.

'Very well then,' he said. 'But this is the last time I give in to you. And I won't be answerable for the consequences.' Miriam purred and linked Pyke's arm more closely in her own. She leant against him friendlily and looked up into his face.

'Who do *you* think is doing all this, Pyke?' she said. 'You might tell a girl what you think, and not be so pompous.'

Pyke considered. His struggle was over; he was now engulfed in Miriam's life again. He had accepted (but only temporarily, he told himself) her dangerous, elastic standards.

'V-very well,' he said. 'I suppose either Rucksack or Bognor, or one of the Robinsons. Or that terrible old cook. Or the bank manager. It's a sw-sw-sweepstake as far as I'm concerned.' Miriam continued to purr.

'You *are* nice, Pyke,' she said. 'You join *in* so.' Their feet echoed strangely on the pavement. 'But it would clarify things,' she added suddenly, 'wouldn't it, Pyke, if Reggie were to murder his uncle, Colonel Rucksack?'

'Or *vice versa*,' said Pyke.

III

Later the moon came up and shed its watery mist and the whole town was laid bare in broad washes of evil silver and black.

And the depraved shape of the Rialto Hotel, and the absorbing menace of the Oranmore stood etched against a shining horizon, where the track of the moon (or so it was said) had tempted the late Mrs Fortescue-Sykes over so many unhappy months towards the cliffs and her last despairing plunge towards the spiky breakwater below.

Colonel Rucksack and Major Bognor paused at the gate of the Oranmore Hotel. The Colonel was aware of the depression that engulfed them, almost immediately.

'Very well, then,' he said gloomily. He spoke very slowly, as though each word possessed an intolerable weight of its own. 'You have the whip hand. Put the thing in *The Times* if you wish. *What* did you say the girl's name was again?'

'Rosemary,' said the Major. 'Rosemary Cathcart.'

But he did not sound very well pleased about it.

Interlude

'H'r'm. H'r'm.'

Mr Justice Mayhem was by now well into his summing-up. His face, built up around his fine, arched, nose, rather like the Sydney Harbour Bridge, and about as unemotional, only showed passion over a truly knotty point of law. He was passionate now, demanding that the jury should concentrate upon facts and clear their minds of cant.

'You will appreciate,' said His Lordship, 'that money (or the lack of it) was possibly the motive that lay behind all these happenings. And so, alas, it often is; the root of evil. The Rucksack Bequest Trust Fund, left by the late Charles Rucksack, the elder, ensured that his estate should pass in equal parts to his children in their lifetime. The implication of this should be obvious to you. At the time that Mrs Bognor died, her brother Charles directly benefited, and later than night he benefited again, following the death of Robert, his younger brother. This left him (as you may see) in full control of the estate.

'But only a person in possession of (or with access to) arsenic and a hypodermic syringe that might be used to inject the oysters in question should be considered as the author of this outrageous crime.

'Now with regard to hypodermic syringes . . .'

BOOK FOUR

'AND MADE THEM TROT SO QUICK!'

'It seems a shame!' the Walrus said.
'To play them such a trick
After we've brought them out so far
And made them trot so quick!'
The Carpenter said nothing but
'The butter's spread too thick!'

LEWIS CARROLL: *The Walrus and the Carpenter.*

CHAPTER TWENTY-FIVE

Tomkins leant confidentially across the counter of Graham Micah, Pharmaceutical Chemist, and suggested that they had a private word together. Near Tomkins' elbow the rubber hot-water bottles, in their several sizes, trembled on their display stands; and the piles of tinned spinach and rose-hip syrup shook and tinkled. Graham Micah, looking nervously at his toppling stock, suggested that the inspector should step into the dispensary.

It was a gloomy morning. The electric light burnt here, deepening the darkness that seemed to press down on the shrouded skylight. Tomkins marched in, saying 'Good morning' to Mrs Graham Micah (he made a mental note that, anyway, there was one woman left in Brunton-on-Sea with good legs), and plunged at once into his interview.

'It's information I want,' he began. 'You've been very 'elpful to me already, I must say, and you're an intelligent chap'

'Thanks very much,' said Graham Micah. But he simpered and looked pleased.

'Well now, look here, can *anyone* buy a hypodermic syringe?'

'Yes, of course they can,' said Graham Micah, surprised. 'But

people don't often want them. We don't have a big stock . . .?'
His voice rose to a question and Tomkins rubbed his sandy
head. He had laid his hat down on the smooth, marble counter
where Graham Micah still kept a pestle and a mortar and other
objects of a sinister and compelling charm.

'Got any in stock now?' he asked.

'I don't suppose so,' said Graham Micah. He moved
towards his mysterious wooden drawers. He opened several
of them and shut them again, and Tomkins wondered (and
not for the first time) why chemists kept patent medicines
in alphabetical order in drawers palpably labelled *Bism* and
Sulpht and *Parald*.

'Mrs Tony Robinson had the last one,' he said vaguely. 'I
think. Yes, she did. She had it the week before last, I remember;
I was in two minds whether to re-order or not . . .'

Tomkins' little blood-shot eyes became more than interested.

'What would she want a hypodermic for?' he asked. 'Cut out
the professional ethics and let's have some facts.'

'Well, she has anaemia, see,' said Graham Micah. 'And so
she has to give herself injections of liver. Has had to since—'

'But surely she oughtn't to be working so hard if her anaemia
is as pernicious as all that,' interrupted Tomkins.

Graham Micah shrugged his shoulders.

'That's her business, isn't it?' he said.

'All married women overwork, anyway,' said Mrs Graham
Micah, poking her lovely head through the doorway. 'Who's
this? Celia Robinson? She's had anaemia ever since a kiddie.
I remember her mother telling me when she was in last week
for Icky Bicky Pegs for the twins. Pardon. I hear a customer.'

And Mrs Graham Micah bobbed out again, a fresh and

delicious sight in her white overall, her golden head like a daffodil in the dark dispensary.

'Poor girl,' said Tomkins involuntarily. 'Anaemia's a nasty thing. Or so they say. I suppose one uses a hypodermic for lots of things. Legitimately, I mean?'

Graham Micah considered.

'Well, of course, morphine addicts use them, I believe. And cocaine.' He smiled a little bleak smile. 'But I wouldn't know about anything like *that*. Asthmatics, certainly, and bronchial cases.'

'Why would *they* use them?' asked Tomkins idly. 'Bronchitis and asthmatics, I mean. Extraordinary this is; I'd no idea—'

'Oh,' said Graham Micah kindly. 'If you haven't had occasion yourself, and you a healthy man, there's no reason why you should know, now is there? Asthmatics for example. They sometimes have to give themselves Adrenalin to relieve a really bad spasm. And bronchial cases, you know, they give themselves injections (or inoculations I believe is the right term in that case) of their own self-infecting bug. Their system fights it out, you know. It's really very clever. Colonel Rucksack, for example, *you* know, the old Colonel—'

Tomkins said that indeed he knew the old Colonel.

'He's a chronic bronchitis. Now every year he has a new *brew* of his own *bugs* (that's what he calls it). And every autumn he's in here to get a new needle. Starts the year fresh in October, so to say. He's really a game old card is the Colonel.'

Tomkins said yes, wasn't he? He wandered delicately to the glass-fronted shelves of sleeping pills and near poisons that stood above the marble prescription table. He opened the cupboard door.

'What's this?' he said. He lifted out a bottle of white powder.

It stood next the bottle of Secconol on the top shelf. He turned it slowly round to look at the label.

'What is what?' said Graham Micah reasonably. He came across the room and took the bottle from Tomkins' hand. He frowned, deeply puzzled. Lines ran suddenly from his nose to his chin. 'That's really very funny,' he said. '*That* oughtn't to be there at all. That ought to be locked up . . .' He went to the door, raising his voice to chide Mrs Micah.

'But *what* is it?' said Tomkins, vexed.

'Oh.' Graham Micah turned lightly back. 'Arsenic. White arsenic.'

CHAPTER TWENTY-SIX

The office at the Oranmore Hotel was more hopelessly untidy than ever. Although April and May had been returned to their nursery (notwithstanding the awful effect that this might have upon them), a litter, obviously of their making, remained behind them: of torn rag books, of half Icky Bicky Pegs and (April's particularly favourite toy) a much-battered, much-chewed silver spoon. The desk overflowed with papers, accounts owed to the Oranmore Hotel by Mrs Bognor and Mrs Greeb for their accommodation, and Ministry of Food papers relative to licences for caterers and casual food consumption. Dust had drifted on all these things and Major Bognor stood amongst them, disdainful and sombre in his neat black suit, in the middle of a complaint to Celia Robinson about his bedroom.

The desk light was on, making a faint yellow nimbus in the gloom. It was bright enough to show that Celia had a long, oily smudge down one pale cheek.

'You see,' continued the Major firmly, 'it's my asthma. I really *do* need to be in a big, airy room. Now that you have so *many* on your hands, what? I mean, the police *have* finished with Mother's sitting-room, haven't they?'

Celia Robinson was very shocked. She did not consider that the Major reacted in a suitable fashion. She coughed and said she would see. Her face showed her feelings plainly.

'Yes, but look here, Mrs Robinson,' said the Major. 'I'm frightfully sorry to bother you ... but we are both bereaved. I mean, aren't we? So we're both in the same boat, what?'

Celia Robinson's face suggested that she hardly considered a boat to be the proper vehicle for a bereaved person. The Major ploughed on.

'No, but honestly, Mrs Robinson, let's face facts, shall we? That little room over the boiler. The Slot, I believe you rather amusingly call it, eh? Well, seriously the fumes from the boiler *alone* would be enough for any healthy man. And though of course, we asthmatics' – the Major, tugging at his moustache obviously linked himself spiritually with King James I, Bernadette and Ranjitsinjhi – 'like to think of ourselves as healthy, what, we aren't. At least actually we *are*. Healthy, I mean. We need to be eh, with all *that* goin' on in our chests, what?'

Celia Robinson said she had never known that the Major was asthmatic; he had never mentioned it before, she said.

'Well, one doesn't like to make a fuss, does one?' said the Major bravely. 'It only takes me *really* badly in February.' Celia Robinson suddenly relented and said it was a terrible thing, wasn't it, and she had a friend who had had to sit upright for nights on end. *She* had had to have injections of Adrenalin. And she was sorry she had been so short with the Major, but really, lately, *things* ...

'Not at all,' said the Major briskly. 'Yes, it's not much fun injectin' yourself, eh? Not that I've had to do it for a week or two, thank God.'

They were interrupted by the front door-bell, which rang shrilly above their heads; it shook their lacerated nerves and made Celia shiver like a half-drowned dog. Outside, the Major saw Tomkins, his little pink face grim, his gay sports jacket somehow pathetic, his waterproof over one arm. Behind him the black police car as usual provided a sombre background. He stood on the door-step and looked up at the eaves. When Celia went to open the door, he didn't smile.

'Look, miss,' he said. 'I'm sorry. I've come to search the hotel. This here's my warrant.'

II

Tomkins followed Celia Robinson into the hotel. As the tramping feet of Constable Beatty and his colleague filled the hall with the echo of the law's delay, he realized that the carpet was up. Perhaps the broker's men were imminent and Tony Robinson had removed it and sold it? Or perhaps they were cleaning the place? Certainly the empty shell of the hall and staircase gave such an appearance of desolation that Tomkins, the unimpressionable, shivered and nearly put on his waterproof. Dust was everywhere, seeping into little piles, making everything gritty, and filling the air with a tickling, acrid unpleasantness. The dark ceiling above the stair-well should have been white, but (where Jo Mabberly's successor had replastered 'after' the Army) a damp, yellow-edged stain had been slowly spreading there all through December and January. Celia, following Tomkins' upturned eyes, remarked that Mrs Bognor had often commented on it. Then she bit her lip and Tomkins wondered why. He apologized for bothering her and then, jauntily, said he would start with the basement.

III

Connie Watson had decided (oddly enough) to be difficult. She barricaded herself into her bedroom and would not allow anyone to come in. Even Tommy, the kitchenmaid, was barred, it seemed, for she joined them outside the door and added her shrill complaints to the general noise.

'Come out of it, Con, you silly cow!' she screamed, beating fretfully with both fists. She made a disagreeable noise. 'I want my cigs. They're in there ...'

Connie Watson was heard to grunt that she would throw them out of the window, then.

'Oh, don't be a fool. These policemen mean business, I tell you. They can knock the door down, if they wanter. Think of poor Mrs Robinson—'

Connie breathed heavily through the keyhole and said that she didn't care what the hell happened to Mrs Effing Robinson's hotel and Mrs Effing Robinson knew what she could do with it ... Eventually a shoulder charge from Beatty and Tomkins precipitated them into the bedroom, where they rolled on the floor in a heap. Connie cackled. She had of course removed the barricade at the last moment.

The basement bedroom of the Oranmore Hotel, properly intended for a happily married couple, was seldom entered by anyone but Connie and Tommy. There was a large, uncompromising double bed of singular horror that occupied most of the room. There was also a small tin hospital bed in one corner.

The window, below street level, gave very little light; damp stains, like those on the ceiling at the head of the stairs, spread unhappily behind the wardrobe. The double bed was unmade and sheets trailed upon the floor. The sickliness of unaired rooms had always annoyed Tomkins. He had such a mania for cleanliness that it almost amounted to a guilt complex. The hospital bed was covered with a litter of things: old shoes, undarned socks, clothes, cigarette-tins and other rubbish. They had obviously been piled there that moment.

Connie sat on the window-ledge and swung her legs. She was wearing a dirty pink dressing-gown.

'Search away!' she screamed. 'Please yourselves. You're wastin' your time. *You* won't find anythin', *I* can tell you—'

Tomkins asked her to stand up. She sulkily complied. He leant past her and opened the window.

'Well! That's pretty, I must say!' Her voice rose to the extremes of hysteria. 'Expect me to take that sitting down, I suppose. Don't like the smell in here, I expect? Pity some people can't arrange for some people to be fumigated in advance—'

Tomkins said nothing. Outside, on the window-ledge was a battered tobacco-tin. He picked it up and gently opened the rusty lid. Inside there was a hypodermic syringe and several ampules.

'Thank you, miss,' he said politely. 'I don't think I need trouble you further. This is precisely what I was wanting.'

IV

Neither Major Bognor nor Celia Robinson made a fuss when they were asked to part with their hypodermic syringes. Major Bognor, engaged in moving his clothes from The Slot to Mrs

Greeb's 'old' room on the same floor, and (for some reason) strangely lacking in bluster, wondered nervously if (in the circumstances) he might be allowed to buy another one. If it was needed, that was. And Celia, too, asked timidly, if she would be allowed to have hers back. But both of them seemed to realize the grave implications that lay behind the possession of a hypodermic syringe at this moment. The Major, moreover, had twenty-four pairs of hand-made boots tucked into his wardrobe, which Tomkins found fascinating, but irrelevant. So Tomkins left the Oranmore Hotel with three hypodermic syringes, neatly labelled Mrs Celia Robinson, Major R. Bognor and C. Watson. And, later that day, he added two others, labelled Col. Chas. Rucksack and Andrew Cathcart. Andrew Cathcart (oddly enough) was also an asthmatic. But the only person who had truly seemed upset was Connie Watson.

CHAPTER TWENTY-SEVEN

Andrew Cathcart only saw his daughter Rosemary at breakfast-time. Then, two breadwinners equal in importance, they faced each other behind newspapers across a table with a woollen cloth *and* a white damask tablecloth. It showed only too clearly Mrs Cathcart's talent for food production. ('Mother, you've surpassed yourself.') Each morning Mr Cathcart would (in his own phrase) *get outside* bacon and eggs; and Rosemary, more continental, would drink orange juice and black coffee. They were quite hemmed in by comfort, thick carpet, and curtains. Rosemary read the *Daily Mirror* (which Mrs Cathcart also enjoyed) and Mr Cathcart read the *Daily Telegraph* – and they did not speak to each other, except to ask for the sugar or mustard. But this morning the security was split. Mr Cathcart was disturbed.

He had turned from the sports page to the news and back to that section of the paper that he called, in his witty way, Matches, Hatches and Dispatches. Then he approached the Engagements. And here his eyes bulged. He simply did not believe what he read. *Major R. G. Bognor and Miss R. Cathcart.* He shut his eyes and carefully opened them, took off his bi-focals and polished them. Yes, it was still there. He put down the paper and read the offending thing slowly aloud, giving each hideous word its insupportable weight.

'The engagement is announced between Reginald Gordon, only son of the late Admiral Edgar Bognor, CBE, and Mrs Bognor, of Brunton-on-Sea, and Rosemary, only daughter of Mr and Mrs Andrew Cathcart, of West Hartlepool, Old Brunton Road, Brunton-on-Sea.'

'Oh!' cried Rosemary, girlishly leaping. 'It's in, is it? Do let me see—'

And she hurried round the table, slopping her coffee on the damask cloth, to lean confidentially on her father's shoulder and read the announcement for herself. She obviously thought it very fine.

'Does your mother know of this?' Rosemary was unaware of the displeasure in her father's voice. She was thirty-two. This was the first time she had been engaged to be married.

'Oh, rather, yes . . .'

Rosemary was so innocently *pleased*. She gave the impression of long, cosy chats with Mrs Cathcart in her delphinium-coloured bedroom, a bedroom Mr Cathcart no longer shared. (Mr Cathcart saw them in his mind's eye; and Mrs Cathcart's hair was down her back in its rat's tail; and both of them wore satin padded wrappers. Wrappers that Mr Cathcart had paid for.)

Andrew Cathcart slammed down his cup.

'And how is this twopenny-ha'penny Major going to support you, might I ask?'

'Oh, don't be silly, Dad,' cried Rosemary. 'Reginald's a gentleman!'

Andrew Cathcart flinched.

'Where's your mother?' he said, strangled. He stood up, he pushed back his chair. It ran silently back on the thick, smooth carpet. 'Tell her I want her. At least you might have told me. I'll be in the study . . .'

And he stamped from the room, trailing the offending paper with him. It was only when Rosemary saw the bacon and eggs congealing on her father's plate that she realized that all was not well with her engagement to the genteel Reginald Bognor.

II

In the orange tawny light of the study, where the reading-lamp was a macabre carved wooden bird, Andrew Cathcart faced his wife. She came hot from the kitchen, her long-sighted aging eyes maddeningly unable to read the announcement as he trembled it before her.

'Well, Andrew, what is it?' she said; she had diagnosed his state in advance as 'just another of Andrew's fusses'. 'I can't see without my glasses, I'm sure. The doctor says my prescription needs alteration, if you please . . .' She grumbled quietly on, until, eventually, holding the paper at arm's length, she found the announcement and read it slowly out to herself. Each word drained Andrew Cathcart's heart of vitality. When she had finished he was leaning against his desk and his knees shook. They heard the front door slam. Rosemary had bolted.

'Well, dear, what *is* wrong?' said Mrs Cathcart. She pressed the paper flat and held it on her knee. She smoothed it out to a nice, neat little square. 'What's wrong with Major Bognor, exactly? He comes of nice people. He's older than Rosemary of course, but you always said his mother—'

Mrs Cathcart spaced all her words, giving each syllable a great deal of weight, as a North Country woman does. Mr Cathcart groaned. He passed his hand over his forehead.

'Eh, Andrew pet, what is it?' Mrs Cathcart stood up. 'You do look badly, love. Sit down now, sit down ...'

And she guided Andrew Cathcart to the rexine armchair, his knees so wambling that he collapsed, sagging, a pathetic heap of clothes, quite unsupported by bones of any sort.

'What you want's a spot of brandy. I'll get it. Then you must choose words some'ow and tell me what's wrong. My, you do look bad.' And Mrs Cathcart bustled about with the bottle of Hennessy Three Star and the tablespoon, until the heavy colour returned to Mr Cathcart's cheeks and his teeth no longer clattered against the tumbler's rim. Then he gripped his knees with both hands.

'That's it, Mother,' he said. 'This is it. The money I told you of, that I took. I swear to Almighty God I'll pay it back. It was Mrs Bognor's.'

They were both silent, staring at each other. Mrs Cathcart's shrewd and far-sighted eyes were suddenly hard and bright in her heavy face.

'What a damned thing!' she said in her flat, unpleasant voice. 'What a damned thing that she should get herself murdered.'

III

Rosemary bicycled furiously down the Old Brunton Road towards the town and the sea. She always bicycled to work. She said the exercise and the morning air gingered up her liver. Today she was additionally glad of the bicycle, because if she had walked she would have had no time to call in at the Oranmore Hotel. It was a tall, old-fashioned bicycle with a cord skirt-guard and a basket in front, well looked after and oiled; when she jumped down from it and propped it against the gate-post she could not help noticing the general untidiness of the Oranmore. One of the oyster shells above the door had fallen in the night; the year-old dark-green paint on the front door had begun to peel. There was no sign, in all that sad and crumbling façade, of the high hopes of Tony Robinson, when he had first come into the place, and walked over it, through piles of plaster, a year ago this month. Rosemary half hoped she would see Tony. She looked up at the eaves, as Tomkins had done, and she saw the front gutter was disintegrating, spilling down the walls in rust and desolation, dripping sadly from a blockage at the corner joint. Rosemary shrugged her shoulders. Celia Robinson had always been a poor thing.

Rosemary went briskly up the steps and rang the bell. Maggie Button, with a cotton handkerchief twined round her hair, told her that Major Bognor was in the lounge.

IV

And so he was, at an uncomfortable writing-table in the window, savagely constructing a letter in his quick, passionate handwriting. The table was not quite the right height. It pressed down on his knees, and he cursed at intervals as it jumped and disturbed him. When Rosemary came in he started guiltily to his feet, snatching at the ink-pot, as it went skidding away. He did not seem at all pleased to see her.

'I saw it, Reg, I saw it! Oh, it was sweet of you to put it in,' she began impulsively, before she saw the white horror in his face. 'Why, Reg, whatever is it? You look quite sick.' But the tone of her voice hardly changed and she went on, gaily enough, 'Are *you* upset about something, too?'

Major Bognor stepped quickly past her and shut the door, almost as though he expected Maggie Button to be crouched, listening, at the keyhole. Rosemary was disturbed.

'What is it, Reg, for heaven's sake? Why is everyone behaving like this this morning?'

Poor smug Rosemary Cathcart was just like anyone else. She desired the illusion of security. Now she snatched at her lover, in despair, hoping that he would repair the emotional foundations that her father had destroyed. Retreating delicately to the fireplace, looking like an elderly, well-groomed tom cat, the Major resented her.

'What d'ye mean, everyone's behavin' like this this morning?' said the Major. He got a grip of the mantelpiece and stared at Rosemary as though he had not seen her before. She was not (he decided) attractive. In fact she actually looked predatory. Her nose was pink, too ... although that might be the fresh air. 'Who's behaving like anything this morning?'

At this welcome, anyone else would probably have sunk, weeping, on the sofa. But Rosemary stood her ground. She crackled with rage. So Reginald had failed her as well. Well, she had always been alone in the world, she knew that, really ... Her eyes were hard and blue, like cheap semi-precious stones in her white and sullen face. She had even had to fight to gain her position in the post office. The Major looked away very much irritated by her.

'Well, *everyone!*' snapped Rosemary viciously. 'Dad picked up the *Daily Tel.* at breakfast and seems to have a sort of attack. And Mother, so far as I can see, Mother's sympathizing with him. Any old way, no one's exactly rejoicing about our little bit of news. And why are *you* so down in the mouth? You think I'm not good enough for your damned family, do you? Well, what does my *Dad* think's wrong with *you*, I'd like to know?' Rosemary suddenly threw back her head and looked rather fine. 'Though what the hell business it is of anyone else's I'd like to know when it's our own life we're leading, not anyone else's . . .'

It was the Major who gave way first. He sat on the sofa out-faced by the hardness in Rosemary's eyes. He covered his face with his hands. And then – to give her her due – Rosemary's heart relented. She sat beside him and put her arms round him. Suddenly into her rapid South Country whine there crept the flat comfort of the Durham dialect. Her father would have been struck by her sudden resemblance to her mother.

'What *is* it, Reg? What *is* it? Why are you so upset, pet?' said Rosemary in the soft flat accents of Mrs Andrew Cathcart. 'Whatever is the matter? It's all *right*, Reg, Rosie-Posie's here. Just tell Rosie. Oh, Reg, Reg, didn't we say we'd *never* have any secrets from each other, even when it was *you* who didn't want to marry *me*, remember?'

And so, defeated, the Major told Rosemary Cathcart all about it.

CHAPTER TWENTY-EIGHT

Tomkins sat in his office, as he had so often sat in the last week, angry, tired and dispirited. He missed his wife more than he allowed: she had at least in her lifetime provided hot, regular meals. Now he existed on sandwiches snatched at the office, and cups of coffee taken at coffee-stalls. Two half-finished cups with fawn unpleasantness inside them and an old dry piece of bread showed the remains of his tea.

He was angry with the Oranmore Hotel Case, because it did not immediately wriggle into good, sound common sense that any jury could grasp. He felt like a lover, whose mistress, having become wearisome, jibs at truth, refuses half-truths and makes no effort to mend her faults. The simile was about right, Tomkins thought ruefully; he *had* fallen in love with the Oranmore Hotel Case. It had all the ingredients of a real, big-time newspaper splasher that would 'make' him. Sinister hotel, more than sinister oysters, and behind them all a ghoulish phantom – another Haigh say, or Heath, or Crippen, if you like ...

Tomkins had often felt this sort of exasperation over girl friends in the past. On the verge of love, of great discoveries and unknown brightness, he had been held up by some annoying trick, a tiresomeness in the hair-do, a piece of vexing feminine insincerity. He scowled and stabbed with his finger at the ink-pot. It *was* true. He had quite fallen in love with the Oranmore Hotel Case.

Now that he reached this conclusion he began to wish he had not pursued all his post office enquiries alone. *Miss Birdseye* could help him now. He wondered where she was, and what she was doing. *His* mind was very ordinary, he told himself, sucking a pencil and looking very ordinary indeed, but Miss Birdseye was something extra. Now, presented with this jig-saw puzzle, *she* would be able to make something out of the dottiness, *surely?*

The telephone buzzed sharply and he picked it up, sad because he was not self-sufficient, furious because he had allowed himself to be emotionally disturbed by a mere *case*. Perhaps he had drunk a little too much last night, but even so ... And perhaps if he had had a proper breakfast ... It was only a matter of fact, or *facts* rather – to be arranged in the proper order ...

'A bone, a rag and a hank of hair,' he remarked into the telephone.

'I don't call that very polite,' replied a deep, vexed feminine drawl.

'Miss Birdseye!' Tomkins was transported. 'I was wishing for you ... Where *are* you? Can you come up?'

'I am downstairs. Constable Beatty has been teaching me Thimble Rig.' Shocked quackings from the telephone implied that Constable Beatty resented the suggestion. 'Yes,' added Miriam. 'I will come upstairs right away.'

When she arrived she was arresting. She wore a racoon fur overcoat that might have formed a part of Max Miller's wardrobe. She wore a pair of navy-blue trousers and a white polo-necked sweater, embroidered with the flags of all nations. Tomkins brought forward a chair. Where had she been and why had she been so *mysterious*? He offered her tea. He hadn't seen her for three days. He made a great fuss of her. Would she smoke?

'I won't,' she said in deep, disturbing tones. '*Mysterious*, indeed.' She rolled her pale-blue eyes. 'It is *you* who have been avoiding *me*. My life is a book where all who run may read.' She paused to flutter her eyelashes. 'And quite often,' she added inconsequently, 'I read it aloud.'

'Now look here, Miss Birdseye,' said Tomkins. 'What 'ave you been up to?'

'Up to? Up to? I don't know what you mean by "up to".' There was another little pause, while Miriam tried not to laugh. 'Well . . .' she added, suddenly coquettish. 'Unless of course you count my getting engaged to Colonel Charles Rucksack.'

II

'Ah, now, Miss Birdseye, this is no time for jokes,' said Tomkins.

'There is *always* time for jokes,' said Miriam severely. She leered suddenly sideways. 'I am, however, perfectly serious. The Colonel consented to become my husband this afternoon.' She rapped Tomkins smartly on the hand and her opal ring flashed a little challenge. 'And I have hurried round to see you about some lovely police protection.'

Miriam's attitude had always been provoking. But today she concealed an inner triumph that was infinitely disconcerting.

'This is one of your fantasies,' said Tomkins accusingly. He began to pace up and down the room. Miriam sat still in her chair, smiling at him.

'Cross my heart and wish to die and may I never ever play in *The Sea-gull* as long as I live,' she said rapidly. She crossed her fingers and spat on them. (It is probably unnecessary to explain that *The Sea-gull* was Miss Birdseye's favourite play.)

'Oh well,' said Tomkins bitterly. 'If you *mean* it.' He sat down and looked as though he were about to burst into tears. 'But why?' he wailed. And then, 'How could you, Miriam, how could you?'

III

'Don't lose your head, dear,' said Miriam briskly. 'It must have occurred to you that Charles Rucksack is, at present, the one and only beneficiary under the Rucksack Bequest Trust? And should he marry again—' She gestured vulgarly with her thumb.

Tomkins said he was disillusioned. He said he would never have thought it of Miss Birdseye – and her an artist, too. So *mercenary*.

Miriam was most annoyed. She pointed out that it was not the first time that Tomkins had allowed his intellect to be fogged by emotional considerations. Tomkins bit his lip.

'Listen, dear. At the *mome* all this money goes to old Rucksack.'

'Yes.'

'Well, if someone marries him that increases the odds against Reggie Bognor's ever getting any money. So if Reggie *is* the villain behind all this, he obviously wants his Uncle

Charles's new wife out of the way as soon as possible – and he may do something foolish.'

'Yes, miss. That's what I can't understand.'

Miriam's laugh was like the baying of a wolf-hound.

'Is that all?'

Tomkins tried to be firm. 'No,' he said quickly. 'There's a great deal more I don't understand. About the Rucksacks, that is. And I'll thank you not to laugh at me, Miss Birdseye. I can't understand how all that money managed to pass out of the Sussex and Provincial without the manager or the teller seeing it go, for one thing—'

'Well, that's easy,' said Miriam gaily. 'That awful Andrew Cathcart embezzled it himself. I'd believe anything of bank managers. But *anything*. He's been perfectly bloody to poor darling Tony Robinson about his overdraft as well. Foreclosed on him. Oh, there's nothing I wouldn't believe of him.'

'I see.'

Miriam leant back and crossed her legs.

'Anything else?' she said brightly, like the Delphic Oracle coming back for more.

'Oh yes. Plenty. If your Major Bognor is the snake in the grass why did he try to kill his mother before his uncle? And if Charles Rucksack—'

'My fiancé,' said Miriam complacently.

'I shall ignore that,' said Tomkins coldly. 'If Charles Rucksack is the villain, what *opportunity* did *he* have of poisoning the oysters? Although I agree it is sinister that he doesn't eat them. And then if it's anyone else, what possible motive could they have? The cook, for example, Connie Watson. What motive could *she* have for killing Mrs Bognor? *She* doesn't inherit any money from her.'

'Or Celia Robinson?'

'Or Tony Robinson?'

They both sat silent now, staring at each other. Outside the warm office the bitter February evening pressed against the window-pane, until the fog of their breathing obscured it. The light was almost gone and the darkness seemed almost colder than the day that had preceded it. Someone knocked on the door and Tomkins said to come in.

It was a smooth, dark young man, plump and sensible-looking. He wore a white laboratory coat. A stethoscope peeped out of his pocket. He was, fairly obviously, Dr Fawcett-Smith, the police surgeon. He put a little attaché-case on Tomkins' desk and said:

'The hypodermic syringes and contents of same that you sent down for analysis, Inspector.' He raised his eyebrows at Miriam, but Tomkins made no effort to introduce them. Fawcett-Smith sighed. 'I must report that I find arsenic in hypodermic "D"; and though there are finger-print smears both on it and on the bottle of white arsenic you gave me, I can't say if they are those of the same person. Perhaps they wore gloves.'

He was a pompous young man. He took a long time to describe the method of his experiment, and how he had labelled the syringes A, B, C, D and E. Miriam and Tomkins (who would infinitely have preferred that they should continue to be called Mrs Robinson, Major Bognor, Colonel Rucksack and Mr Cathcart) became restive during the recital.

'However, the hypodermic syringe "D" definitely contains traces of arsenic,' said Dr Fawcett-Smith. 'Someone has tried to wash it out, certainly, but there it is. They haven't made a very good shot at it.'

'And what about the syringe "C"?' said Miriam insistently. 'The one that we call Major Bognor?'

'There's no trace of anything in *that*, unless you can count some very dirty drain-water indeed.'

Tomkins was silent, thinking and drawing pictures on his blotting-pad. The hypodermic syringe 'D' was, of course, Mrs Tony Robinson's.

CHAPTER TWENTY-NINE

Miriam got up from her chair and went to the window. The little box of an office was hot. She rubbed a patch in the mist on the glass and looked out at Brunton, spread below her in its monstrous Edwardian and Neo-Georgian nightmare. The domes and minarets of Old Jo Mabberly's imagination climbed (as he had intended they should) against the evening sky in sprawling black silhouettes.

The police station was in the middle of the town. Below it ran bright railway lines, shadowed by the *chinoiserie* of the station itself. Even the police station had not escaped the architectural disease that consumed the town. It had rich Edwardian gables and filthy fretwork eaves. The dim blue light that showed the battered, rusting recruiting posters by the door only increased the foolishness of its insignificant grandeur.

Miriam wondered, looking down; when the street lights came on one by one, star by star, to prick the evening like diamonds, she wondered if buildings really affected people. Could drive them to crime, perhaps. How many people, for example, had robbed a telephone box or a gas meter to pay the rent of a beautiful flat that they loved? Or committed murder to pay the interest on a mortgage on an ancestral home? Brunton-on-Sea would certainly drive *her* to almost any excess to escape the awful domination of its ugliness.

Beyond the domes of the Warhaven Arms, where lugubrious Bob Parsons would already be sweeping down the steps for the evening – somewhere beyond *that* were the Gothic lunacies of Pondicherry Lodge and Burma Villa. They had already (to her certain knowledge) driven two owners to suicide. As the Oranmore Hotel they had accomplished God alone knew what . . .

Miriam turned round. Young Dr Fawcett-Smith still lingered by the door, obviously transfixed by her appearance. She addressed him.

'What would be the effect of an asthmatic person injecting Adrenalin into himself with this very dirty syringe?' she asked. She walked to the desk and held up the instrument. She squinted slightly as she tried to bring it and the young doctor in focus. 'Reggie suffers frightfully from asthma, you know,' she added, as though for Tomkins' information. 'I always used to think he ran up an attack when he didn't want to see *me* . . .'

Dr Fawcett-Smith smiled. His smooth brow was furrowed as he considered.

'Well, I suppose I could say that he would recover from the asthmatic attack all right. Asthmatics are very odd. But obviously he *might* infect his blood stream pretty badly – and if he was in a weak state, one of the infections that are known to exist in sewers – one of them might polish him off.'

'Poor Reggie!' said Miriam with a little sigh as she considered it. She turned back to the window. 'What sort of infections exist in sewers?' She tossed the question over her shoulder, throwing the line away as though it were of no consequence to her.

The young doctor looked surprised and raised his eyebrows at Tomkins. Tomkins nodded at him, obviously inviting a reply.

'Well, all sorts of things,' began Dr Fawcett-Smith cautiously. 'Typhoid fever, for one.'

II

Suddenly there was the sound of heavy breathing in the office. Miriam and the young doctor smiled. It was Tomkins who was so intensely excited, leaning forward on his desk, doodling furiously on the blotting-pad. The shape that he drew was (inevitably) an oyster.

'Look here, Fawcett-Smith,' he said anxiously, 'supposing you wanted to poison someone, you clever old medico you, how would you do it?' Fawcett-Smith smiled deprecatingly, obviously dissociating himself from any such suggestion. 'Suppose you wanted them to die of something quite untraceable and all the rest of it, eh? Wouldn't you give them some disease – some pretty dangerous, virulent thing – like typhoid, for example? And then, in spite of nursing and all, you'd have whoever you wished kicking the bucket?'

'I sincerely hope I should not.' Dr Fawcett-Smith had all the prig's rigid horror of imaginary hypotheses.

'Oh, come off it, old pomposity!' Tomkins was still overexcited and still doodling. 'Suppose for the sake of argument that I asked you to kill someone with typhoid, how would you do it?'

Fawcett-Smith went to the window in his turn, collecting

his thoughts as he went. He did not find inspiration in the architectural splendours outside. He spoke dubiously.

'Well, I could inject them with it, of course. But I wouldn't care to do it.'

Miriam thought viciously that he had a ridiculously over-inflated idea of his own responsibilities, and then told herself bitterly that it was just as well, in his job.

'No, you old ass . . .' Tomkins was still badgering him. 'Of course we know you wouldn't. Why, you'd be found out. 'Ow would you do it if you didn't want to be found out?'

Slowly Tomkins' criminal purpose penetrated the doctor's brain. Reluctant admiration struggled with his smooth features. He glanced down at the oyster drawn on Tomkins' blotting-paper and then glanced up at Miriam. His movements were suddenly quick and easy, as though he understood the implications of everything, and was no longer bogged in his professional prejudice (and other Stirling qualities).

'I see what you mean,' he said slowly. 'By injecting some quickly assimilated food. Yes, it would be perfectly possible. And the chances against anyone being found out would be infinitesimal. They *really* would. I believe one might get away with it. The patient (I suppose I had better call the victim that) would probably die in about ten days if neglected enough. One couldn't guarantee that, of course. Typhoid is largely a matter of nursing, as you probably know—'

'We don't know, dear,' said Miriam suddenly. 'And you two clever boys have forgotten something.'

They both turned towards her. Neither of them spoke. Disappointment and bitter intelligence turned Tomkins' piggy eyes hard and angry.

'It was Mrs *Greeb* who died of typhoid. Not Mrs Bognor. Mrs Bognor died of *arsenic* poisoning. Remember?'

III

'Well, there you are,' said Tomkins wearily, throwing himself back in his chair. 'Your guess is as good as mine. Here's poor Mrs Robinson's syringe with arsenic in – the bottle from the chemist that *her husband* had access to – and Mrs Bognor dead. And not a shadow of motive *why* Mrs R should do away with the good lady.'

'I don't know,' said Miriam doubtfully. Tomkins was instantly angry with her.

'What don't you know that I don't know?' he demanded explosively. His sandy hair was on end where his stubby hands had ruffled it into a brush of displeasure and annoyance.

'I don't know that she hadn't a motive,' said Miriam reflectively. 'Those two are so hard up and that awful old hotel is such a terrible old *drain* for the poor darlings – it absorbs *everything* – vitality, everything. And, of course, any money they can lay their tiny hands on ...'

'What do you mean?' said Tomkins. This time he sat still, determined that he should not react to Miriam's histrionics.

'Well, nothing much, dear. But just *what* became of the two hundred pounds that old Mum Bognor drew out of the bank that Saturday morning?'

IV

Tomkins whistled gently and said sure, yes, what about them? He had the serial numbers somewhere.

Dr Fawcett-Smith had completely dropped his semi-patronizing manner. He was hardly recognizable as a first- (or even second-) class prig. He said surely two hundred pounds was in itself a perfectly good motive for murder?

'In working-class 'ouses,' said Tomkins bitterly, 'I suppose it would be. *We're* supposed to be dealin' with the awful immoral middle classes round 'ere.'

Miriam said that when hotel-keepers had reached the sort of financial extremes that these ones had reached, they could be considered two-hundred-pound-murder-worthy, too. In fact, just like the working classes. Tomkins scowled and began to read out the serial numbers of the notes, which began C 28 D 271454 and ended (of course) C 28 D 271653.

'Well,' said Miriam, 'the thing is, if you can find a number of those in someone's possession (I mean, I don't think *one* or *two* would be enough), surely your precious jury – that you're always nattering about – would swallow it, dear?'

When she had concluded her maddening little speech and was standing with one elegant hand on the knob of the door to the outer office, Tomkins was bright red in the face and *glowing* with fury. When she felt she had her audience nicely under control she paused.

'Oh, and Char-les and I,' she continued, drawling maddeningly, 'we will be so glad if you will *both* come to our betrothal party tonight at his house: Cherry Pickings. Six-thirty. Don't be late. And don't dress.'

Tomkins regained control of himself with a magnificent effort of will.

'Oysters,' he said nervously. 'I suppose it will be an oyster party?'

'But of course,' said Miss Birdseye severely.

And the door banged behind her. The room seemed quite empty without her.

CHAPTER THIRTY

Miriam left the police station and stalked up Station Road towards the Warhaven Arms, the Sussex and Provincial Bank and Mr Twiggs, the greengrocer. Her hands were sunk deep in the pockets of her racoon overcoat. Her mind was obsessed by her theory that bad buildings make people behave badly. She paused on Station Corner, where the shiftless navy-blue population of black market taxi-drivers idled with its (collective) hands in its pockets – and where the great golden trolley-buses swept round the corner from Bexhill and Cooden, flashing like meteors as the wires swayed and dipped.

Miriam looked up at the Warhaven Arms, at the twin domes at the massive iron balconies that connected them. The effect was amazingly meaningless. She clicked her tongue. What responsibility for what social indiscretion could the architect of the Warhaven Arms accept? Alas, thought Miriam, her eyes straying down the impossible façade to the mysteries of Station Road; alas, the Gothic revival was not always controlled by the muscular hands of Sir George Gilbert Scott. Old Jo Mabberly had merely become drunk on Gothic: as lesser men become drunk on Pimms or Hock and Seltzer. Miriam thought of him reeling, hiccuping homewards with the plans of the Warhaven Arms sticking out of his pocket.

It was at this moment that she was arrested by the extreme beauty of Mr Twiggs' Greengrocery. The oranges had just come in and he had piled them high inside the windows to the roof, where they glowed like five hundred little suns. The chrysanthemums, too (their white and gold and orange heads as magnificent as those of prize poodles), were massed in splendour above the silver celery and the purple beetroot. The electric light blazed from the little shop to make a place of enchantment. It eclipsed everything on each side of it. Ali Baba ... thought Miriam confusedly, crossing the road, coveting oranges ... And then, thrown in sharp relief by all this beauty, she saw Celia Robinson.

Celia was at her worst. She wore a turban round her head, constructed from a grey woollen scarf. She hesitated on the threshold. Then she plunged into the shop and Mr Twiggs walked forward towards her. Miriam saw the fluttering of banknotes.

So Miriam turned round and went back to the police station.

II

Celia Robinson hurried on, through the evening as it darkened, her brown waterproof gathered round her. She was compelled by the urgency that possesses people of integrity about to pay their debts. Bodger's the Butcher's swam up before her, looking like a great bland cave. Charlie Bodger was washing down the tiles with a mop and a pail of water. He was a savage young man, very virile, in a white overall and a blue apron. He had bad teeth and his hair was curled in a hook.

'Come about your account?' he said rudely. He scattered sawdust from a zinc pail. 'Can't let you 'ave any more meat, y'know, until you let *us* 'ave somefing, Mrs Robinson. Can't run a butcher's on *air*, you know – nor a hotel neither, eh? Expect you're just findin' that one out, eh?'

For Charlie Bodger was not such a bad young man as he appeared, and he was sorry for poor little Mrs Robinson, who had married that shyster and had those two blooming great kids, though, Godamighty, couldn't she even find time to get her shoes heeled? If there was anything more slovenly about a woman than shoes swabbling over at the heel, Charlie would like to know it.

'No, no, I quite agree. As a matter of fact, I've come to *pay* the account.'

'Good God!'

Charlie was much moved.

'I don't know quite *how much it is* ...' Celia stumbled on her self-appointed task. 'Tony usually deals with all *that*. You know it's only recently I've ...'

Charlie Bodger, recovering from his astonishment, slowly wiped his sawdusty hands down his dirty, meaty dark-blue-and-white-striped apron. He went into the little glass office where old Mrs Bodger reckoned up the books and (between whiles) rested her fine bust on the till. Above his head an electric clock, with *Bodger* written large upon its stomach, jerked forward, chopping off the minutes with a hand as unrelenting as a knife. He picked up a neat bill with *Final Demand* stuck all over it on a red-and-white label.

'There you are,' he remarked compassionately. 'Was just sendin' it off. I got mad at Ma allowin' Tony to bounce 'er into givin' 'im that sirloin that weekend. Pardon me.' Charlie coughed and covered his mouth. 'Firty-five pound seven shillin' and sixpence.'

Celia bit her lip. She fumbled in her shopping-bag. She produced a wallet. And she counted out, note by note, thirty-six brand-new pounds. She laid them down on the marble slab outside the little glass cage.

'Just a tick,' said Charlie. 'I'll give you a receipt. I'll give you change.'

'Oh no,' said Celia, very rapidly. 'Don't do that. *Post* the receipt. I've got the fishmonger to settle before he shuts . . .'

'But your *change?*' Charlie was horrified. 'Here.' He slapped and banged at the till, produced a very dirty, crumpled ten-shilling note (held together with stamp paper) and half a crown. 'Sorry it's not up to *your* standards, dear,' he said gaily. He pressed it into her hand. 'You must've got these notes special, eh? Hot from the Mint?'

And he looked down at the thirty-six smooth, hopelessly virgin notes where they lay in his hand. And in spite of himself he observed the serial numbers . . . which were C 28 D 271494 to C 28 D 271529.

III

Celia went on, slapping sadly through the dusk towards the fishmonger's. It was not *quite* half past five, she thought. She hoped that April and May had settled down properly. Tony could not always be trusted to listen for them when they screamed And of

255

course Tony did not know that *she* was out, and he might well not listen at all – or *he* might even have gone out *himself*.

Once April had nearly strangled herself, squeezing in between her crib bars – before Celia (out to get a pint of milk ... or was it the fish ... or veg ...?) had come back to find her scarlet in the face and screaming herself sicker ...

Celia prayed that the fishmonger's was not shut. They owed fifteen pounds there. Then after she had paid *that*, she could start thinking of the new shoes that were needed for April and May. They grew so *fast*. Or perhaps she had better find out what *was* the right time. There was no one in Station Road who looked as though they could tell the time, even. Really, this was such an awful place; it made one feel so awful.

There was never enough time – never quite enough, ever, for anything. She mustn't panic. Oh, dear! She pulled up short, putting her hand on her side where she sometimes had that stitch that Dr Stalag-Jones said was anaemia. She was all confused. She was *always* like that nowadays. What was it she had to do? She had forgotten.

Tony had said she must be changed and bathed and at this party of Miriam Birdseye's and the Colonel's by six. She only had half an hour, then, however early it was. Then she wouldn't really have time to have a bath at all. Unless, of course, it was only *five* and not half past five at all. Oh, how lovely it would be if it were only five! But even then she would just change and scramble into her dress in any old way.

When Celia arrived at the fishmonger's it was twenty minutes to six and the shutters had been up for ten minutes.

CHAPTER THIRTY-ONE

A number of people considered it in questionable taste (particularly as Colonel Charles Rucksack was known to dislike oysters) that Miriam and he should give an oyster party to celebrate their engagement. Cherry Pickings, Colonel Rucksack's wholly oriental house in Pondicherry Parade, was, somehow, a house that no one entered by daylight. It was uncomfortably furnished (elephants' feet and Chinese gongs and Tibetan sporrans), inefficiently looked after by a slippered, whispering married couple with a perpetual (and collective) cold in the head. Tonight it blazed with light. The old homestead (for so Colonel Rucksack put it, rubbing his hands briskly palm to palm) was quite transformed, what? And then he added, in a lower tone, that Reggie's nose would be properly out of joint, by Jove!

And Major and Mrs Bandarlog, who occupied No. 17 Pondicherry Parade (the house next door with the frieze of sacred cows), were perturbed. Particularly was this true of Major Bandarlog, the steel plate in whose head was apt to drive him to emotional excess when heated up. He felt that the good, sombre tone of the neighbourhood would slip sideways if Miriam came to live in it in any capacity whatever; and this heated up the plate in his head no end. The light that streamed out from Cherry Pickings, shining on the gunmetal pavements, reflecting and twinkling as far away as the dark esplanade, was beautiful. In spite of herself (and her fear of her husband, which made her timid), Mrs Bandarlog furtively drew aside the lace curtains and the bead curtains in her sitting-room, fascinated to see the guests arrive one by one.

II

Tomkins came first, smooth and shaven and altogether horrified by the plate of oysters that Miriam pressed on him.

'God bless me, miss,' he remarked, 'I never touch the things. You see,' he went on, backing nervously to the fireplace, 'I was born and brought up in Whitstable.'

Colonel Rucksack could not, it appeared, have agreed with him more. He followed him to the fireplace with a plate of biscuits that had been lightly coated with anchovy paste.

'Someone put in some work on *those* this afternoon,' said Tomkins gaily.

'*Yesterday* afternoon,' said Colonel Rucksack. Tomkins' jaw, which had been moving up and down quite briskly on the biscuit, was suddenly arrested. He seemed to find himself unable to swallow. Miriam, most splendid in long-sleeved purple velvet, her yellow hair piled high upon her head, clasped her hands together and looked almost beautiful as she congratulated Tomkins on his punctuality. They were caught in the cold five minutes before a party takes light, when anything might happen and hostesses are apprehensive. Miriam seemed brave, however. Her eyes danced with the clear light of naughtiness as she advanced to greet Reginald Bognor. He was, she remarked, 'her new intended nephew-in-law'.

'Oysters, Reggie?' she went on, with a superb gesture. 'You know everyone, I'm sure. Your *uncle* you know. *Myself* you know, only too well. Tomkins you know. And the oysters you *had no hand in opening whatsoever.*'

Tomkins gulped his drink. He too moved bravely forward. Off the record, he was going to enjoy a conversation with Major Bognor. And, on the record, fancy anyone growing a moustache that size! Just like an RAF type. No wonder the fellow looked so hot under his collar. Why, all one's strength could be absorbed by a moustache *that* size ...

'Good evenin', Major,' he said. The Major glanced at him nervously. 'I can see you're a great oyster-eater. Can tell 'em at a glance. Now me, I was brought up in Whitstable. Born an' bred there.'

Behind him Tony Robinson came into the room, alone. He began an elaborate Edwardian flirtation with Miriam Birdseye. She waved her purple gloves and even rapped him sharply on the wrist. His dark head was very sleek and caught the light as he bent towards her. Their laughter seemed truly unforced and gay.

'Well, Major ...' Tomkins teetered on his heels. 'We have the whole thing worked out, as you might say ...'

His eyes followed, without awe, a particularly large, succulent oyster as the Major lifted it slowly towards his moustache. The room seemed to be warming up a little.

'Nasty thing, typhoid,' said Tomkins. The oyster stopped and trembled half-way. The Major slowly returned it to its plate. Tomkins was chatty. 'It would kill a horse. Ah,' he went on, 'there's someone who's been longin' to meet you. Fawcett-Smith. I want you to meet Major Bognor, a particular friend of mine.' He nudged Fawcett-Smith vulgarly in the ribs. 'You know, old boy,' he said under his breath. 'The man with the dirty syringe.'

The situation developed farcical intensity. Major Bognor gulped and flushed.

'How do you do?' He glared quickly from one to the other. 'Shockin' bad form,' he muttered. His eyes were red and sparkling. He seemed about to break a blood vessel somewhere. He put his plate down on a Benares brassware tray. It was supported on carved oaken legs, shaped like camels' feet. He shivered, although the room was now really quite warm. Dr Fawcett-Smith advanced, neat and unspectacular in his well-brushed navy-blue suit. He seemed somehow (like Inspector Tomkins) to treat the Major cosily, as a member of the criminal classes. 'About that dirty syringe—' he began gaily.

The door opened and cold air came into the room with Celia Robinson. After her, apologetically stammering, came Pyke.

'Why, Reggie, you aren't eatin' anythin' ...'

Uncle Charles Rucksack appeared at his elbow and pressed another vast plate of oysters into his hand.

'And you so fond of oysters, too,' remarked Tomkins, grinning at Colonel Rucksack, who grinned back. 'Now, as you may know,' he turned again to Fawcett-Smith, 'I was brought up in Whitstable myself.'

'So you'd be afraid of typhoid,' said Fawcett-Smith. 'Nasty thing, typhoid.' And he finished his drink and set down the glass.

Major Bognor was now suffused and crimson. He made one more effort to eat an oyster.

'What we'd *hoped*,' said Tomkins, 'was that you bein' a gentleman – and it's a wonderful thing, education, I don't attempt to deny it, I can assure you . . .' The Major returned the oyster to his plate for ever. 'We hoped that you would think the whole thing over and decide to speak up—'

'I'm sure *I* would never sleep in my bed if I were to eat all those oysters, Major Bognor,' said Fawcett-Smith mildly. 'And *I* only went to Lancing.'

'This,' said the Major, and put his plate carefully down, 'is pure lunacy.' He expelled all his breath in little, gasping shouts. 'No, no, no, no, *no!*' he cried. He stamped furiously from the room.

'Reginald gets more and more eccentric every day,' said his Uncle Charles. He looked quite young. His false teeth gleamed discreetly behind his moustache, which seemed neater than usual. Perhaps Miriam had made him trim it. He moved over to Inspector Tomkins and spoke severely. 'They should never have sent him *East*, y'know.'

'Thins the blood,' said Tomkins.

III

When the Major left so precipitately and without apology to his hostess, everyone went nearer to the fire, as though that would protect them from each other. It was a gas-fire set in a gaunt, Victorian blackleaded frame that showed the influence, also, of Sir G. G. Scott, and it threw disconcerting heat outwards on the unprotected legs of the ladies. Miriam did not mind this but Celia Robinson (who wore rather a short afternoon dress) shied constantly, moving from one foot to the other. Miriam, looking at her with compassion, urged her to 'drink up and have another'. Celia laughed. She said, poor dear, that she did not wish to be tiddly.

'I should think you'd need to be, later,' said Miriam unguardedly.

'What?' said Celia, distracted.

'I said I thought you looked as though you needed it,' said Miriam in a louder voice.

'She certainly does,' said Tony unkindly. 'Always has been a little spoil-sport.'

And Celia's eyes filled with tears.

IV

Pyke also found himself a spoil-sport at this party: censorious and disapproving of the whole thing. His mouth curled downwards in rococo lines. Inspector Tomkins looked up at him confidingly.

'You look pretty well fed-up.'

Pyke nodded.

'Not goin' to honour Brunton-on-Sea much longer?'

'No,' said Pyke. 'No.'

Then he realized his lack of graciousness and bent his head to talk on easier terms with the little inspector.

'The South Coast p-palls a little in February. Or don't you think so?' he said. He waved vaguely. 'All this ... *w-wind*,' he finished madly.

'Lookin' forward to gettin' back to London, I'll be bound,' said Tomkins. 'Booked yer seat?'

'Promised Miriam I'd stay until you made an arrest, damn it.' Pyke was lugubrious. 'N-now l-look what she does – m-making a f-fool of me like this, getting engaged to that *b-buzzard* . . .'

Pyke's caution and good breeding suddenly disintegrated altogether under the strain and the influence of Black Velvet. Stammering passionately, he began upon what he thought of Miriam's behaviour.

'Or *l-lack* of it!' he cried. 'Anyone who has been d-decently b-brought up (to k-keep their word, for example) is at everyone's mercy nowadays. Why should *I* keep my word to stay? While Miriam amuses herself and g-gets engaged to someone else?'

Inspector Tomkins murmured soothingly that he saw what Mr Pyke meant.

'But you needn't worry, sir,' he added brightly. '*You'll* be goin' back to London tomorrow all right.'

'Why are you so sure?' Pyke was bitter.

'Oh!' The inspector spoke lightly, it was suddenly of no consequence to him. 'We're going to make the arrest tonight,' he said.

V

And so it was that Major Bandarlog of No. 17, returning with his unpleasant corgi (that so much resembled him, except of course in that it had no steel plate in its skull) after taking it for its last run before bedtime, was able to observe Inspector Tomkins, Constable Beatty and Constable Briggs making an arrest at the bottom of Pondicherry Parade, under a street light. Major Bandarlog was so much moved when he came in that Mrs Bandarlog bolted herself in the bathroom for three-quarters of an hour while he recovered. He then (of course) wrote a letter to the *Brunton Observer* signed 'Outraged Citizen'.

Interlude

'H'r'm. H'r'm. H'r'm.'

Mr Justice Mayhem drank half a glass of cold water slowly and carefully, after he had cleared his throat, dryly and conscientiously. Everyone in the Court, pleased, leant forward as though His Lordship intended a health measure. When he put his glass back on his desk a little fluttering sigh ran round the room.

'You will observe,' said His Lordship precisely, 'that the weight of evidence collected by the Crown against the accused, as you have heard it, is circumstantial. Without something concrete to support it you will consider it valueless . . .'

BOOK FIVE

'I WEEP FOR YOU,'
THE WALRUS SAID

'I weep for you,' the Walrus said,
  'I deeply sympathise.'
With sobs and tears he sorted out
  Those of the largest size,
Holding his pocket handkerchief
Before his streaming eyes.

LEWIS CARROLL: *The Walrus and the Carpenter.*

CHAPTER THIRTY-TWO

Tony Robinson, as he sat on the top of the bus that jolted him through the beauty of a serene June morning, thanked God for the lovely trees in Hyde Park. Unmoved, blue and misty in triumphant sunlight that had nothing to do with the horror pushed from his heart. Nothing to do with Brunton-on-Sea. For Tony believed in God. He thanked God, too, that he had seen the last of the Oranmore Hotel, Brunton. How oddly it had made them all behave – and Celia, Celia most of all. It was best not to think of Celia ever. He was going to have an ordeal all right, talking to her today.

Now the Holloway Road, in all its purposeful beastliness, swam past, a blur of dirty grey and brown. There was a flash of green at a corner. Surprisingly, a tree. It had been a warm June so far. The trial would come off in a week, the lawyer said. That would be an ordeal, too. He would break down. He knew he would. He wouldn't think about it. This would be the first chance he had to get up to see Celia, since they took her away.

Well, he had so much to *do*. That was it. Selling up the place. Settling April and May at Celia's Aunt Myrtle's (now, she'd been unpleasant all right, more or less implying Celia hadn't the brains to poison a few oysters); and, come to think of it, wouldn't the Judge and the whole blooming jury decide that Celia hadn't the brains to poison a few oysters? For it *did* take brains to work out a scheme like that, surely? He wouldn't think about it.

He took a packet of cigarettes out of his pocket and looked at it. No. He wouldn't smoke one. Damn it, he'd got them for *her*! She said she'd sell her soul for them. But perhaps that had only been a joke. Funny sort of joke. Celia didn't believe in God, or anything. Or so she said. Though that Methodist upbringing must've taught her something. Celia said it just taught her God was ugly. It made her hate everything.

She had always been afraid of jail. That was the funny thing. Maybe all law-abiding (ugliness-fearing) Methodists were afraid of jail. And afraid of the Law and of the Prophets and hanged by the neck till you are dead and all the rest of it. He wished he didn't think about it so much. Funny thing. *He* wasn't a law-abiding citizen, not he. Far from it. Black Market Tony, every blooming thing. Yet he'd never been afraid of jail, not he, nor the shame of it, nor any of those things that Celia was afraid of.

There was a chance Celia would get off. After all, there was only circumstantial evidence against her. And even if they found her guilty, they'd never hang her. They'd only give her life. So Tony Robinson consoled himself as he got off the bus.

Good God! What a gloomy, awful place a jail was! Well, what d'you expect? People don't get put in jails for rest cures. No, but honestly. Those gates. That wicket. The bars. The keys, locks, warder, letting him in. Oh God!

'Robinson? What relation? Husband. Sign here. Just a minute.'

And shuffling feet and dragging feet and someone laughing. And *that* was quite out of place, like the heartless sunlight in that awful square in the middle of the grey buildings. And women prisoners, going somewhere at a half trot in overalls. Oh, Celia . . .!

Tony Robinson groaned and covered his face with his hands. Thank God, thank God it wasn't him. He could never, never, never bear it.

'Don't take on, now,' said the warder. 'She won't like it if you take on. Make it much worse for her, you know. She's very good, they say. Model prisoner.'

II

There was a corridor that was dim and grey. It echoed now and then with feet, walking fast, marching. The feet must have steel tips on their heels because, otherwise, why did they make so much noise? And now the noise rang and thundered in that little, little space. And the room, with glass sides, like a tank. And one deal table. One window, not much light. Celia, outside in the corridor. A wardress. Celia looked grey, too. *Dirty*.

'As you know, I must stay.' The wardress was kind. 'Don't upset yourselves.'

It was surprising that she was kind. She turned her back. Beyond the dirty grey window there was all the blue and gold of June. Tony kissed Celia. What the hell to say?

'Hello, Celia.'

'April and May?'

'Your Aunt Myrtle. She has them. She said not to worry. She thinks they're great kids. Here.' Tony blushed. He pushed the cigarettes across the table. They sat down. The wardress was still turned away. That was kind, too.

'Oh, thank you!'

How grateful Celia was! This was terrible. He could never bear this. Far worse than he thought. Why was she looking at him like that? She had never had those cold, accusing eyes before. After all, it wasn't his fault she'd been fool enough to pinch Mrs Bognor's two hundred quid to pay those bills. *That* was what had landed her here, paying bills. Everyone knew one didn't settle monthly accounts by the month ... Everyone knew ... Oh, damn it! Celia, don't look like that.

'Tony, I know, you see. I worked it out.' Celia spoke slowly. She was bitter, then? That was odd, too. What was she bitter about?

'I love you, Celia.' That was true as far as it went, whatever it meant, whatever anyone meant by a thing like that. 'I do love you, darling. It'll be all right, dear. You know it will.'

The words tumbled over themselves. To hell with words! 'God, I admire you. Don't know how you can be so calm.' Tony gulped. He felt very sick indeed. 'Proud of you I am,' he said.

Celia shrugged her shoulders. She didn't look exalted or self-pitying or agonizingly crusading. All these things he had expected. Instead she was dull, flat, bored, looking at him as though he didn't exist.

'I'm sick of it,' she said. No more than that? She got up, turned to the wardress. 'Can I go back now?' she said.

The wardress was surprised. She mouthed 'Sorry' to Tony. Celia went away, round-shouldered, resigned, leaving him with his horror in that glass-paned waiting-room.

CHAPTER THIRTY-THREE

All that June the heatwave continued in London.

The sun rose each morning, surrounded with little mauve mists, to give little promise of the copper, clanging horror to follow. By eleven the sun had truly almost begun to *thud* upon the wastes of bombed ground at Smithfield and on the debris, like an evil, aching seashore, that still wasted by Cripplegate and the Charterhouse. Soon the thudding blood in each person's head answered the relentless sun, until the byways of the City (from St Paul's and Bart's Hospital to the Old Bailey itself) was one vast, red-hot, aching desert. It was as though the fires of hell had suddenly gone out and had left only cold cinders for the dead to pick through. And the dead (without exception) had shocking headaches.

Since seven that morning they had queued for the public gallery at the Old Bailey to overhear the case between *Rex* and *Celia Robinson*. A skirmishing photographer from an evening paper turned up at 7.30 to photograph the early ghouls, for the lunch-time edition. There were six people who said they had been there all night: a young man in a waterproof (who said he was a criminologist), two Russian ladies with shopping-baskets (who said they were from High Wycombe) and three persons who said they did not wish to be photographed and hid one behind the other. They were Major Bandarlog, Mrs Bandarlog and Johnstone, their parlourmaid.

At ten minutes to ten the Black Maria drove up. At five minutes to ten the witnesses were all there and were shut into a hot wooden box alongside the courtroom. It was like a changing-room at a municipal swimming-bath, thought Miriam.

She sat miserably on a form between Tony Robinson and Major Bognor. Tomkins, who occasionally appeared at the door and winked at her, seemed exactly the same as usual. He was miraculously unimpressed by the heavy magnificence of English law at its most powerful and most traditional. Miriam was more uneasy. Unusually sensitive to atmosphere, she was quite over-powered by the wording of her summons to appear as witness. Also, she was convinced in her heart that Celia Robinson was perfectly innocent. She bitterly regretted the part she had played in collecting evidence for Tomkins against her arrest. Colonel Rucksack, too, had rocked her self-confidence. He had been so distressed when she had broken off their engagement. One might almost imagine that he had taken the thing *seriously*. Miriam began to wonder if there was not something present in the atmosphere here, too, that she should not mock.

Major Bognor was equally overcome by the general malaise and the heat. He gnawed his moustache and sometimes smoked. He did not speak to anyone, but he often screwed in his eyeglass and glared at Tomkins. Tommy the kitchenmaid and Connie the weird old Chef sat, somewhat huddled, beside each other on the other side of the room. Connie, astonish-ingly enough, read *Zuleika Dobson*, by Max Beerbohm. Miriam wondered what she thought of it. She wished that she, too, had brought a book.

Tomkins gave her a daily paper. He smirked. It showed quite good photographs of himself, Celia Robinson and Mr Justice Mayhem.

'And I tell you somefing,' he whispered hoarsely, leaning very near to her. 'Dunno what it means, I'm sure. Freddie Pyke, your ol' boy friend, 'as been briefed as Junior Counsel for the Defence.'

A spurt of hope (as bright and sharp as the flame of a match) struck suddenly in Miriam's tender heart. That could only mean that dear Pyke believed that Celia was innocent. She had always regretted Pyke's rage about her final, inconsequential pre-matrimonial entanglement. Perhaps Pyke, too, had wished to take her seriously?

'What happens next?' she asked.

For Miriam, in spite of the number of murders with which she had been *mixed up*, had never yet achieved the distinction of an Old Bailey trial. All the other murderers that she had apprehended had been found unfit to plead.

'Judge arrives,' said Tomkins briskly. 'Jury is sworn in. Mrs Robinson pleads. Not guilty, I suppose. *Our* lawyer, Acton Park, KC, announced himself an' his learned friend an' junior, Mr Eddie Pearl – he's a clever devil too. And then he wags his nut at his learned friends Gracchus-Tiberius, KC, and F. Pyke, for the defence. Then they start.'

The room was quite certainly full of an unhappy amalgam of dust and carbon dioxide. Miriam decided she would demand compensation of the State for the harm done to her lungs and larynx.

'What do they start with?' She felt quite numb and dead.

'Look, miss, there's no call for *you* to worry. All *you* do is remember the truth and nothing but. And answer the questions. It's just like at the Magistrates' Court, Mr Park'll lead you through your deposition. An' Mr Gracchus-Tiberius will try to break you up.'

Tomkins was more than ever like a neat little sparrow, hopping firmly amongst the massive mansions of the law of England.

'But suppose Freddie tries to make me look a fool?'

Miriam's pale-blue eyes were suddenly wide and fearful.

'Suppose nothing.' Tomkins was quite calm and confident. 'Don't you fuss, Miss Birdseye. You'll be a match for Mr Pyke, I *don't* suppose. A stammer like that'll be a terrible handicap for a barrister. That's why he give it up, they tell me. Doesn't stammer in Court at all, but it's terrible strain concentrating on that as well as everything else. Now just you tell the truth, miss, that's all, miss.'

Miriam was not pacified, even by his adoring use of the word 'miss'. She glared round the room.

'If *everyone* here tells *all* the truth and nothing but,' she cried passionately, 'Mrs Robinson will get off!'

And this did not improve the atmosphere in the room at all.

II

In the court the Judge, his chaplain and the Clerk of the Court took their places. Mr Justice Mayhem was a grand and frightening figure. His robes were red, like blood. The Clerk of the Court, on his feet, in a voice like the sighing of the south wind, asked Mrs Robinson if she were guilty or not guilty; she replied, even more quietly, 'Not guilty.' Mr Justice Mayhem testily demanded, 'What did she say?' His chaplain whispered in his ear and he seemed pleased.

Then the jury, standing, swore they would 'well and truly try and a true deliverance make between our Sovereign Lord, the King, and the prisoner at the bar, according to the evidence'. The jury were an unspectacular lot. There were two women, one rather obviously married; the other, as obviously, a spinster. The ten men were so beige and unremarkable as to create a general blur of navy-blue suits and pink faces. The foreman of the jury was aggressive, but only mildly so. He had a row of fountain-pens clipped into his navy-blue waistcoat. He was a little bald on the top of his head.

The clerk told the jurors (which they already knew) that Mrs Robinson had pleaded not guilty.

Acton Park, his jaw out-thrust, addressed the Court in tones that might have been heard in the Charterhouse. His was a splendid bass voice, almost grand opera in quality. Only his fine blue chin and his well-carved mouth could not have belonged to a horse. Everything else about his appearance was embarrassingly equine.

'*May it please your lordship?*'

He introduced himself and his learned friend, the white-faced Edward Pearl, whose neat parrot-face peered up with great keenness from the table where the briefs lay scattered.

Acton Park swung a flat white hand at his equally learned friend Gracchus-Tiberius (a Roman emperor bass-baritone of a barrister) and *his* learned friend, F. Pyke. Somehow, Mr Park contrived to make this part of his introduction insulting. Pyke bit his underlip and wondered if the Court could hear the thunder of his heart against his ribs. But no. No one, of course, had ever been able to hear anything else while Acton Park was speaking ...

If it pleased Mr Justice Mayhem and the jury, Mr Park would now show (by means of witnesses) that on the night of the 23rd the late Mrs Bognor met her death by eating poisoned oysters.

Moreover, he would produce specimens of oysters that showed traces of arsenic deposit, and expert witnesses (and here Mr Justice Mayhem sighed and his chaplain looked disapproving) to show that this was so. Furthermore, he would make it plain that the accused had in her possession (on the night in question) a hypodermic syringe that contained traces of arsenic.

And he would demonstrate that the accused had access to arsenic on this same night. And (subsequent to the death of Mrs Bognor) how the accused was found to have in her possession a number of one-pound notes known to have been issued to Mrs Bognor by the Sussex and Provincial Bank on the Saturday previous to the 23rd.

At this point Gracchus-Tiberius, twinkling with pleasure, and (in spite of his fine big florid head) looking rather like a fighting-cock about to enter the pit, muttered from the corner of his mouth to Pyke, 'In fact, he'll do everything, old boy, but *actually* produce a witness who *saw* her inject the bloody oysters ...'

'Qu-qu-qu-quite,' said Pyke, and wished that the floor might open for him.

III

Acton Park's first witnesses were oyster experts and the eminent pathologist Sir Godfrey Pawson-Hailsam.

The jury, Mr Justice Mayhem, the accused (and everyone, indeed, but Acton Park and Gracchus-Tiberius) went nearly mad with anxious concentration, heat and final exhaustion as they battered their brains in an attempt to arrive at proof of the cause of death.

Dr Stalag-Jones of Brunton-on-Sea made a short spectacular appearance in the witness-box when she delighted everyone by her monosyllabic and uncompromising replies.

'Certainly,' 'Mrs Bognor died of arsenic poisoning,' and 'Absolutely.'

The jury obviously preferred her to Sir Godfrey. For such, alas, is the fundamental instability of the human brain faced, in a June heatwave, by the cautious, the scholarly, and the painstakingly accurate approach.

His Lordship then adjourned the Court for luncheon.

The six early ghouls opened (and rustled in) paper bags. Indeed, Mrs Bandarlog produced a thermos flask of coffee. She was so thankful for something to keep Major Bandarlog *amused.* For, in spite of his much-overheated steel plate, he had behaved like a perfect angel ever since this trial had been announced.

IV

After luncheon the prosecution ploughed on with its witnesses. Dr Fawcett-Smith appeared in heavy horn-rimmed glasses. He scowled furiously at the Court as he gave evidence about (*a*) the oysters and (*b*) the hypodermic syringe given him by Inspector Tomkins of the Sussex CID for analysis. The public sighed, for they had already read all about the oysters and the syringe in the press as a result of the hearing before the Magistrates' Court. They considered it mere repetition of extremely dull stuff, and they were, I suppose, quite right. However, at the end of Fawcett-Smith's dissertation, Gracchus-Tiberius raised his heavy eyebrows at Pyke, who nodded and rose to cross-examine. Pyke now found his beating heart had risen into his mouth. He swallowed it (and it made a most unpleasant lump in his chest). The intense concentration that was needed to control his gabbling tongue made a hot dew start out on his forehead.

'When you were given these oysters to examine, how many were there *exactly*?'

'Exactly?' Fawcett-Smith seemed horrified.

'What is the matter?' Mr Justice Mayhem obviously wished to be helpful. He struck the terror more deeply into Fawcett-Smith's heart.

'The matter is, my lord,' he said unhappily, 'that there were so many oysters – I really cannot estimate – perhaps a hundred.'

'But surely a record was kept?' Pyke purred unpleasantly at Fawcett-Smith, who became more and more unhappy.

'A record was kept of those which I found to be poisoned . . . I have told you of those . . .'

'Quite, quite,' said Pyke. But he had made his point. He was well pleased at the quick humiliation of Dr Fawcett-Smith.

'I am anxious that we should be as accurate as possible about the hypodermic syringe, my lord,' said Pyke.

'Quite, quite,' said Mr Justice Mayhem.

'Perhaps you *can* say how many hypodermic syringes you were given for analysis?' The sneer, implicit in Pyke's controlled and measured tones, did not seem to distress Dr Fawcett-Smith.

'Oh yes,' said Fawcett-Smith happily. 'Five.'

(Sensation in court, instantly suppressed.)

'Perhaps you would like to tell us how you identified this syringe as the prisoner's syringe? Whose were the other four?'

'I *didn't* identify the other four syringes. That is Inspector Tomkins' business. I can't say whose they were, any of them. I labelled them A, B, C, D and E. The inspector will tell you more. My department is scientific.'

Pyke passed all these statements.

'Yes,' he said at the end of it all. 'Were the other syringes free from – um – *taint?*'

'All except one. This was infected with typhoid.'

For some reason Dr Fawcett-Smith was pleased at the turn that events were now taking. He beamed all over his face. Sensation in court, again suppressed. Acton Park, somewhat ruffled, agreed under his breath to call Tomkins immediately, rather than any other witnesses.

'Can you then tell the Court something about hypodermic syringes from the purely scientific point of view?'

Dr Fawcett-Smith looked up at Mr Justice Mayhem, who nodded, bright-eyed. He waved Mr Park's tentative complaints on one side. He could see no objection to this.

'What do you want to know?' said Fawcett-Smith glumly.

'Is it a matter of great difficulty to use one of these things?'

'No. It is very simple.'

'The fact that a hypodermic syringe was in a household would not necessarily mean that the *owner* would always use it?'

'Anyone could use a hypodermic syringe.'

'If they had access to it?'

'Yes.'

'In fact, the only *proof* that a person had used this syringe would be that someone else actually *saw* them do so?'

'Unless there were some other trace – finger-prints, perhaps – that would be so.'

'That visual evidence would be required, in default of the finger-prints? That other evidence, that the syringe belonged to Mrs – I mean to the prisoner – is purely circumstantial?'

'Yes, I think so.'

'That is all, my lord.'

Fawcett-Smith left the box, clattering his feet noisily. In a hush as compelling as that hush which falls before the curtain rises on a Noël Coward first night, Mr Park, then the usher, called Inspector Tomkins of the Sussex CID.

CHAPTER THIRTY-FOUR

Tomkins took the oath, briskly and precisely. He admitted his identity. Then he began one of those reports in police jargon which (as even the police are aware) have no relation whatsoever to the English language.

Yes, his name was Harold Tomkins. Yes, he was an inspector attached to the Sussex CID. On the morning of the 23rd he *proceeded* to the Oranmore Private Hotel, Brunton-on-Sea, in answer to a telephone call. Here he had found the body of the deceased. (Tomkins then described the scene in Mrs Bognor's bedroom.) He examined the body and effects.

He found that two hundred pounds (property of the deceased) was missing, likewise a sable fur coat.

He *interrogated* (for no policeman *ever* questions) various members of the hotel staff and household, including the accused, as to the manner in which the deceased had met her death.

He *ascertained* that an oyster party had been held on the premises on the night of the 23rd. He then descended to the kitchen parts of the hotel, where he found two dust-bins, full of oyster shells. These were removed to the police station.

Later that week – after several authorities had satisfied themselves about the cause of death – he returned to the hotel with a search warrant. He had the *intention* of discovering whether any member of the household *was in possession of* a hypodermic syringe. He found that the prisoner was. The syringe was removed and tested.

He made enquiries in the town and discovered that a bottle of white arsenic, forming part of the stock of Graham Micah, chemist, had been temporarily displaced.

He then proceeded to interrogate Charles Bodger, butcher; Ephraim Twiggs, greengrocer; Connie Watson, cook at the Oranmore Hotel; and Margaret Button, chambermaid at the same establishment. He found that these witnesses were all in possession of one-pound notes answering to the serial numbers of the two hundred pounds missing from the deceased's handbag. They had, they said, received the money in payment of certain outstanding debts of the prisoner's.

Charged with theft of this money and cautioned, the prisoner broke down and admitted she took it.

Here Tomkins coughed and took a small note-book from his bosom.

'She said,' he remarked, gazing trustfully up at Lord Justice Mayhem – 'she said: "Oh, officer, I knew it was wrong of me to take the money, but this hotel is so difficult to keep running I don't know which way to turn. I shouldn't have done it but for the kids." I then formally charged her with the murder of Mrs Bognor, deceased, and took her into custody. She then said, "I didn't do it."'

II

Gracchus-Tiberius rose as though he were a panther and police officers in plain clothes his normal prey. All through his cross-questioning he seemed about to spring up at Tomkins, who remained quite gay and faced him untrembling.

'Ah . . .' said Gracchus-Tiberius. 'This hypodermic that you removed from the hotel. There was only one?'

'No, sir.' Tomkins' bright little face suggested that he thought mud of all lawyers and that he knew a great deal to Gracchus-Tiberius' discredit. 'There were three in the hotel.'

'Ah . . .' Gracchus-Tiberius closed his eyes. 'Perhaps you can tell the Court to whom these belonged?'

'Yes, sir.' Tomkins referred to his notes, unmoved. 'Three hypodermic syringes: the property of Mrs Robinson, the accused; Major Bognor, a guest in the hotel; Connie Watson, the cook.'

'Was that the total number of hypodermic syringes given to your analyst?' Gracchus-Tiberius continued with his pouncing, purring manner.

'No, sir.' Tomkins was unhurried and still quite gay. 'The total number of syringes the contents of which was analysed was *five*. In addition to those removed from the hotel there were two from other sources. One, the property of Andrew Cathcart, bank manager. Another, the property of Colonel Charles Rucksack. Five in all.' And Tomkins beamed round the Court.

'I see,' said Gracchus-Tiberius wearily.

Mr Justice Mayhem leant forward.

'Are these – may I call them *owners* of hypodermic syringes – to be called as witnesses?' he asked anxiously.

There was a difficult little moment when Mr Acton Park intervened and said that they were ready and waiting to be called.

'Thank you, my lord,' said Gracchus-Tiberius, still with his eyes shut. Mr Justice Mayhem scowled. Gracchus-Tiberius began again on Tomkins.

'These pound notes, now. Is it not *unusual* for a bank (in 195–) to take a tally of the serial numbers of pound notes issued?'

'Yes. I believe it is.'

'Is there any explanation as to *why* it occurred on this occasion?'

A faint shadow of worry passed across Tomkins' face.

'The manager, Mr Cathcart, told me that he had some trouble with this particular account and therefore made a note of the numbers of these notes. He is giving evidence.'

'Thank you.'

And Gracchus-Tiberius sat down.

III

Andrew Cathcart hurried into the witness-box. He was dressed in a neat navy-blue suit and a wine-red tie. His nose and cheeks were also wine red and his hands trembled slightly. He put them in his pockets and hoped for the best.

'You are Andrew Cathcart?' suggested Acton Park.

'I am,' said Cathcart reluctantly.

'You are the manager of the Brunton branch of the Sussex and Provincial Bank?'

'Yes.'

'Perhaps you will tell the Court, in your own words, of the

money that Mrs Bognor withdrew from the bank immediately before her death?'

Andrew drew a deep breath and clutched the edge of the witness-box. Almost one might have supposed it to be the dock, and Cathcart the accused.

'Yes,' he said. 'Well, it must have been about half past eleven.'

'A moment.' Acton Park was vexed. 'What day would this be?'

'I said. Saturday.'

'You did not say. Saturday the . . .?'

'Saturday the day before Mrs Bognor was – um. Saturday before Mrs Bognor died.'

'I think we have established that it was on Saturday the 23rd of February,' said Mr Justice Mayhem.

'Yes, my lord,' said Andrew Cathcart, well pleased. 'Well, I saw Mrs Bognor come in, and I said to Eddie, my teller, I said to him, "Eddie," I said, "you keep a tally of those notes, now, will you? Two hundred pounds," I said, "is a lot of money to draw out." And I think I also passed the remark that it *was* a lot of money and wondered what she would do with it.' Andrew Cathcart now recovered his *bonhomie* and beamed at Acton Park. 'We could all do with two hundred smackers, I dare say?' he remarked outrageously.

'Pray confine yourself to the matter under discussion,' said Acton Park cruelly.

'Oh, sorry, I'm sure,' said Andrew Cathcart, very hurt.

'It was unusual, was it not, to make a note of the serial numbers?'

'Well, since the war, yes, it *is* unusual. But before the war I wouldn't have called it unusual. No. Before the war we often used to keep a tally.'

'I see. Thank you, Mr Cathcart.'

'Oh. Is that all?'

Gracchus-Tiberius did not wish to cross-examine. And Mr Cathcart slapped down from the stand quite aggrieved. He had only just begun to enjoy himself.

IV

Ephraim Twiggs, Charles Bodger and Maggie Button made their appearance; all confirmed the fact that Mrs Robinson had paid an outstanding account with money coinciding with the serial numbers. Ephraim Twiggs was monosyllabic. Maggie Button was terrified. Charles Bodger made an attempt to tell the Court (without invitation) how matters had stood at the Oranmore Hotel, and was sternly returned to the point by Acton Park. But Gracchus-Tiberius in a fine rage rose to cross-examine. He was obviously determined to imply (wherever possible) that his learned friend was suppressing the truth, the whole truth and so on.

'You say that *"matters weren't easy"* at the Oranmore Hotel?'

'That's right, sir.'

'Well, why not?'

'The place was too big for the Robinsons, to my way of thinking, sir. And Robinson didn't pull his weight. Everything fell on the missus, to my way of thinking. Sorry. I mean the accused.'

'We know whom you mean. You suggest that Mrs Robinson was overworked?'

'Oh, definitely. Properly washed out, always—'

'Thank you.'

And Charles Bodger clumped down, quite bewildered by the law and fed-up with the whole business generally, baulked of his determination to 'tell them'.

V

Graham Micah, too, was angry. He was vexed at the amount of time he had already spent away from his business and was determined to get through this 'pantomime' (for this is what he called it) as fast as possible, and back to Brunton-on-Sea by the first train. Before Mrs Micah could leave any more arsenic lying about.

'You say there was a bottle of white arsenic in your shop?' said Acton Park.

'Yes.' Graham Micah tried to justify himself. 'We use it in prescriptions and so on. We keep it under lock and key.'

'You told the police inspector it was displaced. How was that?'

'My wife did not put it back in the proper place after making up an ointment.'

(Several of the jury were hostile. 'Putting the whole thing on his wife.' 'I don't believe a word of it.')

'Where did she, then, put it?'

'It was on an open shelf. Very wrong. I told her so.'

'I see. So anyone who came into your dispensary would be able to help themselves?'

'Yes, if they wanted to. If they came into the dispensary.'

'And the prisoner came into your dispensary during that time?'

'Yes. She is a friend of the family. She was in the dispensary on the 22nd February.'

'Thank you.'

Gracchus-Tiberius observed Mr Justice Mayhem's nose and chin about to meet with displeasure. He hurried on, biting off his words as though they were little pieces of cotton.

'I wonder if you can tell us,' he suggested, purring gently, like a great cat, 'how many other people from the Oranmore Hotel came to your dispensary?'

'Oh yes. All of them.'

'*All* of them?' Gracchus-Tiberius' astonishment was general. It rippled round the court. (The jury rippled, too.)

'Certainly.' Graham Micah was savage and fed-up. There was now no chance of his catching the 3.40. 'We're the only chemist's in Brunton-on-Sea. Only chemist's for *miles*, for that matter.'

'So ...' Gracchus-Tiberius referred to the list in his hand. 'Major Bognor would come in to you for his prescriptions?'

'Oh, definitely.'

'And Major Bognor, too, was actually in your dispensary, let us say?'

Graham Micah frowned. Something stirred at the back of his mind.

'As a matter of fact,' said Graham Micah slowly, '*yes*.'

'So *he*, even, had access to this white arsenic?'

There was another little pause while Graham Micah thought that one out. Finally he said, 'Yes,' in so small a voice that Mr Justice Mayhem bawled out, 'What did he say?' and was told, 'He said *yes*, my lord,' by Gracchus-Tiberius in tones of equal thunder. ('No need to shout,' muttered His Lordship, aggrieved, to his chaplain.)

'And this would also be true of anyone else who came to the dispensary during the time when the arsenic was displaced?'

'It would.'

'Can you suggest to the Court any other person who came into the dispensary and therefore had access to the poison?'

Mr Micah screwed up his face and tried to remember.

'Robinson,' he said finally. 'I can remember Tony Robinson coming.'

'And he is the prisoner's husband?'

'Yes, he is.'

Gracchus-Tiberius sat down, exhausted. Pyke passed him a note. It was written in his flourishing Oxford hand, Greek e's and all:

Nice work. Keep it up. We're half-way to a Not Guilty already.

CHAPTER THIRTY-FIVE

Acton Park, by now a little white about the gills, stepped forward to take Anthony Robinson through his deposition. Away from the Oranmore Hotel (it was understood that the arrangements for selling that evil place were now in the solicitors' hands), Tony looked (and indeed *was*) quite different. He held his shoulders back. His colour was fresh. The navy-blue pleats round his eyes, a permanent feature of his general Brunton appearance, were gone. Now his eyes were mildly shaded with pale baby blue.

Celia Robinson sat listlessly in the dock. She had been unaware of much that had gone on all round her. She took no notes, and most of the time she looked down at the floor. She seemed to have no interest in her existence, nor in her chance of freedom, nor even in the terrible black square that hovered (in everyone else's imagination) above Mr Justice Mayhem's head.

When Tony took the oath, at the sound of his voice she raised her head. That was all, but it was so remarkable a thing that the wardress who was with her stepped half a pace forward.

Mr Park turned to the Court. He had ventured (he said) to

bring Mr Robinson into the court to explain how the oysters had been opened for the party. He did not propose to ask him for any other evidence, and he would not have done so had not Mr Robinson offered it in the first place. Mr Park was sure His Lordship would wish the Court and jury to arrive at an accurate picture of the oyster-opening?

'Quite so, quite so,' said His Lordship.

And Tony took the oath, looking so handsome that Celia's heart turned right over. For one intolerable moment she most maddeningly wished she were alive and with him once more. It was misery, however, she recollected, being alive. Apathy, and therefore death, alone were peaceful and tolerable. And she relapsed once more into lethargy.

'*You are Anthony Robinson?*'

'I am.'

'You are the proprietor of the Oranmore Hotel?'

'Y-e-es. Yes, I am ...'

'The arrangements for this oyster party were therefore under your jurisdiction?'

'It was my hotel. Yes.'

'Who opened the oysters?'

There was a great pause while the Court awaited Tony's reply. They wanted sensation, and Tony didn't disappoint them. He shrugged his shoulders.

'I can't say,' said Tony.

'Do you mean you *don't know*?'

'I can't remember.'

Acton Park was dumbfounded and furious. The reporters, scribbling in their little box, were gleeful.

'But, Mr Robinson,' Mr Park exploded, like an atom bomb,

'didn't you, on a former occasion, volunteer the information that you had opened some of the oysters yourself? That you had opened about a dozen? And that you left the remainder to be opened by Major Bognor and a guest in the hotel? And possibly your wife?' A little cloud seemed to hang, threatening, upon Mr Park's fine and horse-like brow.

'Oh yes,' said Tony.

'And what have you to say now?'

'I was drunk when the police inspector took that down. I'm terribly sorry. I was drunk when I signed it. I never can remember what I do or say when I'm drunk, and I can't really be relied upon. I'm terribly sorry; I often tell lies, too.'

Tony's ingenuous blue eyes rolled comically round the courtroom and instantly everyone liked him. His blue eyes rolled back to Mr Acton Park, KC, who did not like him at all.

'But do you mean to tell the Court—' spluttered Mr Park. He pulled himself up short. 'Are you drunk this afternoon?' he suggested.

'No,' said Tony coolly. 'Are you?'

Mr Justice Mayhem banged sharply on his desk in the howl of laughter that followed this and reminded Mr Robinson that his wife was facing a charge of murder.

'I am sorry, my lord,' said Tony. He was all grace and humble pie and careful apology. 'Most sincerely sorry.'

'Perhaps you will tell us what happened on the afternoon of the 23rd,' said Mr Justice Mayhem sternly. 'Unless, of course, you were drunk then also?'

'I am afraid I was,' said Tony. 'Blind drunk. I really am most terribly sorry.'

And that, as Gracchus-Tiberius muttered to Pyke, was

certainly that. Mr Robinson was hustled from the witness-box with indecent haste, while Gracchus-Tiberius loftily shook his head from side to side, patently refusing to have anything to do with so 'hopelessly volatile' a witness. He was surprised (his wig appeared to say, bobbing serenely, refusing his right to cross-question) that the Crown should have *called* so unstable a witness. And:

'Major Bognor!' called the Clerk of the Court.

II

The Major bent down and peered through his eyeglass at the oath where it was inscribed on fine ivory. He held up the Book in his right hand, where it shook ever so slightly.

'Your name is Reginald Bognor?' started Acton Park at a hand gallop, determined to have no nonsense. 'You were resident at the Oranmore Hotel, Brunton-on-Sea, on the 23rd February? It was your mother's birthday? You had ordered some oysters to give her a treat? You opened these oysters? How? And when?'

Acton Park began to breathe more easily as Major Bognor answered his questions with careful, soldierly variations on the affirmative theme. 'Yes,' said Major Bognor, and, 'That is so,' and, 'It was,' and, 'I did.'

'Perhaps you will tell the Court in your own words, then, how, when and where these oysters were opened?'

'Certainly,' said the Major. He straightened his shoulders, and in the pious, pompous tones of one who has been falsely accused of nameless indecencies, he began:

'I went down to the basement and found they had put the

oysters in the housemaid's pantry. I was angry because there wasn't a proper light there and I couldn't see what I was doin'. I only had a potato-peeler, y'know, to open the bivalves with. So I began to open 'em, and after a bit I found I'd lost the knack. I cut me thumb . . .' said the Major, whining slightly.

'A moment,' said Mr Justice Mayhem. 'How do you open an oyster?'

'Well, sir,' said the Major, 'you feel around the edge of the shell for two little teeth, and then you nip in yer knife an' press like *mad* and the oyster kind of gasps, and you can get it open, what?' The Major grinned, and it was evident that he enjoyed opening oysters.

'Thank you,' said Mr Justice Mayhem, and shuddered. 'And you only have a knife for this? No other instrument?'

'No, sir. It is rather tough, but if y' have the knack, y'know . . .' began the Major patronizingly.

'Exactly,' said Mr Justice Mayhem, looking down his nose, 'the knack which you had lost. Proceed.'

Abashed, the Major also looked down his nose. Acton Park leapt to pick up the threads.

'You found this job too big for you?'

'Yes,' said the Major. 'I went upstairs to see if I could find Robinson. But he was in his office (er, I think he was *asleep*), and I went along to the lounge, and one of the guests – feller called *Pyke* – agreed to help me.'

Pyke looked down and simpered.

'He was jolly good at it, actually. We both got jolly tired, what, and we finished by puttin' the oysters on the top of the kitchen stove. That saves time, y'see, m'lord, they gasp for air . . .' explained the Major, gazing up despairingly at Mr Justice

Mayhem, who seemed no longer interested in the opening of oysters. Aggrieved, the Major continued, 'Er – our hostess was in the kitchen *cryin'* when we went in there.'

The Major paused, as who should say what now?

'You left the oysters alone when you went upstairs to find help?' suggested Acton Park smoothly.

'Yes,' said the Major, surprised.

'So for about ten minutes, say, they were unguarded?'

'Yes.'

'How did they look when you returned?'

'No different. There were about a dozen open. Pyke and I opened the remainder.'

'Thank you.'

III

Gracchus-Tiberius stood in a sanguine and gracious manner and interrogated Major Bognor.

'You say that the oysters were deposited in the housemaid's pantry?'

'That is so,' said the Major.

'By whom?'

'By Mr Robinson, I think, and two employees of the Rialto Hotel. They had been delivered there in error. There were about two crans, I think—'

'*Cran?*' cried Mr Justice Mayhem, as though it were an agony to him.

'It is a term among oyster dealers, my lord,' said Gracchus-Tiberius soothingly. 'It means a gallon or so, I believe.'

'Oh!' But His Lordship was fretful. It had been a long day

and he was eighty-one and he wished to go home now. More than one person quite agreed with him. Only the accused seemed unmoved and unperturbed by the wranglings and delays of the law.

'And the oysters remained there all the afternoon, untouched, so far as you know?'

'Yes.'

'*You* didn't go down and look at them yourself, for example?'

'No. Not until I went to open them.'

'Are you an expert on oysters, Major Bognor?'

The Major smirked.

'Yes. I believe so. Yes. I have that reputation in the Regiment, I believe, what?'

'I see. Thank you, my lord. That is all.'

IV

And so His Lordship, most thankfully, adjourned the Court until the following day.

Outside in the streets the fiery summer sky had turned a vague lilac green. The sun had hardly set. The fading heat seemed to steal away from the pavements in a warm smell of roses. The papers were selling on the street corner.

'*Robinson – Oyster Murder Sensation!*' cried a newspaper man. Miriam, fed-up with her long, hot day, wasted in the unpleasant confines of the witnesses' waiting-room, paused with Connie Watson to buy one.

Together they walked to the Underground station. A plane tree etched a pattern against the sky and threw a coolness down towards the street.

'Well, I'll be—' said Connie suddenly. She was reading the paper, spread at arm's length in front of her. 'My God! So Tony's gone back on his police-barracks homicide-squad statement, has he?' Connie was suddenly shown in her secondary (or Humphrey Bogart) role again. 'That shows he's got guts, by damn! "*Terribly sorry . . . I was drunk*", indeed! Pity he didn' think of that months ago. Might not've arrested 'er then . . .'

And Connie seemed indignantly deep in thought when Miriam left her. Miriam left her to spend a gay evening with some theatrical friends in Kinnerton Street. Here she gained considerable *cachet* from her connection with the sinister 'Oyster Case'. She hated to disappoint her friends by admitting that she had only sat all day in a sort of turkish-bath waiting-room.

CHAPTER THIRTY-SIX

On the second day of the trial Miriam arrived prepared for anything. She carried a large, bulging bag (somewhat like that of the Fairy Blackstick). It contained two novels (one light and one medium-heavyweight), a rubber pillow, some sewing, a piece of unpleasant mauve knitting that she took a pleasure in unravelling, and a thermos flask containing iced coffee. Thus encumbered, she sat on the bench in the witnesses' room, removed the pillow from her bulging bag and blew it up. Major Bognor watched her, aggrieved. He obviously wished that he, too, had a pillow.

'Surprised at you takin' this thing s' seriously, Miriam,' he said crossly. 'I'm also surprised I've been called for a second day. They had everything in me deposition yesterday. Terrible business gettin' here by 10 a.m. Nearly kills me.'

Miriam nodded at him briefly.

'I believe in doing everything as *well* as possible,' she said. 'I once became a house mistress, quite by mistake, for the same reason. Also, I'm expecting some shocks.'

'Oh?' growled the Major. 'What makes you think that? What?'

And he stabbed with his furled umbrella at the rough, splintery floor between his nicely polished shoes.

'Don't know,' said Miriam. 'Don't know at all.'

But her pale-blue eyes strayed towards Connie Watson, where she sat in the opposite corner. Connie was alone today. She was dressed, surprisingly, as the owner of Whortleberry Down. Her clothes were of good cut and cloth. They seemed brown, sad relics of her better days. Round her neck, on a broad, black watered-silk ribbon, hung a single eyeglass. With this in her eye she outfaced the Major's scrutiny. There was a frightening similarity between them as they glared through their monocles. It was an unnerving thing.

At that moment the usher called, '*Myfanwy Constance Hildegarde Watson!*' Connie stood up and lurched towards the door. She had suddenly gone chalk-white and her features seemed very overdrawn. Miriam wondered idly if it were the effect of the euphonious roll of her unaccustomed Christian names.

II

A narrow runway, like a dirty ski-ball alley, led down to the witness-box at an obtuse angle. Connie took it at a half-run and was brought up short by the alarming appearance of the Court swimming before her eyes, and by the Judge in his death-robes. For in this manner Connie thought of him.

She took the oath, miserably, in a whisper.

'Are you Myfanwy Constance Hildegarde Watson?'

'Yes,' said Connie. She admitted her address.

Mr Acton Park took her, glibly enough, through her deposition. Connie testified that, on the afternoon of the 23rd, three barrels of oysters were delivered to the hotel and placed in the housemaid's pantry. There was some trouble over the washing-up and Connie (being tired) had gone into her bedroom 'for a lie-down'. When she came out of her bedroom, later on, the oysters were open, ready for the party. Also, the washing-up had been done. She agreed that Mrs Robinson had probably been downstairs during the ten minutes when Major Bognor went to get help. She had heard her crying. The jury turned to one another, surprised that a woman in tears could even be suspected of directing a hypodermic syringe.

Mr Park was displeased with his witness. Why had she never mentioned before that Mrs Robinson was crying? Mr Park sat down.

III

Pyke stood up and Connie gave him a broad grin of welcome and recognition. She looked like a grey and smiling toad, and Pyke was horrified. He nevertheless proceeded bravely with the cross-examination.

'I am interested in the period that you spent lying down. Did you sleep?'

Connie chuckled rudely.

'No,' she said. 'I have to sing to hide the drumming underneath.'

'I see,' said Pyke hastily. 'You were awake?'

'Oh yes.'

'Did you lie down all the time?'

'No. I moved about a bit. And being restless I wondered whether to have a shot of my stuff—'

'What's that?' said Mr Justice Mayhem.

'The witness was wondering whether to take some medicine, my lord,' said Pyke. He sounded a little anxious.

'I see.' Mr Justice Mayhem, however, did *not* see. He frowned angrily.

'So—' Pyke turned to Connie.

'So I leant out of the window.'

'You did *what?*' Mr Justice Mayhem was outraged.

'She kept her medicine outside the window, my lord,' said Pyke soothingly.

'Oh. How very odd. Oh!' said His Lordship.

'Yes. That's right. I kept it on the window-sill,' said Connie. She nodded away in the box, becoming every minute more toad-like than ever.

'Now here is a plan of the front basement of the Oranmore Hotel,' remarked Pyke smoothly. 'I have several copies of it. They have been drawn by a surveyor.'

A copy was handed up to His Lordship, who was promptly entranced. He began to measure it with a little rule. Connie was not quite so entranced.

'Do you recognize this as the Oranmore Hotel?' asked Pyke.

'Oh yes,' said Connie doubtfully. 'There's my bedroom. And the housemaid's pantry right next door. And then, t'other side of the house altogether, there's the dining-room, ex-cetera, *ex*-cetera. Oh yes. This is the Old Graveyard all right.'

'What's that?' Mr Justice Mayhem glared down at Connie Watson. At that moment she seemed the personification of antisocial behaviour.

'It is a slang term, my lord. The witness invented it for the hotel. The graveyard.'

To everyone's alarm His Lordship laughed. 'Very apt,' he said. And returned to his little plan.

'Now I want you to describe very carefully to the Court what you did when you leant out of the window.'

'Well, there was a light waggling up and down in the house-maid's pantry. That's the window on my lef' when I got out of me own window, see? And I know there's no electric bulb in there because I took it for the scullery. So I go and have a butcher's hook—'

'What?' His Lordship was fascinated.

'A look, my lord.'

'Oh, I see. This is rhyming slang, is it?'

'Yes, it is. Butcher's hook, look, see?' Connie leant expansively on the edge of the witness-box. She was by now quite at her ease. Although the jury did not care for her they were nevertheless riveted to her words, fascinated by evil. Pyke gently prompted her.

'And what did you see?'

Connie screwed up her toad's eyes.

'There was a feller in there. With a big flashlight. He had it in 'is teeth, *which* I saw by going across to the other side of the window. And he had a hypodermic whatname. You know. One of these – like for . . .' She began to gesture.

The Court knew what she meant, and Pyke told her so.

'Yes. And he was injecting something into these oysters. There was about two dozen oysters open, see? I could see quite plain, although there was only the flashlight in there. Everything else was dark except his face, and where the light shone, see? I expect he could only have been seen from where I was.'

'You are quite sure it was a man?'

'Yes.'

'It was not a woman?'

'No.'

'It could not have been the accused?'

'Oh no.'

'Do you know who it was?'

'Oh yes. It was—'

'You are on oath, remember . . .'

Mr Justice Mayhem had been galvanized into speech.

'Yes, my lord.'

Connie was transfixed by the drama in her control and the breathless intake of breath all round the Court. If these people were going to take her seriously she would take herself seriously. For a moment or two she became the sober, undrugged householder, the ex-owner of Whortleberry Down, with a Glory of a partner and all the world once more at her feet. She glared round at the Court.

'This is the whole truth and nothing but. The man was Bognor. Major Bognor.'

CHAPTER THIRTY-SEVEN

'But why did she never come forward before?' Miriam was very seriously angry. 'That's so awful of her. Letting us all make fools of ourselves. That's what I shall *never* forgive ...'

Miriam sat back in one of her tartan armchairs in her Baker Street flat. Below her window the buses sighed. It was a beautiful summer evening. Her bag (not even unpacked) containing the two novels, her sewing and the rest of her painless time-killers, lay where she had thrown it in her fury beside the statue of the little black boy, who held the electric lamp by the door. She passed a hand through her pale-yellow hair. It stood up in an angry brush. Pyke smiled, unrepentant, at the window.

'*You* knew, Pyke, too, you *knew*. Otherwise they would never have let you appear for the defence, you old ...' Miriam paused and searched round in her mind for some really frightful insult. '*Nark!*' she found eventually.

Pyke's stammer returned to protect him.

'F-f-funny, isn't it,' he said, 'h-how the t-taxis go down Baker Street j-just like the h-hansoms used in the old days? S-so many of them, too. When W-Watson and H-Holmes used to h-hail them. I often wondered how they got fixed up so quickly and how the hansoms c-came c-c-cl-clopping up.'

'Pyke!' Miriam was petulant. She pushed forward her under-lip and scowled through her yellow fringe, like a Toulouse Lautrec. 'It *was* you. You did it *all* . . .'

'Well, not entirely.' Pyke was still by the window. He was remote and strange. But there was triumph in his voice. (Perhaps it had not been *too* bad, his return to the Bar? Perhaps it was more fun, after all, than the theatre?)

'Connie Watson came round to my chambers after the f-first day,' he said slowly. 'She had been f-frightened because she was a drug addict, you know. B-but when Robinson b-behaved so well and told the truth and said he was *drunk* that afternoon, she thought she would have another g-go and risk getting another job. It wasn't pleasant for her, either, you know. Old P-Park was allowed to re-examine, and he gave her an absolute *p-pasting*. Suggested it was a m-morphine pipe-dream. To say nothing of that d-damned old fool Mayhem droning on with his s-summing-up like that. I was surprised the Crown didn't withdraw, I m-must say.'

'You don't smoke morphine,' said Miriam angrily. 'Even I know that, and I never even touch *aspirin*. I was so angry not to be called, after getting there every morning at ten o'clock. I think I shall sue the Crown – or Tomkins – for my expenses. Think of the time I've wasted. *Two whole days*, when we might have been writing our play . . .'

'Oh, quite,' said Pyke, and smiled his wry, rosebud smile. He turned his back again and looked down on the street. It was nearly empty and the street lights came on one at a time. It must be quite late. 'You might damn' well have thought of writing our play in Brunton-on-Sea,' thought Pyke. 'H-how b-beautiful Adam houses are,' he said.

'But what will happen *now*?' cried Miriam. 'Now that Mrs Robinson is not guilty and plans to go to Canada with Tony like it says here ...' And she tapped the evening paper with her forefinger.

'W-well. They've arrested Bognor ...'

'But did he do it? How awful it all is – so muddling. What will the Crown (Rex or whatever it calls itself) and that wretched Tomkins try to prove *this time*?'

'Simply that he m-murdered his m-mother, I think. B-but apparently he's also confessed that he m-murdered his Uncle R-Robert (you know, the dotty, whom we never saw) and his father (the Engineer Rear Admiral) and his Aunty Rucksack ... and he intended to give his mother typhoid and his Uncle Charlie Rucksack arsenic all in the one night. *He's* very pleased with himself for nearly having got away with it, evidently. He told that bank manager's daughter too – but she didn't believe him.'

'He always had vitality,' said Miriam wistfully.

'Ch-Charlie would have died first, you see, of the arsenic,' went on Pyke, 'and his mother would have died in ten days' time. And the Rucksack Bequest Fund would all have been Bognor's. But evidently the plates got switched and Uncle Charlie never t-turned up. Bognor is quite cross about it evidently. He won't stop talking ...'

'My *God*!' said Miriam. 'My God! And that was the man I once thought of marrying!' There was a long pause while Miriam rubbed her nose with her forefinger and became slightly less angry.

'Well, I didn't really *think* of it,' she said. 'I toyed.'

Pyke came across the room and stood opposite her. He was very grave. It would take a long time to rehabilitate Miriam in his affections. Yes, he loved her, but with reservations. Once he had loved her unreservedly.

'My dear Miriam,' he said, 'he is really very odd indeed . . . I b-believe they think he is unfit to plead, l-let alone to *marry* . . .'

Miriam's face slowly lit up.

'Surely,' she said, 'they will need me in a witness-box to prove *that*?'

And then Miriam looked up and saw the expression on his face. And it struck her that her dear Pyke was, perhaps, a little displeased with her.

THE END

VIRAGO MODERN CLASSICS

The first Virago Modern Classic, *Frost in May* by Antonia White, was published in 1978. It launched a list dedicated to the celebration of women writers and to the rediscovery and reprinting of their works. Its aim was, and is, to demonstrate the existence of a female tradition in literature, and to broaden the sometimes narrow definition of a 'classic'. Published with new introductions by some of today's best writers, the books are chosen for many reasons: they may be great works of literature; they may be wonderful period pieces; they may reveal particular aspects of women's lives; they may be classics of comedy, storytelling, letter-writing or autobiography.

'The Virago Modern Classics list contains some of the greatest fiction and non-fiction of the modern age, by authors whose lives were frequently as significant as their writing. Still captivating, still memorable, still utterly essential reading' **SARAH WATERS**

'The Virago Modern Classics list is wonderful. It's quite simply one of the best and most essential things that has happened in publishing in our time. I hate to think where we'd be without it' **ALI SMITH**

'The Virago Modern Classics have reshaped literary history and enriched the reading of us all. No library is complete without them' **MARGARET DRABBLE**

'The writers are formidable, the production handsome. The whole enterprise is thoroughly grand' **LOUISE ERDRICH**

'Good news for everyone writing and reading today'
HILARY MANTEL

VIRAGO MODERN CLASSICS

AUTHORS INCLUDE:

Elizabeth von Arnim, Beryl Bainbridge,
Pat Barker, Nina Bawden, Vera Brittain, Angela Carter,
Willa Cather, Barbara Comyns, E. M. Delafield, Polly Devlin,
Monica Dickens, Elaine Dundy, Nell Dunn, Nora Ephron,
Janet Flanner, Janet Frame, Miles Franklin, Marilyn French,
Stella Gibbons, Charlotte Perkins Gilman, Rumer Godden,
Radclyffe Hall, Helene Hanff, Josephine Hart, Shirley Hazzard,
Bessie Head, Patricia Highsmith, Winifred Holtby, Attia Hosain,
Zora Neale Hurston, Elizabeth Jenkins, Molly Keane, Rosamond
Lehmann, Anne Lister, Rose Macaulay, Shena Mackay, Beryl
Markham, Daphne du Maurier, Mary McCarthy, Kate O'Brien,
Grace Paley, Ann Petry, Barbara Pym, Mary Renault, Stevie
Smith, Muriel Spark, Elizabeth Taylor, Angela Thirkell,
Mary Webb, Eudora Welty, Rebecca West,
Edith Wharton, Antonia White

CHILDREN'S CLASSICS INCLUDE:

Joan Aiken, Nina Bawden, Frances Hodgson Burnett,
Susan Coolidge, Rumer Godden, L. M. Montgomery,
Edith Nesbit, Noel Streatfeild, P. L. Travers

Don't let the story stop here

Virago was founded in 1973 as *'the first mass-market publisher for 52 per cent of the population – women. An exciting new imprint for both sexes in a changing world.'*

Today Virago is the outstanding international publisher of books by women. While the cultural, political and economic landscape has changed dramatically, Virago has remained true to its original aims: to put women centre stage; to explore the untold stories of their lives and histories; to break the silence around many women's experiences; to publish breathtaking new fiction and non-fiction alongside a rich list of rediscovered classics; and above all to champion women's talent.

Join the Virago Community!

For our latest news, events, extracts and competitions, visit
www.virago.co.uk

@ViragoBooks   ViragoPress   @ViragoPress
ViragoPress   virago.co.uk/virago-podcast

virago

To order any Virago title by telephone, please contact our mail order supplier on: +44 (0)1235 759 555.